Love was indeed blind, Emily thought bitterly.

She had once seen Jim Keegan as some kind of perfect man. She'd seen someone tender, someone kind and sensitive, someone who loved her as much as she loved him.

Wrong.

Seven years ago, her vision had been clouded.

But now there was nothing to keep her from seeing James Keegan clearly. Over the next few weeks, she would have an opportunity that most women never had—she would be able to see, *really* see, this man she had once loved so desperately. She would get a chance to see, firsthand, that he wasn't the perfect man she'd once thought him to be. She would be face-to-face with the real man—the selfish, insensitive bastard he truly was.

Maybe then she would stop longing for the sound of his laughter and the warmth of his touch.

Maybe then, finally, she would be free.

Dear Reader,

Welcome to another month of fabulous reading here at Silhouette Intimate Moments. As always, we've put together six terrific books for your reading pleasure, starting with *Another Man's Wife* by Dallas Schulze. This is another of our Heartbreakers titles, as well as the latest in her miniseries entitled A Family Circle. As usual with one of this author's titles, you won't want to miss it.

Next up is *Iain Ross's Woman* by Emilie Richards. This, too, is part of a miniseries, The Men of Midnight. This is a suspenseful and deeply emotional book that I predict will end up on your "keeper" shelf.

The rest of the month is filled out with new titles by Nikki Benjamin, *The Wedding Venture;* Susan Mallery, *The Only Way Out;* Suzanne Brockmann, *Not Without Risk;* and Nancy Gideon, *For Mercy's Sake.* Every one of them provides exactly the sort of romantic excitement you've come to expect from Intimate Moments.

In months to come, look for more reading from some of the best authors in the business. We've got books coming up from Linda Turner, Judith Duncan, Naomi Horton and Paula Detmer Riggs, to name only a few. So come back next month—and every month—to Silhouette Intimate Moments, where romance is the name of the game.

Yours,
Leslie Wainger
Senior Editor and Editorial Coordinator

Please address questions and book requests to:
Silhouette Reader Service
U.S.: 3010 Walden Ave., P.O. Box 1325, Buffalo, NY 14269
Canadian: P.O. Box 609, Fort Erie, Ont. L2A 5X3

NOT WITHOUT RISK

SUZANNE BROCKMANN

Published by Silhouette Books
America's Publisher of Contemporary Romance

SILHOUETTE BOOKS

ISBN 0-373-07647-9

NOT WITHOUT RISK

Books by Suzanne Brockmann

Silhouette Intimate Moments

Hero Under Cover #575
Not Without Risk #647

SUZANNE BROCKMANN

wanted to be a cowboy, an astronaut, a spelunker and a rock-and-roll singer when she grew up. Allergic to horses, too nearsighted for NASA and slightly claustrophobic, she took up writing instead and has successfully gone with her characters on trail rides, into outer space and deep beneath the earth. She actually was a rock singer, forming and fronting an original band while attending college in Boston. Suz still lives in the Boston area, surrounded by the best family and the coolest group of friends in the world.

For the *real* Marshalls

Chapter 1

Emily Marshall was in the bathroom. No, not the bathroom, the head. On a boat the tiny bathroom was called the head.

And as long as you're correcting yourself, Emily thought as she leaned closer to the mirror to reapply her lipstick, *this floating castle with sails can't really be called a boat.*

Boats were unassuming, functional little things you sat in and used oars to row. Or they were things with sails attached that gave you calluses on your hands, sunburn on your face and a healthy lungful of fresh ocean air. Sometimes they took you from point A to point B, but mostly from point A to nowhere, and back again.

Despite the fact that there was, indeed, no destination for this evening's sail, there was nothing unassuming about the sailing vessel Emily was standing on. True, the *Home Free* wasn't large enough to be called a ship, but somehow the word *boat* didn't fit, either.

Yacht, thought Emily as she adjusted the straps of her new black party dress. Alexander Delmore's boat really had to be called a yacht.

She looked at herself critically in the mirror. She'd picked up this dress in a fancy department store's bargain basement. Even marked down the way it had been, it had put her out nearly half of one of her weekly paychecks.

Spending that much money was a big deal to her. It meant she'd have to watch her grocery money for the next few weeks, and really try to keep her expenses down. But to real estate tycoon Alexander Delmore, the amount she'd spent on the dress would have been laughably small. When Alex took her out to dinner, he spent that much on one bottle of wine.

Of course, he made significantly more money wheeling and dealing in real estate than she made as a high school English teacher. That was just one of the simple facts of life. And it was typical of Emily to have fallen in love with a job in a city school system that couldn't afford to pay a decent salary. Sure, she could have applied for a job in a more affluent district. Or she could have stuck to her original college major and gone into business or gotten a job working with computers. It was her own fault that she never seemed to have enough money.

Emily made a face at herself in the mirror. But even with her tongue sticking out, she still looked sophisticated, thanks to the elegant lines of the dress.

Earlier this evening, Alex had asked her out again, for next Tuesday night. He wanted to take her to a party at a local country club. If she spent the other half of her paycheck on yet another expensive dress, she'd be eating pasta or tomato soup until the end of the month.

Emily didn't like eating pasta day in and day out. She liked lobster. And veal. And expensive cuts of filet mignon. She liked asparagus, regardless of the season. She liked watermelon in the winter, and imported chocolate.

She liked houses like Alex's, houses that overlooked the clear blue water of the Gulf of Mexico. She liked houses like Alex's, with six bedrooms and four and a half baths. She liked fluffy new towels that weren't fraying around the edges. She liked cleaning ladies and dinners out. She liked big floating weekend parties on Alex's yacht—parties like this one that started early in the afternoon on Saturday and didn't end until late Sunday night. She liked big-screen stereo TVs and state-of-the-art compact disc players.

She liked the thought of having enough money that she'd never have to worry about the phone bill or the electric payment. She liked the idea of vacations and cruises and trips to Europe.

She also liked Alexander Delmore.

But she didn't love him.

It was clear that he was interested in her. He had as much as told her that he was looking to settle down, to start a family. He was one of Florida's most eligible bachelors, and Emily was flattered that he found her attractive.

But... she didn't love him.

Her neighbor, Carly Wilson, said so what if you don't love him? Love was overrated. A good strong case of like could outlast the most passionate love affair, particularly if it was combined with an enormous bank account. How often does real love come along, anyway? Carly had asked. According to Emily's neighbor, the answer was usually never.

Emily stared at herself in the mirror, searching the familiar blue of her own eyes. She was amazed that she could be wearing this gorgeous, expensive dress that made her look like a million dollars, and be standing here, in the bathroom—head—of millionaire Alexander Delmore's luxurious yacht, thinking about... James Keegan.

After seven years, you'd think she'd be over the man. And she *was* over him, Emily told herself firmly. Her affair with black-hearted Jim Keegan was dead and buried, deep in the past. Jeez, it had been over almost before it even began.

So what the heck was she doing thinking about him?

Because of love. She was thinking about Jim because she had honestly loved him. As rotten and cruel as he had been, as badly as he had hurt her, the fact remained that Emily had loved James Keegan with all of her heart and soul. And deep inside she knew that never, not in a billion years, would she ever love Alex Delmore even half that much.

Still— Carly's voice seemed to echo in her head, as if she were a little devil perched on Emily's shoulder —*who says you have to love Alex to marry him?*

"I do," Emily said out loud to her reflection, then winced at her poor choice of words.

She gave the short skirt of her new dress one more yank southward and quickly ran her fingers through the short, blunt-cut of her chestnut hair. She took a deep breath to further exorcise James Keegan's too-handsome ghost, then turned to open the door that led out into Alexander's tiny shipboard office.

She heard the angry voices as soon as her hand was on the doorknob, but it was too late to pull back. The door swung open, and the arguing men immediately fell silent. Alex and another man—Vincent something—looked up at her, and she could see surprise and annoyance in both pairs of eyes.

"I'm sorry," she said. "I didn't mean to interrupt...."

Alexander Delmore shook his head. "No problem," he said, crossing the tiny cabin with a smile on his tanned, handsome face. "I didn't realize you were using the head." He glanced back at the other man as he took Emily's hand. "If I'd known, we would have gone somewhere else to have our...chat."

Emily couldn't remember the other man's last name. They had been introduced earlier that evening, when all the party guests first boarded Alex's yacht. Vincent what? she thought. Martino? Or was it Medino?

Whoever he was, he was a heavyset man. His dark complexion and body-builder's physique offset Alex's golden slenderness. And, unlike Alex, Vincent still looked annoyed at the interruption.

"If you don't mind..." Vincent said pointedly.

Emily slipped her hand free from Alex's. "I'll get out of your way," she said.

"It'll only be a second," Alex promised. "I'll meet you up on deck."

The office door closed tightly behind her.

Emily was halfway down the hall when she realized that she'd left her purse in the head. She turned back, but when she got to the door to the office she could hear that the two men were arguing again. They were keeping their voices low, but there was no mistaking the underlying current of tension.

She had just lifted her hand to knock when Vincent's voice rose slightly.

"If you don't like *that* deal," she heard him say quite clearly, "how about *this* one—I waste you and take *all* of your profits."

Waste? Had he said *waste?* As in . . . *kill?*

Alex's voice rose enough for Emily to hear him, too.

"I had a deal with your uncle that worked out fine for years," he said, his voice shaking with emotion.

"My uncle's dead," Vincent said. "And *I'm* in charge now. You want to deal, first you gotta deal with me."

"Fine," Emily heard Alex say. "In that case, you can deal me out."

Vincent laughed, but there was no humor in it. "You don't expect me to believe that you'll get out of the business just like that, do you?"

Emily could almost see Alex's shrug. "Believe what you want, Marino."

There was a loud thump from inside the office, as if someone's head had hit the bulkhead, hard. Emily's heart was pounding, but she couldn't move, couldn't run away.

"I *believe*," Vincent's voice growled, "that I just might break your face. I *know* that there was a snowstorm somewhere off the Gulf Coast last night, and I *know* that this pretty little boat of yours was there to intercept. You cut me my share, or you're dead. That's your deal. Take it or leave it."

A snowstorm? In July? In *Florida?*

With sudden clarity, Emily remembered waking up in the early hours of the morning to the sound of a small outboard motor. The yacht's motorized dinghy had quietly pulled up alongside the bigger boat, and even as she watched out her cabin's tiny porthole, the gentle throbbing of its engine had been cut.

Someone had been out on the deck. Emily hadn't been able to see who it was, but she had heard the sounds of movement. The little boat had been secured to the side of the yacht with a rope, and a ladder had been thrown down. The person in the boat had turned, and in the early dawn Emily had had a clear view of his face.

It had been Alex.

When she asked him about it at breakfast that morning, he'd apologized for disturbing her, and told her that he'd been out fishing.

Fishing? Fishing for what? Something Vincent Marino would threaten to *kill* Alex for?

Snowstorm. Snow. *Snow* was slang for cocaine, wasn't it?

God in heaven, was it possible that Alex was dealing *cocaine?*

Emily turned and ran.

Chapter 2

Emily sat at the interrogation room table in the St. Simone police precinct, her hands clasped tightly in front of her.

The police officer who had first taken her statement had called this the interview room, but Emily knew better. It was an interrogation room. A mirror lined one wall. It was clear that it was really a window, and that people could stand on the other side and observe and hear the conversation without being seen.

The clock on the wall was covered with a protective grid, like the clocks in the gym at the high school where she taught English. The walls were a drab cross between beige and green, and the tile on the floor was gray. It was pitted and cracked from age.

Yes, this was an interrogation room. And after three hours, with seven different police officers asking her the same questions, she could safely assume that she was being interrogated.

The room smelled like stale cigarette smoke—until the police detective she'd been talking to came back into the room, carrying two ceramic mugs of steaming coffee.

"We have those foam hot cups," he said, in his gentle Hispanic accent, "but I don't like to use them—not now that I know what they do to the environment. But these mugs are okay—I washed them myself, and I am very careful to get them clean."

Emily could believe it. The detective—Felipe Salazar, he'd said his name was—was neatly dressed and meticulously well-groomed. He was a young man, probably even younger than her own twenty-five years, with short dark hair and a face with high, exotic cheekbones that might have looked dangerous if not for his open, friendly smile. He reminded her of a puppy—a Doberman puppy who had potential, but hadn't yet learned to be dangerous. With the exception of the few minutes he'd spent getting coffee, he had remained with her for the duration of her questioning.

Six other police officers had come into the room, and she'd told her story over and over and *over* again. She realized they didn't believe her when she told them that Alexander Delmore—one of the pillars of St. Simone society— was running drugs. She knew that was why she had to tell what she had heard and seen again and again—the police were waiting for her to slip up, to make a mistake, to mess up on the details, to change her story in some way.

All the other police officers and detectives had expressed their doubts about what she was telling them. Some had said she must have misheard the conversation between Delmore and the man she'd IDed as Vincent Marino. Some had said she must have mistaken someone else for Marino, allegedly the new kingpin of a statewide crime syndicate. Others had implied that her story was a load of baloney. They had implied that she had some dirty, rotten motive for wanting to smear Delmore's good name.

Emily had been asked countless personal questions about the nature of her relationship with Alex. Had they recently had an argument, a falling-out? How long had she been seeing him? How long had she been *sleeping* with him?

Emily couldn't see how those questions had anything to do with Alex's involvement in drug running. But she'd answered them truthfully. And the truth was, she wasn't intimately involved with Alex. When they went for weekend sails on his boat, his crew had always been on board with them, and she had always had her own cabin. She had *not* slept with him.

But she could tell that none of the other police officers believed her about *that,* either.

But young Detective Salazar had been nothing but kind. He'd said he *did* believe her. He'd asked her to be patient and put up with the skeptics. He said that if Delmore was guilty of distributing cocaine, then Delmore should go to jail—regardless of the amount of money the man had donated to the widows-and-orphans fund over the past few years.

As Emily took another sip of black coffee, Salazar shuffled the pages of notes he had been taking throughout the three hours of questioning.

"Do they believe me yet?" she asked him bluntly.

He smiled at her apologetically. "My boss, Lieutenant Bell, will be coming in to talk to you," he said. "And my partner is around here somewhere. He'll be in soon, too."

The door opened, and Emily looked up to see a woman come into the room. She, like most of the others, wasn't wearing a police uniform. She was wearing a dark blue jacket and skirt and a utilitarian white shirt. She was short and wire thin, and she could have been anywhere from forty to sixty years old. Her brown hair was streaked with gray, and she wore a pair of half glasses on her thin nose.

She peered over the tops of them at Emily. "Emily Marshall?" she said. "I'm Lieutenant Katherine Bell."

The older woman didn't hold out her hand to shake, so Emily stayed in her seat and didn't uncross her arms. Bell sat down next to Salazar and appropriated his notes. "I understand you believe Alexander Delmore is involved in some sort of illegal activity," she said, looking down through her glasses to read Salazar's perfect handwriting.

Emily didn't say anything. She waited for Bell to finish reading through the notes.

"You claim that your relationship with Delmore is casual," Bell commented. She glanced up at Emily, with one eyebrow elevated in an expression of disbelief.

"It's more than a claim," Emily said, keeping her voice at its usual controlled calmness. But her blood pressure was rising, and she was long past the point of merely being annoyed. "It's a fact. And I fail to see exactly how that question pertains to my suspicions that Alex is bringing cocaine into the country."

Bell sat back in her seat. She tapped her fingers on the table as she studied Emily carefully. "We're asking these questions because we're trying to figure out what you're doing here," the police lieutenant finally said. "These are serious accusations you're making. We need to be sure you're not a jilted lover, or someone out for revenge. For all we know, you're psychotic. For all we know, you've never even *met* the man, and—"

"Do I look crazy?" Emily asked.

Bell shrugged. "Believe me, honey, it takes all kinds."

Emily leaned forward. "I'm here, Lieutenant, because I teach high school in the seventh district."

Bell actually looked surprised.

"I assume you're familiar with that part of the city," Emily said.

The seventh district was in the part of St. Simone located on the wrong side of the proverbial tracks. There were guns and crime and drugs in the poverty-stricken seventh district, and those guns and crime and drugs didn't stay politely outside the high school doors. Emily had seen students arrested at gunpoint in the corridors of her school. She'd seen students sick and shaking from withdrawal, desperate to get their hands on more of the drugs that would temporarily ease their pain. She'd had students, mere children themselves, bring their babies into class with them, unable to afford day care. She'd seen empty seats, desks made suddenly vacant because some kid had overdosed on crack and died the night before.

"I know what crack does to people—especially to children," she told Lieutenant Bell. "If Alex is selling drugs, he needs to be stopped. I refuse to just sit by and do nothing."

"And you think he *is* selling drugs," Bell said.

"How else can you explain what I overheard?" Emily asked.

"She correctly identified Vincent Marino from a photo lineup," Salazar murmured to Bell.

"Marino doesn't exactly keep a low profile," Bell replied, with a shrug of her narrow shoulders. "Any number of people could ID him."

"Still, it's worth checking out," the detective said. "I have to wonder what Vincent Marino—a man nicknamed 'the Shark'—is doing on Mr. Delmore's guest list. *Someone* is bringing drugs into town. We have been trying to trace the source for years. Maybe it's Alexander Delmore. Maybe not. But we won't know if we don't at least investigate."

Bell was shaking her head. "It would take months to set up that kind of investigation," she said. "Months, and more money than it would be worth spending on a wild-goose chase. No, I don't think so."

Bell pushed back her chair, about to stand up and leave.

But Salazar caught her arm. "Wait, Lieutenant. I have an idea," he said. "Look at Ms. Marshall's eyes. They are the same shade of blue as Diego's."

Bell looked pointedly at her watch. "Is there a reason you're telling me this, Detective?"

"I say we get Diego to go undercover as Ms. Marshall's...I don't know...brother, I guess. With those eyes, they look like they could maybe be related," he said. "And if Ms. Marshall keeps on seeing Delmore, she can get him to take her on another one of those floating parties, and Diego, playing the part of her big brother, can tag along. Then he can check this guy out." He glanced at Emily. "Diego is my partner," he said. "He's the best in St. Simone. And probably all of Florida, too."

Bell was silent.

Salazar continued. "Provided Ms. Marshall is willing to cooperate—and I think, from what she has told me, she is—we have got a quick and easy way to pull off this investigation. If Delmore is smuggling drugs, wham—we nail him. If he's not, we pull out, and no one ever needs to know we suspected him in the first place."

Bell's flinty gray eyes flicked over to Emily. "*Are* you willing to cooperate?" she asked. "Are you willing to put up with one of my detectives moving into your apartment for a week or two, posing as your brother?"

The thought was not at all appealing. Emily's apartment was tiny, with only one bedroom. But if she needed to do this to help catch Alex... She lifted her chin. "As long as your detective is willing to sleep on my couch and share the bathroom," she said.

"And what about the risk?" Bell asked. "If Alexander Delmore *is* responsible for bringing shipments of cocaine into the country, he could be an extremely dangerous man."

"I think it's worth the risk," Emily said.

The door opened, and Salazar broke into a wide grin. "Hey!" he said. "Diego! Just the guy we were talking about...."

Emily turned to get a look at the man Salazar thought so highly of, and froze.

His name wasn't Diego. It was James. James Keegan.

For the first time in over seven years, Emily Marshall was face-to-face with Police Detective James Keegan.

"Ms. Marshall, meet Detective Keegan," Salazar said.

But of course. Diego was Spanish for James.

"Emily?" Jim said, his voice hardly more than a whisper.

Emily tried valiantly to regain her composure. But it was hard. It was terribly hard. He was standing there, staring at her as if he couldn't believe his own eyes.

His brown hair was shaggy and long—longer than it had been seven years ago, when he was a newly recruited detective on the Tampa police force. His hair was long enough to pull back into a ponytail at the nape of his neck, but he wore it down around his shoulders. It gleamed, thick and wavy, in the overhead light. And soft. Emily couldn't help but remember how incredibly soft his hair was to touch.

His face was instantly familiar, yet there were visible changes. His nose was still crooked, his lips still full, his mouth still generous. But his cheekbones were a little more pronounced, adding a ruggedness and maturity to his face that hadn't been there before. The crow's-feet and laughter lines around his eyes and mouth had gotten deeper.

His deep blue eyes, though, were exactly the same. They still seemed to sparkle and burn with life and heat. And they still were shadowed by some inner darkness his quick, easy grin couldn't hide.

She'd forgotten how big he was. At six foot four, he seemed to fill the room. His shoulders were broad underneath the thin cotton of his T-shirt, and the muscles in his arms stretched the sleeves. His faded blue jeans were the new, loose-fitting kind, and they somehow seemed to emphasize his lean, muscular physique. Emily wondered if he still ran five miles every day, rain or shine.

She exhaled noisily, realizing she'd been holding her breath. "What are you doing here?" she asked.

"I transferred down from Tampa, about three years ago," Jim said. His deep voice was still husky. And he still hadn't lost that slight trace of a New York accent. "What are *you* doing here?"

Jim Keegan had been living in St. Simone for three years. Emily had trouble catching her breath again. Only chance had kept her from running into him before this. St. Simone wasn't *that* big. . . .

She was silent as Salazar quickly sketched out his plan, realizing with a sudden icy shaft of fear that James Keegan was the man they'd all been talking about. James Keegan was the man who would be posing as her brother. He was the man who would come and live in her apartment for a week or two.

No way. There was no way on earth she'd ever agree to *that*. She couldn't even handle seeing him for a minute or two. No way could she put up with him for two whole weeks.

"No way," Jim Keegan was saying, shaking his head. "It wouldn't work."

"Are you kidding, man?" Salazar said. "It's a great way to gain Delmore's confidence."

"And it would provide Ms. Marshall with round-the-clock protection," Lieutenant Bell pointed out.

"May I speak to you, Lieutenant?" Jim asked. He opened the door. "Out in the hall?"

He glanced briefly at Emily as Lieutenant Bell pushed back her chair and stood up, and Emily knew that Jim Keegan didn't want to spend the next two weeks with her any more than she wanted to spend the next two weeks with him.

Jim politely held the door open for his boss, not daring to look back at Emily again. Damn it to hell, what was she doing here in St. Simone? He'd been so sure that she'd returned to her parents' home in Connecticut after she finished her four years at the University of Tampa. Whenever he thought about her—and, damn it, he tried hard not to make a habit of it—he imagined her happily married to some well-mannered business suit, living somewhere in New England.

So what was she doing here in Florida? And what the hell was she doing dating a well-known playboy like Alexander Delmore?

And—God!—how had she managed to become even *more* beautiful in the past seven years?

She'd been eighteen when they first met—and eighteen when they'd said good-bye.

She'd been a college student. A freshman, a lousy *freshman,* at the University of Tampa, with waves of long reddish brown hair that fell down past her shoulders and blue eyes he was convinced were the color of heaven. Her heart-shaped face had been soft looking, and she'd had full, beautiful lips that were usually curved upward into a smile. She'd looked exactly like what she was—a nice young girl. Too nice. And way too young. And, God, how he'd loved her....

Lieutenant Bell's raspy voice interrupted Keegan's thoughts. "Was there something you wanted to discuss, Detective?"

"Yeah," he said. "You've got to find someone else to take this case. I can't do it."

"Can't?" Bell said.

"I was once involved with Emily Marshall," he said bluntly. No use beating around the bush. "I'm sorry, Lieutenant, but there's no way I can play house with this woman."

"Involved," Lieutenant Bell repeated. "Intimately, I assume, or this wouldn't be an issue."

The muscles in his jaw tightened. "It was a long time ago," he said.

"Who dumped whom?"

"I was the one who broke it off," Jim said. "She was just a kid, and—"

"Spare me the sordid details," Lieutenant Bell said, "and just tell me if you think she's here right now because of you."

It took Jim a solid ten seconds to understand what she was suggesting. "You mean, do I think she's concocted this story about Delmore because..."

"She wants to get your attention?" Bell finished for him. She watched him, waiting for an answer.

He shook his head. "No. You saw the look on her face when she recognized me," he said. "She was surprised as hell."

She'd been so surprised, she forgot to hide the hurt that still glimmered in her eyes—hurt from the way he'd treated her all those years ago. God, he could still close his eyes and see her standing outside that University Boulevard bar, shock and pain and disbelief on her sweet face.

"Besides," he said, shaking his head slightly to banish the image from his mind, "what happened between us—it was over seven years ago."

"Good," said the lieutenant. "Then you shouldn't have any problem working with her on this case, right, Keegan?"

She started back toward the interview room.

"Lieutenant," Jim said, "give me a break here. Please."

Lieutenant Bell turned back to face him, crossing her arms. "You and your partner are the only detectives available right now, and I suspect that Alexander Delmore won't buy into believing that Felipe Salazar is Ms. Marshall's brother," she said. "If you tell me you're still emotionally involved with this woman, I will have you removed from this investigation. But that will mean waiting a number of weeks before another detective is available. And *that* means there will be a number of weeks that Ms. Marshall is out there, by herself, with a man she suspects is running drugs." She pinned Jim with her stern gaze. "I am not keen on the idea of Emily Marshall being a part of this investigation in the first place, but Detective Salazar is right. If we start immediately, we can get this done quickly and easily. And then Ms. Marshall will be out of your hair, Detective.''

She was watching him closely, and Jim knew that she was unerringly reading the tension in his shoulders, neck and jaw. The idea of Emily being in danger was making him crazy. God, it was even worse than the picture that kept flashing in his head of Emily together with her new boyfriend, Alexander Delmore....

"Now," Lieutenant Bell said. "Are you telling me that you are still emotionally involved?"

Emotionally involved? No way. Impossible. Not after seven years. Yeah, sure, he'd thought about Emily Marshall now and then, but that didn't mean he was emotionally involved. And yeah, sure, seeing her again was a real surprise, so it was only natural that he should feel so off balance. And add to that the amazing fact that she was still so damned pretty. He'd always thought that imagination and memory tended to exaggerate things, that he'd somehow built up his memory of her until he remembered her as some staggeringly gorgeous woman. But she was even more beautiful than he'd remembered.

But so what? He still found her attractive. Big deal. That didn't mean he was emotionally involved.

Besides, what good would being emotionally involved do you, a little voice inside of him asked, with more than a slight trace of sarcasm. You dumped her, pal. It's not likely she'll come back for more.

"Are you, Keegan? Are you emotionally involved?"

"No," Jim said, but his voice sounded unnaturally hoarse, unusually raspy.

He hoped to God he wasn't lying.

Chapter 3

James Keegan.

Didn't it figure that it had to be James Keegan?

Ever since Emily had overheard Alex's argument with Vincent Marino, ever since she'd first come to realize that the wealthy society man that she was starting to think of as her boyfriend might be a drug runner, she'd felt as if she were living in some kind of dream world.

Last night on Alex's sailboat, she'd numbly pretended that nothing was the slightest bit wrong. She'd smiled at Alex as he came up beside her on the main deck and draped his arm casually around her shoulders. She'd kept up a steady stream of conversation as he drove her home in his BMW after the sailboat returned to its yacht-club mooring. She'd even let him kiss her good-night the way he always did.

It had been late—long after two in the morning—when she unlocked the door to her tiny apartment.

She would have gone to the St. Simone police right away, but she'd suddenly gotten scared. What if Alex suspected that she'd overheard his conversation with Marino? What if he was watching her apartment that very moment? If he saw her leave in the middle of the night, and if he followed her to the police station, then he would know for sure that *she* knew he was involved in something rotten.

So she had waited for morning, then showered and changed into her favorite pair of khaki shorts and the T-shirt that was on top in her T-shirt drawer.

Morning had taken forever to come. The hours between three and five-thirty had seemed centuries long. But then, finally, it had been six and then seven o'clock. Cars had started moving on the street. People in her building had woken up. Emily had managed to wait until eight-thirty before she left her apartment.

Talking to the police detectives had been just another unreal part of that horrible, weird dream.

And then James Keegan had shown up.

That had been the final bizarre touch to an already surreal experience. Boy, how many times had James Keegan appeared out of the blue in her dreams at night? Too many to count.

She would be having some nice, friendly, soothing dream. She'd dream she was out shopping with Carly, or having dinner with some of the other teachers from the high school. But then everything would shift, and Jim Keegan would suddenly be there. Sometimes he would just look at her, with that familiar hunger in his eyes. Sometimes he would touch her, the way he'd touched her that one weekend they'd shared, the weekend he'd made love to her. But sometimes she'd see him, not in his own bed, but in that horrible hospital bed, after he'd been shot, with all those awful tubes and wires connecting him to all kinds of monitors and respirators. She would beg him not to leave her, not to die, but he would never even open his eyes.

Never, not even in Emily's wildest dreams, had James ever gotten assigned by his boss to move into her apartment and pretend that he was her brother.

And that made *this* funky real-life dream a true nightmare.

She was trapped. Sure, she could say no, she didn't want Jim to move in, she didn't want him to invade her life again. Of course, that would leave Alexander Delmore free to bring as many kilos of cocaine as he wanted into the city.

Emily stumbled on the rough blacktop of the parking lot outside of the police station. Brother, she was exhausted. And this nightmare was only beginning.

The hot July sun beat down on her mercilessly as she fished in the pocket of her shorts for the keys to her car. She dropped the key ring twice before she realized there was a reason her hands were shaking and her vision was blurred.

She was crying.

She'd held up so well while the police asked all their questions. She hadn't lost her temper even once—she had remained calm and cool, even when she felt insulted and embarrassed. And, most importantly, she hadn't screamed hysterically when Jim Keegan walked into the room. She hadn't burst into tears. She hadn't even looked more than surprised.

This must be a delayed reaction, she thought dazedly. She'd felt like crying ever since she'd found out that she had misjudged Alex so completely.

Emily futilely wiped her eyes with the back of her hand and tried one more time to get the car key into the door's lock. The lock popped up, and she opened the door. The inside of her car was hotter than Hades, but she got in anyway and started the engine. She opened all four of the power windows and cranked the air-conditioning.

Why James Keegan? Why *now?* What had she done to deserve this?

Emily gave in to the flood of tears. She rested her arms against the hot plastic of the steering wheel, put down her head and let herself cry.

Jim Keegan broke into a run as he headed down the corridor, Emily's purse in his hand. He pushed open the door that led out into the municipal parking lot and braced himself for the almost solid impact of the humid outside air.

Damn, Emily was nowhere in sight. He hadn't been *that* far behind her, had he?

As he scanned the rows of cars parked in the lot, he was well aware that he didn't have a clue what kind of car she drove. Something expensive, no doubt, he thought sourly, a gift from her millionaire boyfriend.

But then he saw her. She was sitting in the front seat of an unassuming little Honda, slumped forward, her arms and head resting on the steering wheel.

As Jim walked toward her, he realized almost immediately that she was crying, and his heart lurched. Calm, collected Emily, who never lost her temper, who never was rattled, who never allowed any of her anxieties to show, was crying as if the world were coming to an end.

He'd only seen her cry one other time before. It had been in the hospital, about a week after he was shot. She'd stayed with him for days, first waiting outside ICU while he was in critical condition, then sitting beside his bed after he was out of immediate danger.

He'd been unconscious most of the time, but the few times he came to, she'd been there, smiling at him. He'd felt reassured by her serenity. He hadn't noticed the lines of strain and worry on her beautiful face. He hadn't noticed—until the night he woke up to find her crying inconsolably.

She'd thought he was asleep, and she was weeping as if her heart were breaking.

That had been the beginning of the end. Jim had known that he was the cause of Emily's unhappiness. Of course, he'd already known that he was poison, that he didn't deserve her. Seeing her cry like that had just hammered it home.

Yet here it was, seven years later, and he'd made her cry again. He had to assume he had something to do with her tears. Damn, seeing her again made *him* feel like crying.

She didn't hear him as he walked up to the open window of her car. She didn't hear him when he stopped, either. So he crouched down, making his face level with the window, and cleared his throat.

"Emily?"

Emily jumped. She lifted her head and found herself staring directly into Jim Keegan's dark blue eyes.

"You okay?" he asked.

Emily tried to dry her face, but she was perspiring from the heat inside the car, and she succeeded only in smearing her wet face with her damp arm. Thankfully, the air coming from the air-conditioning vents began blowing cold.

"I'll live," she said shortly.

His mouth twisted in what might well have been an apologetic smile. "You left your purse in the interview room," he said in his rich, husky voice as he handed it to her through the window. "Some things never change, huh? You should get one of those belt packs, and just never take it off. That way, you can't leave without taking your purse with you, you know?"

"These days I don't usually leave my purse behind," Emily said stiffly. Then she remembered that forgetting to take her purse out of the bathroom on the *Home Free* was what had made her overhear Alex's conversation with Marino. "At least not all the time."

She glanced over to find Jim studying her. He was close enough that she could see the soft, dark fans of his thick eyelashes, and the specks of green and gold mixed in with the blue of his eyes. He was close enough for her to see the roughness of his two-day-old five-o'clock shadow, and the supple smoothness of his full lips. He looked tired. The lines of laughter that creased his face and wrinkled the edges of his eyes seemed more like worry lines in the harsh afternoon light. She could read his tension clearly by the way he clenched and unclenched his teeth, making the muscles move in his jaw.

"You look good, Em," he said softly.

Oh, sure. If he was standing close enough for her to count the stubble of his five-o'clock shadow, then he couldn't help but see that her eyes were red and swollen from tears, and that her face was puffy and pale from crying and lack of sleep. Frankly, she looked like hell. And she knew it.

"Don't cry anymore, okay?" he said. "I know that working with me isn't going to be a lot of fun for you—it's not going to be easy for me, either—but we'll do this quickly and get Delmore in jail, where he belongs. Then everything will be back to normal."

Emily actually laughed. "Normal?" she said. "I'm going to help send my boyfriend away for twenty years to life. Do you think he's still going to want to go steady with me after that?"

Jim was silent. God, what an egotistical bastard he was. Here he'd gone and assumed that she was crying because she was upset about seeing *him* again. But she wasn't. She was crying over *Delmore.*

"I'm such an amazingly lousy judge of character," Emily continued. And it wasn't as if this were the first time she'd misjudged a man. Seven years ago, she'd totally misjudged Jim Keegan, too. "I thought Alex was nice—I thought he was basically a good man. A little stuffy, maybe. A little pompous. But basically good."

God, maybe she'd loved Delmore, Jim thought, feeling an odd twist in his gut. Maybe she *still* was in love with him. Yet she believed so strongly in right and wrong that she felt compelled to turn him in. That couldn't be easy. In fact, it had to be torture.

"I'm sorry, Em," he said.

"Don't call me 'Em,' Detective," she said sharply, putting her car into gear. "You don't know me well enough anymore."

She pulled out of the parking lot and was gone.

There was a message from Alex on the answering machine when Emily got home that afternoon.

"My twelve-o'clock appointment cancelled," he said without ceremony, and without introduction. It was clear he expected Emily to recognize his voice. Of course, she did. "If you get back from wherever you are before noon, give my secretary a call. She'll page me, and we can meet up for lunch. If not, I'll see you on Tuesday."

See you on Tuesday.

Emily didn't want to see Alex on Tuesday—or any other day, for that matter. She didn't want to see him ever again.

She didn't want to see Jim Keegan ever again, either, but he was going to show up at her apartment in a few hours and she was going to have to spend the next week or two seeing him every single day. He was going to be the first person she saw every morning, and the last person she saw every night.

Emily opened the sliding glass door that led out to a tiny deck overlooking the courtyard of her apartment complex. The courtyard held a modest-size swimming pool filled with sparkling-clean blue water, but it was the lush plants and trees that grew on the tiny grounds that Emily loved.

She sat down on one of the two lounge chairs that just barely fit on the minuscule deck. Emily put her head back, listening to the relentless buzzing and sawing of disgruntled insects protesting the day's heat. It had to be a hundred degrees in the shade, with humidity that hung almost visibly in the air, creating a haze that seemed to magnify the power of the sun.

It was summer in Florida, and Emily loved it. The droves of winter residents had migrated north, and the streets seemed empty, the pace so much slower. Of course, as a teacher, she had most of her summers free, which added to the sense of laziness. She had the time to kick back, to walk instead of run, even to stroll instead of walk.

Emily had loved Florida from the start—from the first time her parents took her family here on vacation. When Emily was twelve, Dr. and Mrs. Marshall had bought a beach house on Sanibel Island. From then on, school vacations and a hefty part of the summer had been spent on Florida's Gulf Coast. It had seemed only natural that Emily would attend college at the University of Tampa.

The university. She had only been there about a month when it became clear that a serial rapist was stalking the campus. Emily had joined a student organization formed to promote student safety. She'd helped get the word out that there was a serious danger to young women walking alone on campus—at any time of the day, and particularly at night. She'd helped set up an escort service so that no one would have to walk anywhere alone. And she'd worked closely with the Tampa police force as they'd tried to catch the rapist.

Many of the kids on the committee had been in awe of the police detectives. Although they were barely in their mid-twenties, the detectives were so obviously men compared to the college boys. And Detective Keegan—he looked like a cross between Mel Gibson and Kevin Costner, with his charmingly crooked grin and smoldering blue eyes—was the number one topic of conversation on the girls' floor of the dorm. Emily had been determined not to be one of the many who developed a schoolgirl crush on the man.

Still, she often looked up during meetings to find him watching her. He'd smile at her, then look away, but moments later, he would be watching her again. Staunchly she tried to ignore him. She always left the meetings quickly, careful not to dawdle, wary of the strange attraction that seemed to spark between them—afraid it was all due to wishful thinking on her part.

Wishful thinking, because Detective Keegan was more than just an incredibly handsome man. He was sharp and funny and smart and so electrifyingly *alive*. But deep in his eyes, and hidden behind his boyish grin, Emily could see real sadness and pain. No one else seemed to notice it, but she knew it was there. She imagined he'd seen awful things on the street, even in the few short years that he'd been a police detective. Rumor had it that he'd recently moved to Florida from New York City. No one seemed to know why.

Despite her resolve to steer clear of James Keegan, the truth was, Emily *would* have given just about anything to spend more time with him.

She could still remember the first real conversation she'd had with Jim. The rapist had been evading the police for weeks, managing to attack four more women, despite the added security measures. Emily had been sitting in on a task force meeting between the police and campus security, and it had suddenly occurred to her that the rapist could very well know their every plan and every move if—and this was an awful thought—he was one of the campus security guards.

After the meeting was over, Keegan's partner left before Emily could approach him. That meant she'd have to share her theory with Jim Keegan.

He was surrounded, as usual, by a crowd of adoring coeds. Emily waited in the doorway, leaning against the frame. He glanced up at her, and somehow he knew that she wanted to talk to him.

"What's on your mind, Emily?" he called across the room.

Emily was surprised. She hadn't realized he even knew her name.

"I was hoping to have a word with you," she said.

He glanced at his watch. "I'm late for a meeting downtown," he said. "Can you walk me to my car while we talk?"

Emily nodded. "Sure."

"Excuse us, ladies," Detective Keegan said, smiling at the other girls.

The girls disappeared down the hall, with more than one catty look thrown in Emily's direction. Jim noticed, and grinned.

"It's nice to be so popular," he said.

"Watch out," Emily said dryly. "You just might find yourself voted this year's homecoming king."

Keegan laughed, coming to stand next to Emily. He was outrageously tall—at least eight inches taller than she was. She had to tip her head back to look up at him. And he had a nice laugh, rich and full and husky. It was sexy, just like his speaking voice. Emily felt her pulse kick into a higher gear, and she chastised herself, determined not to let him know how much he rattled her.

He opened the door that led to the outside and stood back to let Emily go through first.

"So, what's up?" he asked.

Praying that her voice wouldn't give away her nervousness, Emily explained her theory about the possibility of one of the security guards being the rapist as she walked Jim Keegan down to the back campus parking lot.

He was silent for a few minutes after she finished talking. They arrived at his car—a battered silver Chevy—and he leaned against the door and just looked down at her from his intimidating height. Somehow, she managed to hold her own, calmly meeting his eyes. Somehow, she managed not to blush under his scrutiny.

"I'm going to let you in on a little secret," he finally said. "Meyers and I came up with that same idea just yesterday." His blue eyes became even more serious. "You can't talk about this with *anyone,* okay?"

She nodded, her own eyes wide.

"That meeting we just held?" the detective continued. "It was a setup. We're not going to have our patrols and our stakeout teams in the places we planned to have 'em. Instead, we're going to send out decoys in the areas we told campus security that we *weren't* going to be tonight. If this son of a bitch *is* working for the campus security, and if he decides to have some of his twisted idea of fun tonight, we have a good chance of nailing the bastard."

"That's an awful lot of ifs," Emily said.

"Yeah, I know." Keegan reached up to rub the back of his neck, as if it ached.

"Is there anything I can do to help?"

"Yeah," he said, pushing himself up and off his car and aiming the full intensity of his neon blue gaze at her. "Stay in your room and lock your doors and windows. Until we catch this bozo, you—and every other woman on campus—are not safe. Don't forget that, Emily."

He reached forward to push a stray lock of her long brown hair off her face. Emily stepped backward, startled by the heat of his touch, and then embarrassed that she had reacted so obviously. But Jim looked away, as if he were embarrassed, too, and murmured an apology. He stared down at his boots, scuffing them slightly in the dust of the parking lot.

"Remember what we know about this guy," he said, glancing back at her. "He's partial to brunettes. And we think he stalks his victims. We think he picks them out in advance, then follows them around to get their schedule, to find a time they're regularly alone and vulnerable. If you get the sensation that someone's tailing you, don't ignore it, okay?"

Emily nodded, unable to keep from smiling slightly. "That's *my* speech, remember?" she said. "I've just spent the past two weeks visiting all the floors of all the dorms, saying those exact words."

Keegan smiled, too, a quick flash of white teeth. "Yeah, I know." His smile faded. "It's just... if this guy *is* somebody we've all been working with, he might get a real perverse kick out of hurting somebody like you—you know, one of the women on the student committee. And I'm afraid, 'cause you... I don't know... you really stand out in the crowd, you know?"

Emily had to laugh. "Me?" she said in disbelief. "I don't think so. Kirsty Conlon or Megan West, maybe. They're always the center of attention. Not me. I don't get noticed, not the way they do."

"What, you think bouncing around the room and monopolizing the conversation is the only way to get noticed?" Jim asked, almost fiercely. "You're wrong. Because I noticed you. I noticed you the first time you walked into that meeting room."

Emily felt her pulse skip a beat. He'd noticed her. This grown man, this real-life hero, this undercover cop, with a body to die for and the face of a movie star, had noticed *her.* But she was quick to scoff at her reaction to his flattering words. Because they were surely just that—flattery. He'd probably said similar things to Kirsty and Megan and all the other girls who followed him around, fluttering their eyelashes at him.

But his next words surprised her.

"I can't believe you're only a freshman," he said, looking down at his boots again, talking almost as if to himself. "You seem so much older than the other girls." He glanced up at Emily, his eyes frank and honest. "You know, if you were a senior, I would've asked you out. Hell, if you were a *sophomore,* I would've.... But a *freshman...*" He shook his head in disgust, as if being a freshman were her fault.

"What makes you think I'd go out with you?" Emily asked.

"When I first noticed you," he said frankly, "I also noticed that you noticed me, too."

"You're outrageously self-confident, Detective," she said, crossing her arms, determined not to let him see how his words were making her heart pound.

"You're outrageously pretty," he countered.

Her heart leapt higher, but then reality intervened. Inwardly Emily rolled her eyes. More blatant flattery. She knew darn well what she looked like. Sure, she had pretty eyes. And her hair was an exceptional shade of brown. But there was nothing special about her face, nothing that made her qualify as outrageously anything.

Keegan leaned back against his car again, looking for all the world as if he were preparing to stay right there, flirting with her, all afternoon long.

The man's smile was way too charming, and his eyes seemed to hold a warmth and an intimacy that implied that she was the only woman in the world worthy of his attention. Emily knew that couldn't possibly be true. Still, the heat in his eyes was intoxicating. She could get addicted very easily—she was already wondering when the next task force meeting would be, when she'd next see James Keegan. That, combined with the fact that she had discovered she truly liked the detective's open honesty, not to mention that mysterious sadness in his eyes, could be very dangerous. If she stayed here, talking to him much longer, she would develop a full-fledged crush on the man. Assuming, of course, that she hadn't developed one already.

"Didn't you say you were already late?" she asked him. "You better get going."

"Yeah, I should," Jim said. He unlocked his car door. "Hop in."

Her surprise must have shown on her face, because he laughed.

"Don't worry, I'm not trying to kidnap you," he said. "I'm just not about to leave you all alone out here in this parking lot."

Emily looked around. It was broad daylight. Of course, three of the seventeen rapes had occurred during the day—one of them in the back seat of the victim's car, in the north campus parking lot. She shivered. And climbed into Jim Keegan's sedan.

"Thanks," she said.

"My pleasure," he said, with his quick grin.

He drove her the quarter mile back to the main campus building and pulled over to the sidewalk. She started to open the door, but he reached out and held her arm.

"You know, I was serious about what I said before," he told her. "About wanting to ask you out."

Emily didn't know how to answer, so she said nothing.

"I was wondering—" Jim stopped, then shook his head and laughed. "This is going to sound really stupid, but... can I call you? In about a year or two?"

He was still holding her arm, and Emily gently pulled herself free. "You're right," she said, getting out of the car. "That *does* sound really stupid."

But in the end, Emily thought, closing her eyes as she lay on the lounge chair on her tiny deck, *she* had been the stupid one. Seven years of hindsight made that more than clear.

From inside the apartment, she heard the faint sound of the doorbell ringing, but she didn't open her eyes. She wasn't expecting Jim for another few hours, and she didn't feel like talking to anyone right now, not even Carly. Maybe especially not Carly.

But the bell rang again, and then again, and Emily pushed herself to her feet and went inside. Carly had probably seen her car in the parking lot. She knew Emily was home, and she wasn't going to give up until they talked.

With a sigh, Emily opened the front door.

"I *thought* you were home," Alex said, with his smooth, charming smile. He leaned against the doorframe. "I didn't wake you, did I?"

What was he doing here? Emily's heart was in her throat as she stared at him, and she swallowed, trying to push it back down where it belonged. Just because Alex was here, that didn't mean that he knew she'd gone to the police. Just because he was here, that didn't mean that he suspected her of anything. As long as she kept her cool and acted normally...

· "No, not really," Emily said, trying to keep her voice even. "I was sitting out on the deck, thinking about dozing off."

"Mind if I come in for a minute?"

Yes. "No, of course not," she said, stepping back to let him into her apartment. "Can I get you something to drink? A glass of iced tea? Some wine? A beer?" Good grief, she sounded like a waitress. If she didn't relax, he *was* going to get suspicious.

"Actually," Alex said, "I can't stay long."

Thank God.

"I just came by to give you this," he continued, taking a slim black jeweler's box from the inside pocket of his suit jacket. He held it out to her with a smile. "I saw it when I was out at lunch, and it made me think of you, so I gave in to the urge to be self-indulgent." He wiggled the box. "Open it."

Emily slowly took the box from him. It was heavy, and it felt cool in her hands. Why was he doing this? He'd never bought her anything before. Was he using this expensive gift as an excuse to drop by, to see how much of his conversation with Vincent "the Shark" Marino she'd overheard?

But he was smiling at her, and his smile seemed genuine enough.

Of course, this was a man who was a suspected drug smuggler. Was *anything* he did or said genuine?

"Go on. Open it," Alex said again.

Emily slowly opened the box.

It was a necklace. It had a simple yet substantial gold chain with a single enormous sapphire pendant in an equally simple setting. It was elegant, and it had surely cost Alex a small fortune.

But what had it cost the people he made his money off of? What had it cost the addicts and the kids looking for a kick, for a high, or for a quick fix for their poverty and depression? How many people had had their lives ruined, how many people had overdosed and died, in order for Alex to be rich enough to buy her this necklace?

"I can't... I can't accept this," Emily said. No way was she going to wear this necklace. No way could she put this piece of gold, bought with Alex's tainted money, next to her skin.

"Sure you can," Alex said. "It's nothing, really."

Emily closed the box with a snap and held it out to him. "I'm sorry," she said. "I'm just... I'm not comfortable accepting this. It's not appropriate."

Alex laughed. "Oh, come on."

"I'm serious, Alex," she said. "I'm not dating you so that you'll buy me expensive jewelry." *I'm dating you so that I can help the police get the evidence they need to put you in jail, where you belong.*

"Think of this necklace as an apology," Alex said. "I thought maybe my conversation with Vincent Marino upset you, and I wanted to say I was sorry about that."

Panic. For one mind-numbing instant, Emily was frozen with fear. He knew. Alex knew she'd been out in the corridor, eavesdropping. But he was still smiling at her. He wouldn't look so calm, so confident, if he thought she knew about his illegal activities, would he?

"Vincent *who?*" she asked, playing dumb, praying he would buy it. "Alex, I'm not sure what you're talking about. I wasn't upset at all last night."

His smile broadened. "Well, good. My mistake. Keep the necklace anyway."

She wanted him to leave, but she wanted him to take the damned necklace with him. If he left it, he'd wonder why she didn't wear it tomorrow night at the country club. And she wouldn't wear it. She *couldn't*.

"I can't accept this," she said, forcing it into his hand. "People will get the wrong idea."

He laughed again, but this time with good-natured resignation. "Can't it be an early birthday present?"

"My birthday's not till October," Emily said. "Even then, it's too expensive a gift. It's just not appropriate."

Alex slipped the box back into his jacket pocket. "Well, then, I'll hold on to it until it *is* appropriate," he said. "Is that okay?"

He'd be holding on to the necklace until hell froze over. And that was just fine with her. Emily nodded.

"I've got a dinner meeting I need to get to," Alex said. "I'll see you tomorrow night."

Emily nodded again.

He stepped toward her, and she turned away, afraid he was going to kiss her goodbye. But then she was even more afraid that he would wonder why she didn't kiss him. She leaned forward and lightly brushed her lips against his, praying that her revulsion wouldn't show.

"See you tomorrow," she said lightly, opening the door.

And then he was gone, leaving behind only a trace of his expensive cologne.

Emily locked the door behind him. She turned the dead bolt and fastened the safety chain.

She went into the kitchen and dug through the cabinet underneath the sink until she found a spray can of disinfectant. Then she sprayed the living room until the last of Alex's scent was wiped clean from the air.

Chapter 4

Jim Keegan sat and stared at the computer screen on his desk. In real life, Emily Marshall's brother, Daniel, was an astronomy professor. She couldn't remember what she'd told Alexander Delmore about her brother, so Jim was taking this crash course on the computer in basic astronomy. He was learning the lingo so that he wouldn't look stupid—or suspiciously unscientific—when someone mentioned pulsars or red dwarf stars or God only knows what else.

He glanced at his watch. He was supposed to show up at Emily's in less than three hours. Three hours to learn ten years' worth of facts and theories. Jim was known as something of a quick study, but he wasn't *that* quick.

No, he was just going to have to pray that Alexander Delmore knew even less about the universe than he did.

Still, he dragged the cursor back up to the explanation of a black hole, and tried to concentrate. A black hole was a collapsed star with such an intense gravitational field that everything around it was irresistibly sucked toward it. Even light couldn't escape its pull.

Jim shook his head. He knew all about irresistible pulls. He'd experienced one himself, seven years ago.

He had been well aware that he should stay away from Emily Marshall. He had been well aware that she was too young, too sweet, too damn *nice*, for a man like him. And after they caught and locked up that bastard who had raped all those college girls, Jim *had* stayed away from Emily—for all of two weeks.

But, just like a stray beam of light bouncing around the universe, he'd found himself constantly pulled in the direction of the irresistible black hole that was the university—and Emily.

One evening, he found himself standing outside her dorm. When he realized where he was, he tried to tell himself that he had no idea what he was doing there, that it surely was a coincidence that he'd ended up on that particular street in this particular part of town.

But the more pragmatic side of him knew that his excuses were a load of bull. He'd come to the university campus for one reason and one reason only—to see Emily.

He could have flashed his police badge to get past the guard at the high-rise dorm's security checkpoint. But he wasn't here on official police business, so he used one of the telephones in the lobby and dialed Emily's room. As the phone rang, he half prayed that she was in, half prayed that she wasn't.

"Hello?"

She was in.

Jim cleared his throat. "Uh, yeah, Emily?" he said. "This is Jim Keegan. How ya doin'?"

There was a brief pause, the tiniest of hesitations. Then: "Fine." Emily's voice was musical, even over the telephone wires. "What can I do for you, Detective?"

"You can start by calling me Jim," he said.

"Jim," Emily repeated. "Thanks for calling that night— my roommate gave me the message that you called to say you caught the rapist. I was glad to hear that he was off the streets."

"You never called me back," Jim said.

There was another pause. "I was going to," Emily said. "In about a year or two."

Jim laughed. "Touché," he said. "Look, I'm in the lobby of your dorm. You want to come down? We could go get something to eat."

"I already had dinner," she said.

"We could get dessert then," he said. "Or, I don't know—a cup of coffee?" All of a sudden, he was positive that she was going to turn him down. "You're still on the student safety committee, aren't you?"

"Yes, but—"

"There are some things I'd like to talk about, if you've got the time," Jim said. It wasn't the truth, but he would have said damn near anything to get a chance to see her again.

There was another brief pause.

"All right," Emily finally said. "I'll be down in a few minutes."

He leaned on the edge of the security desk for nearly twenty minutes before he saw Emily come out of one of the elevators. She smiled as she walked toward him, and his heart started beating so damn hard he was sure the security guard could hear it.

She looked fabulous. She was wearing a pair of faded jeans and a turquoise T-shirt that hugged her slender curves. Her long chestnut hair was shiny and loose around her shoulders, and she wore very little makeup—just a touch of lipstick and some blush on her cheeks. Her eyes were the color of the ocean.

She walked with the poise of a much older woman. But she was only eighteen. He'd have to remember that. She was just a kid.

"How're your classes going?" he asked as they went out the doors into the early evening. In Florida, November nights were still soft and warm. The sidewalks were alive with people out for fresh air.

"Great," she said, smiling up at him as they began to walk.

Her skin was soft and smooth looking, and her features were delicate, almost fragile. Her freckle-covered nose tipped up a tiny bit at the end, and her chin was a touch too pointy, making her look slightly elfin. She was gorgeous— an incredible mix of woman and girl, of sophistication and innocence. The woman in her was emphasized by the peaceful calm of her lovely blue eyes.

Jim took her arm and pulled her out of the stream of pedestrian traffic.

"I lied," he said bluntly. "I didn't come here to talk about the student safety committee. I came because I wanted..."

He couldn't find the right words. Why *had* he come? Because he wanted to see her again? But he didn't just want to see her. He didn't just want to talk to her. He wanted...

"What?" she breathed, looking up into his eyes.

Jim realized he was still holding her arm. He realized he was standing close enough to breathe in her sweet, fresh scent, close enough to feel the heat from her body, close enough to kiss her....

He bent his head, drawn irresistibly toward the tantalizing sweetness of her lips. But he made himself stop, a whisper away from a kiss, giving her a chance to pull away, to pull back. But she didn't move. She didn't use the opportunity to escape. She simply looked up at him, her lips parted breathlessly, a spark of anticipation, of excitement, in her eyes.

So he kissed her. Right there, on the sidewalk in front of the university dorm.

He didn't intend for it to be anything but a sweet kiss, a gentle kiss—a single kiss. But one kiss wasn't enough, and he kissed her again. And again. He pulled her against him, and the softness of her body made him crazy, and he forgot all about gentle and sweet. He ran his tongue along her lips and, God help him, she opened her mouth to him, granting him access, inviting him in.

It wasn't an invitation he needed to be given more than once.

Jim felt her fingers in his hair as he drank her in. He kissed her again and again, long, hard, deep kisses that made the world spin dizzily around him and made the air suddenly thin and hard to breathe.

He might have gone on kissing her for hours, days—hell, even *weeks*—but she pulled back. She was breathing as hard as he was, and her beautiful eyes were nearly molten with desire as she gazed up at him.

Her voice shook slightly as she spoke. "Does this mean you don't want to wait a year or two before you ask me out?"

Jim had had to laugh. With hindsight, he knew that was the exact moment he'd fallen in love with Emily. But at the time, he hadn't recognized the sensation. All he'd known was that she made him smile, that she took the edge off all the pain he carried around with him day in and day out.

Jim stared blindly at the definition of a nebula that was displayed on his computer screen.

He'd never told Emily that he loved her. Not even that one wonderful, exhilarating, *terrifying* weekend they'd spent together, that weekend he'd lost all control and made love to her. He'd never told her, never said the words.

He couldn't. Because if she'd known, she wouldn't have let him walk away from her without a fight. She would've known that the cruel things he'd said to her were said out of fear and pain.

Jim shut the power on his computer down, then went to pack up the things he would need over the course of the next two weeks.

Two weeks that would be spent with a woman who had
every reason to hate him.

What had Lieutenant Bell called this investigation? Quick
and easy? Yeah, right. This was going to be as quick and
easy as a canoe trip around the world . . . without a paddle.

Emily woke up drenched with sweat, with the setting sun
glaring in her face. She pushed herself up from the deck
chair, slid open the glass door and went inside. The living
room was cool and dark, and as she closed the sliding door
behind her she shut out the noise of the traffic and the rau-
cous cries of the seabirds that wheeled overhead. The steady
hum of the air conditioner joined with the gentle throbbing
of her refrigerator, making her apartment seem like some
kind of environmentally controlled spaceship, detached and
separate, independent and remote from the rest of the
planet.

Emily went around the corner into the small galley
kitchen and opened the refrigerator. She poured herself a
large glass of seltzer, and drank it thirstily as she glanced at
the clock on the wall.

It was 5:38.

Jim Keegan would be arriving in less than an hour.

She pushed her sweat-soaked hair back from her face and
searched her cabinets for an aspirin. She didn't have a
headache yet, but she could feel a real doozy coming on.

Of course, it wasn't too late to call off her participation
in the investigation.

Emily poured herself another glass of seltzer and drank
this one more slowly, swallowing the extra-strength aspirin
tablets with the first sip.

What if she had guessed wrong about Alex Delmore?
What if she had misunderstood his conversation with Vincent Marino? What if Alex really had been out fishing in the
dinghy that morning? What if he was innocent? He had
acted innocent enough an hour ago, when he dropped by.

But if he *was* innocent, what was he doing socializing with one of Florida's most powerful mob bosses? And Emily *hadn't* misunderstood that conversation. She knew exactly what she'd overheard. And, come to think of it, why would Alex have bothered to take the dinghy if he wanted to fish? Why wouldn't he simply have done his fishing from the deck of the *Home Free?*

No. Something odd was going on, and her every instinct screamed that Alex was involved.

If she backed out of this investigation now, she'd always wonder how much crack Alex had brought into Florida during the time wasted because she refused to cooperate with the authorities. She'd wonder how many people—how many *kids*—died from drug overdoses, from heart attacks, from knife fights over possession of those drugs.

How many kids would die because *she* was too chicken to spend a little time with Jim Keegan?

This was good, Emily realized, grabbing this course of reasoning as if it were a lifeline. Thinking this way would help her stop focusing on the awfulness of her situation.

True, working with Jim Keegan would be terrible, because she'd be forced to face the embarrassment of knowing that he'd once played her for a fool. She would have to face the fact that she had misjudged him so absolutely, that seven years ago she hadn't really known him at all. True, she'd have to face the constant reminder of the pain he had caused her. And, true, she'd be forced to confront her own stupidity every time she looked into Jim's blue eyes and felt her heart *still* leap and her pulse *still* kick into double time.

But maybe, Emily thought, just *maybe*, it was also true that spending the next two weeks with Jim Keegan would be a good thing. Aside from the fact that helping with the investigation could save lives, maybe two weeks of close, day-to-day contact with this man would be helpful to her. Maybe it would help her see the real Jim Keegan—the same Jim

Keegan who had lashed out at her so cruelly all those years ago....

Emily closed her eyes, remembering with stark accuracy the night she and Jim had broken up. It had been April, early spring, only about three weeks after he was released from the hospital. It had been only three *days* after she went to his apartment, looking for him—and ended up staying overnight. They'd made love for the first time that weekend....

Emily shook her head, unwilling to let herself remember the way he'd touched her, kissed her, *loved* her—and left her. *That* was what she had to remember. Not quite three days after they made love, he had left her for good.

It had been a Wednesday night, and Emily had been standing outside her dorm. She'd been ready for their date a little early, so she'd gone down to the front of the building so that Jim wouldn't have to come inside to get her.

But he was late. Fifteen minutes. Then thirty. She went inside to use the pay phone, but there was no answer at his apartment. He hadn't even left his answering machine on. She called her own machine, checking to see if he'd called to tell her that he'd be late. But there was nothing. No message.

After another fifteen minutes, Emily was well past worried. It wasn't unusual for him to be late, but he'd always left messages before—either on her machine or wherever they were planning to meet. Refusing to think about hospitals or gunshot wounds or the growing number of city police officers who had been shot dead on the streets over the past few years, she walked briskly to the sports bar on the corner, where they had been planning to go that evening. Maybe he'd left a message for her there. Maybe he wasn't lying in some pool of blood somewhere. Maybe—

Jim was there.

He was there, sitting at the bar.

With his arm around a pretty dark-haired woman who had to be wearing the shortest skirt Emily had ever seen in her life. Disbelief flooded through her.

She must have made some sort of sound, because Jim turned toward her. He looked surprised to see her at first. But then he laughed.

He actually *laughed*.

She knew she should turn and walk away. But she was a fool. She just stood there and stared at him, thinking that there must be some mistake....

"What are *you* doing here?" he asked. The woman he had his arm around peered curiously over his shoulder at her.

Emily couldn't speak. She just looked at him, unable to move.

He sighed heavily and turned back to the dark-haired woman. "Don't go anywhere, babe," he said, and kissed her. On the lips. Then he slid off the bar stool and walked toward Emily.

Jim staggered once before he reached her. He laughed again, as if his inability to walk a straight line was something he found funny. He stank of whiskey as he walked past Emily, motioning for her to follow him.

She walked woodenly behind him, out the main entrance and onto the sidewalk in front of the bar.

"What'd I do? Mess up the dates again?" Jim asked, turning to face her. "I thought we were on for tomorrow night."

Emily shook her head no. And suddenly, through all the disbelief, through the hurt and pain of having seen him with that other woman, came waves of relief. At least he wasn't dead. At least he wasn't lying in some ambulance, racing to the hospital while the paramedics tried to keep his heart from pumping his blood out of a bullet hole in his chest....

Thank God.

"What did you say?" Jim asked, his eyes narrowing slightly.

Emily realized she must have spoken out loud.

Her eyes filled with tears as she looked up at him. "I thought you'd been shot again," she said, her voice shaking. "I thought you were dead."

"Oh, God," he said, recoiling as if she had hit him, turning away, covering his face with his hands. But he turned back almost instantly, his eyes flashing with anger, his face nearly contorted with rage.

"I'm *worse* than dead, damn it!" he shouted. "So stay the *hell* away from me!"

He moved toward her. His anger and his sheer size were menacing, frightening, but Emily stood her ground. If there was one thing, and only one thing, that she could hold on to as a truth in all this insanity, it was that, drunk or sober, Jim Keegan would *never* hit her.

"I don't understand," she said. "What are you doing? I love you. And I thought—"

"You were wrong," he said, backing away when he realized that she wasn't going to be the one to move. "Whatever you thought, you were *wrong,* damn it!" He lowered his voice. "Yeah, it's been fun, and last weekend was a blast, but— You don't *really* think that I've slept alone every night since we started dating in November, do you? Get real, kid...."

The shock of his words overcame her relief, and Emily turned and ran.

Last weekend was a blast.

Emily had let him touch her in ways that she'd never let a man touch her before. She'd given herself to him, heart, body and soul. But to Jim, it had merely been "a blast."

She had heard the expression "Love is blind" a hundred times in the past, but before that night she'd never experienced the phenomenon firsthand.

Love was, indeed, blind. She had seen Jim Keegan as some kind of superhero, some kind of perfect man. She'd seen someone tender, someone kind and sensitive, someone she thought loved her as much as she loved him.

Wrong.

Seven years ago, her imagination had obviously clouded her vision.

But now there was nothing to keep her from seeing James Keegan clearly. Over the next few weeks, she would have an opportunity that most women never had...she would be able to see, *really* see, this man that she had once loved so desperately. She'd get a chance to see, firsthand, that he wasn't the perfect man she'd once thought he was. She'd have a chance to dissolve the superhero myth that still surrounded him in her dreams, despite the way he had treated her that awful night. She'd be face-to-face with the real man—the insensitive, selfish, impolite *bastard* that he truly was. And maybe then she'd stop longing for the sound of his laughter and the warmth of his touch. Maybe then, finally, she'd be free.

The doorbell rang as Emily was stepping out of the shower. She quickly dried herself and slipped into a terrycloth bathrobe. On the way to the door, she glanced at the clock. It was only quarter of. It figured that Jim Keegan would be early. It figured that he'd catch her wearing only her bathrobe—

She stopped short, halfway across the living room.

Oh, brother, if she answered the door in her bathrobe, what was he going to think? Stupid question. She knew exactly what he was going to think, and it wouldn't be good.

"Hey, Emily, open up! I know you're home—I saw your car in the lot!" a voice called from the other side of the door.

But the voice didn't belong to Jim Keegan. It was Carly's voice.

Emily opened the door to her neighbor's familiar face and shining... *blond* curls?

"What d'ya think?" Carly asked, needing no invitation to come inside. She turned, posing like a model on a fashion runway, snowing off her new hair color in the middle of Emily's living room.

Carly Wilson, thrice divorced before the tender age of twenty-nine, rarely stood still. And when she *was* standing still, it was usually because she was laughing too hard to move.

Carly had moved into the apartment down the hall from Emily not quite a year ago—after her most recent divorce. At the time, the diminutive woman had had thick, straight, nearly jet-black hair. Since then, she'd gone through a wide variety of perms and cuts and hair colors, the most recent being a not-quite-believable shade of red.

Carly was, of all things, a librarian. With her flamboyant wardrobe and her ever-changing hair color, she was far from the stereotype. But she *did* love books. In fact, she claimed to love books even more than she loved men. And that was saying something.

"Blond, huh? It looks good," Emily said, closing the door. "What's the occasion?"

Carly laughed and plopped herself down on the couch. "No occasion," she said, in her low, scratchy voice, which was incongruous with her petite size and cheerleader-cute face. "Just time for a change. Speaking of changing, I caught you fresh out of the shower, didn't I? Don't let me stop you. Go on, get dressed."

"I'll just be a minute," Emily said.

Carly turned, raising her voice so that Emily could hear her even in the bedroom. "You know what triggered this new color?"

"Nope," Emily called back, pulling on fresh underwear. "What?"

"I was out with Mac again on Saturday night," Carly said from the living room. "We went to the Crazy Horse Saloon, 'cause his band was playing there, and during one of their breaks I found out that that man can really dance. And I mean *really*. So he's leading me around the line of dance like some kind of cowboy Fred Astaire, and I suddenly realize that I'm daydreaming about dancing with him at our wedding reception!"

"Uh-oh," Emily said. She brushed out her still-damp hair as she came back into the living room, wearing a clean pair of shorts and T-shirt.

"Uh-oh's right," Carly said, her brown eyes merry with suppressed laughter. "Now, Mac is undeniably good-looking, and I confess he's got the ability to make my poor heart beat twice as hard as it should, but *marriage?* Good Lord, it wouldn't last a month. Three months, tops. And, quite frankly, I can't afford another divorce. So I figured if I wanted a change in my life that badly, I'd skip the wedding and just color my hair and rearrange my living room furniture instead. Besides, in a few more weeks, after old Alex pops the question, I can help you plan *your* wedding, right? I'll get plenty of vicarious thrills that way—no need to suffer through the experience again myself."

Emily stared out the sliding glass door, her good humor suddenly gone. But Carly didn't notice. She chattered on about the new curtains she was thinking about buying for her kitchen windows until the doorbell rang.

Emily turned then, her hairbrush still in her hand. Oh, shoot. This time it had to be James Keegan.

"Are you expecting someone?" Carly asked curiously.

The smaller woman beat Emily to the door and threw it open wide. Even though she couldn't see who was at the door, Emily knew it was Jim simply by the sudden change in the way Carly was standing.

"Well, hel-lo," Carly said. "*Who* are *you?*"

"I'm looking for Emily Marshall," Jim's husky voice replied. "I thought she was in 6B. Am I wrong?"

Emily stepped behind Carly, and Jim's face relaxed into a smile. "Well, hey, Em, how ya doing?" he said. "The directions you gave me from the airport were great."

It was odd—his words and expression were relaxed and friendly, but the message Emily was getting from Jim's eyes was anything but. Who the hell is this, he was silently asking about Carly, and what the hell is she doing here?

"You gonna invite me in?" he asked.

"Please...come in," Emily said, pulling Carly back with her, out of Jim's way.

Jim lugged a duffel bag over the threshold and closed the door behind him. His long hair was pulled back with a rubber band at the nape of his neck, and he was dressed in a pair of khaki pants and a white polo shirt.

Emily realized that she'd rarely seen Jim wear anything besides jeans and a T-shirt, or the sloppy, army-issue shorts he sometimes wore when it got too hot for long pants. Every now and then he'd worn a suit because he had to. Of course, it occurred to her that Jim was undercover right now. He was wearing what he figured her visiting brother might wear—and he was pretty darn accurate. Except Danny never looked so good in *his* Dockers.

Jim slid a gym bag off his shoulder and onto the floor next to the duffel bag and turned toward Emily. Before she realized what he was doing, he'd put his arms around her.

"It's been a long time," he said, pulling her in close to him.

Damn, she smelled great. She still used the same sweet-smelling soap when she washed her face. She still used the same brand of shampoo. She still didn't bother to wear perfume. She still smelled young and fresh and achingly lovely. Jim let go of her, fast.

Trying to hide how off balance he felt, he turned to the blond woman and made himself smile. "Hi," he said. "I'm Dan Marshall. I'm Emily's brother."

The blonde held out her hand. "I'm Carly Wilson, Emily's neighbor."

"I'll get some iced tea," Emily said as Carly dragged Jim into the living room.

Jim sat down on a couch with pale floral-patterned upholstery. Emily's apartment was small, smaller than he'd expected—proof that Alexander Delmore wasn't subsidizing her living expenses. He was relieved about that, more relieved than he should have been. What was wrong with him? He didn't have any reason to feel jealous of Delmore, and certainly didn't have any reason to feel possessive toward Emily. Seven years was a long time.

As Carly gave him a detailed narrative of exactly when and where she'd met Emily, Jim looked around the place that he was going to be calling home for the next few weeks.

Several framed pictures hung on the white walls. They were photographs—two of the ocean, one of an older man and woman on the front porch of a house, and one of the earth taken from the moon.

There was an entertainment center directly across from the couch, with a small, inexpensive TV and stereo inside a cabinet. A wicker-and-glass coffee table sat in front of the couch. Rows of bookshelves lined one of the other walls. A single rocking chair was the only comfortable place to sit besides the sofa. A small, round dining table and two hard-backed chairs were at the end of the room, in front of a sliding glass door and adjacent to what Jim figured must be the kitchen. He could hear Emily moving around back there, could hear the clink of ice cubes in glasses, the sound of the refrigerator door opening and shutting.

Jim looked up at Carly, suddenly aware that she'd asked him a question. "I'm sorry—?" he said.

"Jet lag, huh?" she said sympathetically. "Where'd you fly in from?"

"Colorado," he lied. "Denver."

"You know, I can really see the family resemblance," Carly said. "It's in your eyes. You're definitely Emily's brother."

Jim looked up as Emily came into the room, carrying three tall glasses. She set them down on the coffee table, then handed one to him. His fingers brushed hers accidentally, but she didn't seem to notice. Hell, he nearly stopped breathing at the slight contact, but she didn't even blink.

Emily offered Carly one of the glasses, but the blond woman shook her head and stood up.

"I'm outa here," Carly said. "You guys have some catching up to do."

"Oh," Emily protested. "You don't have to go...."

"No, no," Carly said. "You don't need me butting in." She smiled at Jim. "Besides, your brother's tired. I'll come back tomorrow, after he's had his rest."

Jim fought the urge to join in with Emily's protests. Having the neighbor there was something of a relief. Having her around meant that he and Emily weren't alone, together, in this tiny apartment. It meant that they wouldn't have to look at each other or talk.

But he knew that Carly's presence would simply put off the inevitable. He and Emily *had* to talk. He had to find out more about her childhood and her parents. He had to find out if Emily remembered what she'd told Alex about her brother.

And, sooner or later, they had to talk about their history. There was no way he could stay here for any length of time without at least *mentioning* their past relationship. It would be too weird.

So he stayed on the couch while Emily walked her friend to the door. He heard them say goodbye. He heard the door close. And then he heard... silence.

Keegan looked up to see Emily pick up her glass of iced tea and sit down across from him in the rocking chair. She met his gaze calmly, and again he felt a stab of frustration. How could she act so cool when just the idea of them alone together was making him sweat bullets?

He covered his discomfort with a smile. "So," he said, "here we are."

She didn't comment. She didn't say anything equally stupid simply to break up this damned silence. She didn't do anything except sip her iced tea. And watch him.

God, she was beautiful. And so damned unaffected by his presence. Jim clenched his teeth.

Emily was holding her glass of iced tea so tightly that her fingers were starting to cramp. She forced herself to loosen her hold and take a sip. She could see the tension in the way Jim was sitting. He was nervous. Well, rightly so. He *should* be nervous. Seven years ago he'd taken advantage of a young girl's trust and love. Quite frankly, he'd used her in the most blatant and obvious way. He'd treated her abysmally.

It was clear that he had never imagined he'd see her again, let alone be forced to occupy the same space for anything longer than a few brief, embarrassment-tinged moments.

She gazed at him, not having to bother to ask herself the timeworn question *What had she seen in him?* She knew exactly what she'd seen in him—she was looking straight at it. Thick honey-brown hair that waved around a lean, handsome face that could have made a fortune on a movie screen. Dark blue eyes surrounded by thick black lashes, a slightly bent, very masculine nose, and a million-dollar smile—although he wasn't smiling now, was he? Still, smiling or frowning, James Keegan was outrageously attractive.

And that was just his face. His body was more of the same story. He looked like he might have put on a few pounds over the past seven years, but they were all pounds put on in the right places. His stomach was still flat, and his hips were still slim and his legs... Yeah. He was in even better shape than he'd been in at age twenty-five.

He cleared his throat, clearly ill at ease. "We've got a lot of ground to cover here," he said, reaching into his back pocket for a small notepad. "Where do you want to start?"

Emily leaned forward slightly to put her glass down on the coffee table. "Where do you want me to start? With Danny? My parents? Our house in Connecticut?"

"How about we start with Delmore?" Jim suggested, flipping to a blank page in his pad.

Her eyes met his suddenly, a startling flash of blue in the grayness of the rapidly dimming room.

"Alex," she said.

"Yeah," Jim said. "Your boyfriend."

Emily crossed her legs with a sudden quick movement. That, and a slight flaring of her nostrils, were the only signs that he had touched a nerve. And he wanted to touch a nerve, he realized suddenly. He wanted her to be as rattled as he was. He wanted to see some kind of evidence that she had missed him these past seven years as goddamned badly as he had missed her. Had she cried the way he had? Had she ached just from wanting to see him, the way he had for her?

He'd imagined her so many times, walking on the beach, staring out at the ocean, feeling so utterly alone and lost— the way he'd felt without her. But he'd also imagined her finding some nice safe guy and settling down. *Settling,* that was the key word. He'd imagined Emily settling for someone else, but still wanting *him.*

"Alex is a little old to call a *boyfriend,* don't you think?" Emily said.

"Maybe we should call him...your lover." Jim added just the slightest tinge of nastiness to his voice. He was needling her on purpose. There was no way she could have missed it.

But she didn't react. No intake of breath, no flicker of her eyes, no tension in her shoulders. She just looked at him. And then she smiled.

"Alex Delmore and I dated," she said quietly. "That's all you need to know, Detective. Anything else isn't your business."

What the hell did that smile mean? It was as if she were keeping score, and she'd just won a point.

Jim reached forward and took a healthy slug of his iced tea, trying hard to keep his cosmic balance. He put the glass back on the tabletop with just a little too much force, and it made a loud noise in the room's silence.

"Mind if we turn on a light in here?" he asked.

Emily shook her head, standing up in one graceful motion and crossing to a halogen lamp.

"Also, you better get used to calling me Dan," Jim added, squinting slightly as the bright light seemed to fill the room. "Or Danny, or whatever you call your brother."

"Danny," Emily said, moving back to the rocking chair and sitting down again. "But he calls himself Dan now."

"I need you to try to remember what you might have told Delmore about your brother," he said. "Any little mention, anything he might remember."

Emily chewed thoughtfully on her lower lip. "You know, I don't know if I've ever even mentioned my brother to Alex," she said. "I guess I must've. We've talked about Guilford, where my parents still live—you know, in Connecticut—so I must've mentioned Danny. But only vaguely. Like, 'I have only one brother, no sisters. My brother lives in New Mexico. He's an astronomy professor.'"

Keegan's eyebrows slid upward. "That's it?" he asked, in obvious disbelief.

Emily shrugged. "Alex and I really haven't talked that much," she said.

"I'll bet," Jim muttered under his breath. If she heard him, she gave no sign, except for another of those damned smiles.

They worked for close to two hours, going through Dan Marshall's background, and the details of Emily's childhood home in Connecticut. A little after nine o'clock, Jim rubbed his hands across his face and stretched.

"I gotta stop," he said. "I'm losing my concentration. I'm sorry, but I pulled a double shift last night—I haven't slept more than two hours in the past forty-eight. Mind if we finish this up tomorrow?"

Emily shook her head. "The couch pulls out into a bed," she said. "There are sheets and a pillow in the linen closet. A blanket, too, but it's pretty hot—you probably won't need one. Feel free to use the shower."

"Thanks," he said.

He looked down at all the notes he'd taken, and cleared his throat. "I know..." he said hesitantly, his voice huskier than usual. He stopped, then started again. "This has got to be difficult for you. Working with me, I mean." He looked up and forced himself to meet her steady gaze. "Especially with me living here like this."

Emily was silent for a moment. Then she shook her head. "No," she said with a small smile, "actually it's not that bad."

Jim couldn't hide his disbelief. He stared at her, and exhaled shortly—a quick burst of doubt that under other circumstances might have been called a laugh. "You're kidding," he said flatly.

Again she shook her head. "No."

"You don't hate me?"

If she was at all surprised by the directness of his words, she didn't show it. She *did* consider his question carefully, though.

"No," she said finally, as if the answer were as surprising to her as it was to him. "I don't. It's true that I dislike you, but dislike is different from hate. Hate's much too strong a word.'' She stood up. ''If we're done for tonight, I'm going to run out to the grocery store. I have a couple things I need to get. Want anything?''

Keegan shook his head. He felt oddly dizzy. Emily didn't hate him. She only *disliked* him. Somehow that was worse. ''No,'' he said, realizing suddenly that she was waiting for an answer to her question. ''No thanks.''

Emily picked up her keys and went out the door, closing it firmly behind her. It wasn't until she was down in the parking lot and sitting in her car that her knees began to shake.

God help her, she was such a liar. She didn't know *what* she felt for Jim Keegan, but it sure wasn't the cool indifference she'd pretended to feel. She wanted to feel indifferent, though. She wanted to be able to look at Jim and feel only mild distaste, not this...jumble of emotions, this mishmash of intense feelings.

She took a deep breath, and then another, and another. She'd seen glimpses of what she assumed must be the real James Keegan tonight. Rude, arrogant, selfish, impatient, conniving...the list went on and on. She was noticing all the imperfections and flaws that she hadn't been able to see when she was dazzled by his rugged good looks and the kind gentleness that she knew had to have been an act.

After two weeks of eye-opening reality, she *would* feel nothing but cool indifference toward him.

Wouldn't she?

Chapter 5

Emily woke up at eight-thirty, and got dressed before she left her bedroom.

But when she opened her door, the rest of her apartment was quiet. Too quiet. She ventured down the hallway and peeked into the living room.

The pullout mattress was back inside the couch, and the sheets that Jim had used were folded in a neat pile on the coffee table. His bags were out of the way, in the corner of the room, and he was nowhere in sight.

The kitchen was just as empty, but there was a note for her out on the counter.

"Emily," Jim had printed in his big, bold handwriting, "I went out for a run. I'll be back before nine." He'd started to sign the note "Jim," but had crossed out the *J* and signed it "Dan" instead, underlining the name twice for emphasis.

His handwriting was so familiar. It brought back a barrage of memories so intense that Emily had to sit down.

Over the course of the five months they had dated, Jim must've left her a hundred little notes like this one. Sometimes the notes had been tacked to the corkboard on her dorm room door. And sometimes he'd sent them through the mail, on silly postcards or even just scraps of paper stuffed into a business envelope. Often she'd opened her mailbox to find more than one envelope with her name and address printed on the front in Jim's neat block letters. She'd opened them to find clippings from newspapers or magazine articles he thought she might be interested in, along with a quick note. Sometimes he'd only send a note, and sometimes it would be only one line. But no matter what he said or what he sent, the message had been clear—Jim Keegan had been thinking about her.

So how did his thoughtfulness fit into the picture now?

Instead of being part of the softer side of a tough man, all those notes had probably just been another way Jim manipulated her into trusting him. And, boy, it had worked, hadn't it?

The fact was, he'd dumped her only days after he got her into bed with him. It seemed safe to assume that, therefore, his sole goal in courting her had been to have sex with her.

When you looked at it *that* way, then yes, all those wonderful little notes did seem nasty and manipulative.

Emily stared down at the paper she was holding in her hand. But what about *this* note? There was nothing manipulative about this one. He had nothing to gain by telling her where he'd gone and when he'd be back. It was simple consideration.

She crumpled it up and threw it in the trash. So what? Even an ax murderer could be considerate now and then, she thought sourly.

The front door opened slowly, and Emily looked up.

Jim poked his head around the edge of the door, saw her, then stepped into the room.

"You're up," he said.

He was wearing a pair of running shorts and a muscle shirt that had more armhole to it than shirt. His skin—and there was so much of it showing—glistened with sweat, and his hair clung damply to his neck and the sides of his face.

He was carrying a white paper bag, and he brought it into the kitchen and put it on the counter. "Breakfast," he explained, with an uncertain smile. "I picked up some bagels at that place down on the corner. You ever go there? It's called Stein's. I walked in and, you know, I thought I was back in New York City."

As he talked, he poured water into Emily's coffeemaker and searched the cabinets for filters. He found them on his second try, then opened the refrigerator and grabbed the can of coffee.

"You want more than one cup?" he turned to Emily to ask.

She was watching him, eyebrows slightly raised, and he stopped. "Um . . ." he said, "you mind if I . . . you know, make some coffee?"

Emily shook her head. "No," she said. "As long as you don't mind chipping in to help pay for the beans. Or whatever else you use."

"Of course," he said.

"Then, by all means," she said, "make yourself at home."

He smiled sheepishly. "I already was," he admitted.

"I noticed," Emily said. But then she smiled. At him.

But it was just a little smile, and it was over nearly as soon as it started. Still, Jim stared at her, momentarily lost in the blueness of her eyes.

He forced himself to turn away, pretending to concentrate on measuring out the scoops of coffee as he regained his equilibrium.

Sure, it was just a little smile, but it *was* a smile. A real smile, not one of those odd smiles she'd given him last night—one of the ones that suggested that she knew some kind of joke and she wasn't going to share the punch line with him.

He pushed the filter into the coffee machine and put the can back in the fridge. As he glanced up, he saw that Emily was still watching him.

"Well," he said, uncomfortable under her steady gaze, "if it's okay with you, I'll take a quick shower while the coffee's brewing, and then we can get back to work."

She nodded. "That's fine."

"Help yourself to the bagels," he said.

Emily watched him walk down the hall to the bathroom. Jeez, he was *still* a hunk and a half. She pulled her eyes away before he could turn around and see her checking out his long, strong legs and his incredibly perfect rear end.

Many men hit their thirties and started losing their hair and developing beer bellies. But not Jim Keegan. No. He had to be one of those men who became more perfect with age. It wasn't fair.

"I'm Dan Marshall," Jim said, looking over his notes. "I'm thirty years old, a professor of astronomy at the College of Santa Fe in New Mexico. I went to Yale for two years, then transferred to the University of New Mexico in Albuquerque, where I got my bachelor's degree. I went to Denver, Colorado, to get my master's, then back to UNM for my doctorate—"

"Have you ever even *been* to Colorado or New Mexico?" Emily asked.

He shook his head no. "I stayed on at UNM for two years, teaching, until I got the offer to head the department in Santa Fe—"

"How can you pretend that you've lived in the Southwest for ten years, when you've never been there even once?"

Jim looked up from his notes and smiled. "I've seen a lot of Westerns," he said.

"I'm serious," Emily said. "Alex's mother lives in Phoenix. And I know that he's been skiing in Colorado, but I don't know exactly where. What if it was near Denver? What if he asks you a question that you can't answer? It won't take much for him to realize you've never been out West."

Jim shrugged. "I'll get by."

Emily was leaning forward slightly, watching him, sitting in the same rocking chair she'd sat in last night. She wasn't wearing much makeup, but her face had that glow that a person could only get from good health and the persistent Florida sunshine. Jim's eyes traveled almost involuntarily down the long, slender lengths of her bare arms and legs. She had one hell of a perfect tan, not too dark, but a delicate golden brown. She sure didn't get that tan from sitting inside, in her living room, all day. She had to be as antsy as he was, as eager to get outside and stretch her legs, work off some of this nervous energy.

Talk about nervous energy. Jim hadn't felt this restless in a long time. Of course, the fact that he'd spent last night only one room away from a woman he'd once felt a powerful and irresistible sexual attraction toward had a lot to do with it. His eyes moved back up Emily's long legs. God, she was gorgeous. She was a knockout, with those killer legs and that body—

Damn, who was he kidding? The attraction he felt wasn't a thing of the past. It was extremely present-tense. It was here and now, and he couldn't deny it. Seven years later, and he *still* lusted after this woman.

But if the attraction was mutual, she sure as hell wasn't showing it.

"You hungry?" he asked her. "I know this great lunch place down by the beach. What do ya say we go get something to eat? My treat." He stood up and put his file of notes into his gym bag. "Come on. It's nearly one-thirty, and I'm starving. This place has the best jerk chicken in the universe." He forced a grin. "And I oughta know. I'm an astronomer, right?"

Emily glanced at her watch. Was it really one-thirty? She hadn't even had breakfast—only a cup of Jim's ridiculously strong coffee. She wasn't hungry, but she stood up anyway. Getting out of the confines of this apartment was a decidedly good idea. "Just let me get my sun hat," she said.

Jim was waiting by the door when she came out of the bedroom. "You wanna take your purse?" he asked.

Emily pretended that she had forgotten her little canvas bag on purpose. "I thought this was going to be your treat," she said.

He smiled. "I thought maybe you'd want your sunglasses."

She knew she hadn't fooled him, and she sighed. "I'm twenty-five years old," she said. "I'm an organized person. I'm relatively neat, and always punctual. Why do I forget my purse all the time?"

"Get a purse that's really heavy," Jim said as they walked down the stairs to the apartment complex's parking lot. "Then you'll notice when it's not hanging on your shoulder. Like, you know, right now I'm really aware that I'm outside without my shoulder holster on. It doesn't feel right. Something's missing, and I know it."

Emily glanced at him. He'd changed out of his shorts when she went to find her hat, she realized. He was wearing long pants and a pair of cowboy boots now, despite the hot weather.

"Are you—"

He finished the question for her. "Carrying? Yeah. I've got a gun in my boot. It's not as easy to get to, but I didn't think it would be believable for your brother to wear a jacket in this weather. And a shoulder holster would look a little funny without a jacket to cover it up." He paused as they left the building's protective awning and walked into the uncovered parking lot. The heat was intense, reflecting off the blacktop and making the air feel thick and suffocating.

"But I've been carrying a weapon for so long, it feels unnatural for me to be without *something*—even a gun in my boot," Jim said, watching as Emily unlocked the door to her little car. "That's how you've got to get with your purse. You've got to feel like it's an essential part of you—that something's missing when you don't feel it there, next to you. You know what I mean?"

"But I hate carrying a purse," Emily said. "I don't *want* it to be an essential part of me."

"Then maybe you *should* get a belt pack," Jim said as he squeezed himself into Emily's subcompact car. He had to recline the seat slightly, and still his knees nearly touched the dashboard. "By the way, *that's* how I do it."

"Do what?" Emily looked away from the rearview mirror to glance at him as she put her car into reverse and backed out of her parking space.

"How I handle questions that I can't answer when I'm undercover," Jim said. "I get around the questions. I answer vaguely, and then I change the subject, like I did with your question. Remember, you asked me what I'd do if Delmore asked me something about Colorado that I couldn't answer, right? I turned around and asked you to lunch."

"Yeah, but what if Alex asks something specific, like have you been to his favorite restaurant in Denver?" Emily said. "Won't he be suspicious if you don't even know what part of town it's in?"

Jim rested his elbow out the open car window as she pulled on to the main road. "I'll say something like 'I didn't get out much when I was living in Denver—not on a teaching assistant's salary.'"

She shot him a skeptical look, and he said, "I'll also do some research. I'll look at city maps, memorize street names, learn the addresses of major attractions . . . and restaurants."

Emily glanced at him again.

"I've gone undercover before," he said, "with much less preparation. I guess I'm just a good liar."

She didn't say a word.

"Take a left up here on Ocean Ave.," Jim said. "You know, I was surprised you live so far from the beach. I thought for sure you'd be within a block or two of the water."

"The only way I could afford to live near the beach was with a roommate," Emily said. "And after all those years of college roommates, I really wanted to live alone."

"I remember you wanted to live in a house *on* the beach," Jim said. "You wanted to be able to roll out of bed, open the blinds and have the ocean be right there, in your face."

Emily laughed, despite her growing discomfort at the easy familiarity of Jim's words. "Yeah, right. Last hurricane season, there was a time or two when the people who owned beachfront property actually *had* the ocean in their faces. Literally."

He was watching her, a smile playing at the corners of his mouth. "You don't really expect me to believe *you'd* be scared away from the beach by a little bad weather."

"No," she admitted. "It was purely a financial decision. If I could afford to live by myself in a place that's on the beach, I would. But, unfortunately, I can't handle a higher rent with my current salary."

"When did you decide to become a teacher?" Jim asked. "You took all those computer courses your freshman year. Weren't you majoring in computer science and business?"

She glanced at him. "Is this more research?"

He was silent for a moment, looking out the window at the rows of fancy condominiums that lined Ocean Avenue. "Yes, I need to know more about you," he finally said, "but no, that wasn't why I asked." He pointed to the public beach's parking lot. "Park here. We can walk to the lunch place."

Emily put on her right blinker and moved carefully into the right lane. Just as carefully, she said, "I'd prefer to continue the type of interview we've been using to give you the information you need to know about my personal life. I'm not comfortable pretending we're old friends chatting and catching up on the past seven years."

She pulled into the parking lot and drove down a long row of cars, looking for an empty space.

"So, what you're saying is, after I get the information I need from you in order to pull off masquerading as your brother, you don't want us to have any other conversations," Jim said. "Is that it?"

Emily glanced at him. His mouth was tight, and he used his left hand to rake his hair back from his face. He wasn't pouting, but maybe if she pushed him, he would start. And she found grown men who pouted extremely unattractive...

"Yes," she replied. "That's what I'm saying."

Ahead of her, a car pulled out of a spot, and she quickly zipped into it. She switched off the motor, took the key from the ignition and turned to look at Jim.

To her surprise, he *wasn't* pouting. Instead, there was very genuine regret in his eyes, and a resigned sadness on his face.

"I'm sorry, Emily," he said quietly. "I'll do my best to respect your wishes."

He smiled at her then—a small, bittersweet smile. Emily could have sworn she saw a sudden glimmer of moisture in his eyes, but he turned away before she got a closer look. He opened the door and hauled his large frame out of the tiny car.

Emily followed him to the lunch stand, where they waited for their sandwich order in subdued silence.

Why couldn't he have pouted? Why couldn't he have been a baby, or acted rudely, or... She would have preferred *anything* to the honest, humble regret she'd seen in his eyes.

"Let's find a picnic table in the shade," Jim said, leading her toward the beach.

Heat waves shimmered over the wide expanse of fine white sand and even over the deep blue-green of the Gulf waters. Emily sat down across from Jim on the bench of a wooden picnic table aged silver-gray by the sun, the wind and the salt air.

She still wasn't hungry, but she unwrapped the chicken sandwich Jim had bought her and took a bite.

"Great stuff, isn't it?" he asked.

Emily nodded. Surprisingly, it was.

"Ready for more questions?" he asked, getting out his little notebook, making their conversation official.

He'd put sunglasses on, and she couldn't see his eyes. She nodded again. "Fire away."

"I pretty much know all the basics," Jim said. "You know, like the year you were born, your middle name, your birthday—"

"You remember my birthday?" Emily was surprised. "And my middle name?"

"October seventeenth, and Sara." Jim smiled. "God, you know, I even remember the name of your favorite elementary school teacher. Mrs. Reiner, fourth grade, right? You used to talk about her all the time."

Emily was staring at him, her sandwich temporarily forgotten. She was frowning, her delicate eyebrows wrinkled in disbelief, her usually clear gaze cloudy with uncertainty.

It was the first real, heartfelt look she'd given him. It was the first glimpse he'd had past her cool, controlled front. And it *was* a front, he realized suddenly. It had to be a front, or he wouldn't be able to see past it, right?

"How can you remember that?" she asked, her tone incredulous. "After all this time?"

"Because I was crazy about you," Jim said. He knew as soon as the words were out of his mouth that it was something he shouldn't have said. His habit of saying what was on his mind, of laying his thoughts and feelings out on the table, had gotten him into trouble before, and he knew right away that this wasn't going to be an exception.

His uncensored comments often got uncensored reactions, but Emily just stared silently at him.

He knew he was in trouble, though. He knew that his words were worthless in her eyes. And there was no way on earth he could back what he'd just said with any proof or evidence. In fact, the very way he'd broken up with Emily seemed proof that he hadn't cared about her in the least.

Jim looked down at his sandwich, sitting on top of its white paper wrapper. Suddenly he wasn't feeling very hungry.

But when he glanced up at Emily again, she was smiling. It was one of those private smiles, though, one where the joke was on him. The uncertainty in her eyes was gone, replaced by confidence and determination.

Her smile disappeared, and her gaze became positively steely as she looked him straight in the eye and said, "You are so full of crap. Don't you dare try to whitewash the past. I know exactly how you felt about me." Her voice was quiet, but her even tone left no doubt that she meant business. "If you insist on continuing to insult my intelligence with further ridiculous interpretations of our...sordid little affair, I'll be forced to go over your head, Detective. I won't hesitate to issue a complaint to Lieutenant Bell."

Sordid little affair. Jim's relationship with Emily had been the greatest, most treasured love affair of his life. Hearing her refer to that time as nothing but a sordid little affair was a slap in the face.

But what could he say? If he stood up and shouted at her the way he wanted to, shouted that he had *loved* her, damn it, where would that get him? She wouldn't believe him, and he'd be off the case—as fast as Lieutenant Bell could say the words "Keegan, get your butt into my office."

Without his participation, the investigation would be postponed and Delmore would be free to continue shipping kilos of cocaine into Florida. Then Emily would have even more reason to dislike him.

And Jim knew with a sudden, startling clarity that he didn't want Emily to dislike him. He didn't know what the hell he *did* want, but he knew for damn sure that he didn't want *that*.

So he didn't shout. He didn't tell her she was wrong. He didn't say anything at all. He simply took off his sunglasses, rested his elbows on the picnic table and tried to relieve the ache that was starting to build up inside his head by pressing his forehead against the heels of his hands. He could hear the seconds ticking by on his watch as they sat in silence, neither of them moving.

After many, many of those seconds had gone by, Jim looked up, running his hands down his face. He rested his chin on his thumbs and his lips against his fingers as he looked across the table at Emily.

She was staring out at the ocean, her eyes soft and unfocused. He nervously cleared his throat, and her gaze flickered toward him before returning to the distant horizon.

"Emily," he said. He cleared his throat again, but it didn't make his voice any less husky. "I'm sorry. Can we . . . maybe . . . start over, here?"

She looked at him dead-on. Her expression was so chilly, he could've gotten frostbite.

"Start over?" she said. "I intend to start over. After Alex is in jail and you're out of my apartment, after I don't have to see *either* of you *ever* again, I'm going to start over. Definitely in a different city, maybe even in a different state."

"That's not what I meant—"

"I know what you meant. And the answer is no. Next question, Detective."

Jim stared at her, shocked by the hard edge to her words and the equally hard set to her usually soft mouth. This was a side of Emily he'd never seen before. It was a side he suspected hadn't existed back when she was only eighteen years old, back before her contact with men like Alexander Delmore had jaded her. Men like Delmore, and—yeah, who was he kidding?—men like him.

He'd left her because he thought the short-term hurt would be better than the pain he would cause her in the long run. He'd felt he didn't deserve the happiness he found with her, *and* he'd thought he would poison her if they stayed together. Instead, he'd managed to poison her by leaving.

But then he saw her lower lip tremble. Her eyes filled suddenly with tears that she couldn't control. She said one choice word, one he'd never heard her say before, as she turned her head away, trying to hide her tears from him. But it was too late. He'd already seen.

Jim reached for her, across the table. But she jumped back, away from him.

She tripped over the piece of wood that connected the bench to the table and went sprawling in the soft sand. Jim was up in a flash, but she was faster. She scrambled to her feet and started running down the deserted beach.

"Emily, wait!" Jim said, but she didn't stop.

Damn, she'd left her purse on the table. Jim dashed back for it, tucked it securely under his arm and went after her.

She had one hell of a head start, but his legs were longer, and he was used to running distances. Still, he had to work hard to catch her.

"Emily, stop!" he said, but she didn't, so he grabbed her arm.

"Leave me *alone!*" She struggled to get away, but he tightened his grip.

She swung angrily at him, but her aim was off and her fist bounced ineffectually off his shoulder. Jim knew the blow had hurt her hand more than it had hurt him.

She was crying—thick, hot, angry tears. She wiped at them as if she were trying to make them go away, but they wouldn't stop. She struck out at him again, and he pulled her in tightly to his chest.

"Emily, come on. *Please . . .*"

Emily felt the fight draining from her as soon as his arms went around her. She couldn't stop crying. Sobs racked her body, and she wanted nothing more than to lean against Jim's warm solidness.

If she closed her eyes, she could pretend she'd somehow gone back in time to when she was eighteen. She could pretend that he really *had* loved her, and—

His fingers trailed lightly through her hair, and she felt the familiar surge of sexual heat she had always felt when he touched her that way. It was his gentleness, his tenderness, that had turned her on—that obviously *still* turned her on.

Brother, what was *wrong* with her? How could she think of Jim Keegan this way? How could she allow herself to be attracted to him now, when she knew the kind of man he really was?

With her last bit of strength and her last scrap of fight, Emily pushed herself away from him.

But she couldn't break free. His arms just tightened around her. Angrily she lifted her tear-streaked face toward his. His face, his mouth, were mere inches from hers. And as she looked up into his eyes, she saw the deep blue of his irises nearly swallowed by the widening expanse of his pupils as he looked into her eyes. She knew without a doubt that he was going to kiss her. Her anger was transformed instantly into fear. Fear, and something else. Something far more disturbing.

"Emily," he whispered, leaning down toward her.

"*Don't,*" she whispered, and he froze, leaving less than an inch between his lips and hers. "Please, if you have even a shred of decency left . . ."

Jim released her immediately. God, what was he doing? What had he been thinking? Apparently holding her in his arms that way had knocked all sense clear out of him.

She stared at him, her eyes big and accusing. She had stopped crying, but her face was still wet, and one last tear hung on her lower lashes. Though he knew damn well that he shouldn't, Jim couldn't resist reaching out and, with one knuckle, gently brushing that tear away.

Emily flinched as if his touch had burned her.

"I'm sorry," he said.

"Don't touch me," she said. "Don't *ever* touch me."

Jim looked down at the sand, out at the ocean, up at the sky, and finally at Emily. "Emily," he said huskily, "I've got to confess—it's hard not to. I can't seem to stay away from you."

"You had no problem seven years ago," she said, and walked away.

What could he say to that? Silently he followed her back to the car.

Chapter 6

Jim was pacing. He moved from the front door to the sliding glass door that led to Emily's tiny deck. He moved back to the small dining table, lingered there for a moment, then went back to the front door. Then he went to the sliding glass door....

Emily brought her eyes and her attention back to the slim Hispanic man sitting across from her on the couch.

"I will be in the room," Detective Salazar was saying in his soft, charming accent, "or at least somewhere in the country club, the entire time you and Mr. Delmore are there."

Emily nodded.

"If you have a problem, Emily..." Jim said, speaking for the first time in nearly twenty minutes. Both Emily and Salazar looked up at him. "Any problem at all, find Phil. He'll get you out of there."

"What kind of problem could I possibly have?" Emily asked, crossing her legs as she coolly gazed up at Jim. "It's a society dinner. I seriously doubt Alex intends to perform any illegal acts in front of the gossip columnists from the local newspapers.''

Jim pushed his hands into the front pockets of his pants and leaned his back against the wall, finally standing still. "You're right. He probably won't," he agreed. "But this is a man you suspect is a felon. You're going to spend hours with him, pretending that you don't know how he really makes his money. That's not always easy. If you find that you can't do it, if you get overwhelmed, if you get scared—"

"I'm not scared," Emily said, raising her chin in defiance. But what was she defying? His words, or their underlying kindness? Or maybe it was the quiet gentleness of his voice...

"Well, that's good," Salazar said, smiling at her. "Now, your goal tonight is not to get any information from Mr. Delmore. You're gonna leave the information gathering to my buddy Diego, all right?"

Diego. James. Emily's gaze flicked over to where Jim was still leaning against the wall. He was watching her, and she quickly looked back at Detective Salazar. "All right," she said.

"Your goal is for you and your 'brother'—" Salazar gestured toward Jim with his head "—to get invited along on one of Mr. Delmore's floating weekend parties. That shouldn't be too hard. It also couldn't hurt for the two of you to get an invitation to Mr. Delmore's home. The investigating we've done shows that Alexander Delmore does most of his business either at home or on board his yacht—" His eyebrows drew together, and a look of concern crossed his face. "Is there some kind of problem? You don't look happy."

Emily *wasn't* happy. "My relationship with Alex is kind of...odd," she said. "He's told me on more than one occasion that one of the reasons he likes dating me is that I never pressure him for anything. I've never asked him when

I'll see him again, I've never asked him for *anything*. He's told me that in that respect I'm different from the other women he's gone out with."

Jim stared down at his cowboy boots, listening to Emily talk about her relationship with Delmore. She might as well have been describing *their* relationship, seven years ago. Because she hadn't pressured him for anything, either, not even his attention. That was what had drawn him to her when they first met—after the initial shock of physical attraction, anyway. She'd been so low-key, so laid-back, so cool and collected. If she had dangled her body at him like bait, if she'd sent him long, meaningful looks and body-language telegrams the way most of the other college girls had, he would never have given her a second glance. Well, he might have given her a second glance, but he wouldn't have become so intrigued by her.

Even after they'd been dating for months, Emily had never assumed anything. She'd never demanded anything from him. Or had she? He could still picture her, that Saturday morning she'd come by bus all the way out to his apartment because he hadn't returned any of her phone calls. He'd been home from the hospital for only a few weeks, and she'd been worried about him. Still, even then, she hadn't demanded anything from him—except maybe the peace of mind of knowing he was all right.

"Do the best you can," Salazar said to Emily, interrupting Jim's thoughts. "Don't say or do anything different from what you would normally say or do. It won't help to get him suspicious."

"*I'll* ask Delmore to take us for a sail," Jim said. "I'll do it when he comes to pick you up tonight, after you introduce him to me, okay?"

Emily nodded, her blue eyes flashing in his direction.

God, he could see wariness in her eyes every time she so much as glanced his way. It had been stupid of him to hold her in his arms like that, down at the beach. What was he, some kind of idiot? Had he really thought that Emily would want comfort from *him?* Yeah, she'd want that about as much as she'd want a pink slip along with her next paycheck.

The truth was, *he'd* wanted an excuse to touch her. He'd wanted to run his fingers through her hair...wanted to feel her body pressed against his. He'd wanted to kiss her. God, he still wanted to kiss her. And she knew it now, too.

Perfect, Keegan, he thought. Just perfect. She was under a ton of stress, and here he was, making it worse for her.

The doorbell rang. Jim glanced at his watch. It was only quarter to four. They had nearly three hours before Delmore was due to arrive.

"Who is it?" he asked.

"I don't know." Emily stood up, uncertainly eyeing the door. "It could be Alex. He dropped by yesterday without calling first."

Salazar got to his feet, too, as the bell chimed again.

"Phil, get out of sight," Jim told the other detective. "Go down the hall, into Emily's bedroom. If it *is* Delmore, we don't want him to see you."

Salazar nodded and vanished down the hall. The bell rang again, this time twice in rapid succession.

"You want me to get it?" Jim asked.

Emily shook her head and went toward the door. Her heart was pounding as she opened the door.

"Thank *God* you're home."

Jim looked over Emily's shoulder at the painfully skinny young woman standing in the doorway. She had long red hair and the kind of pale complexion that burned almost instantly in the hot Florida sunshine. She also had one hell of a black eye, and a grubby little boy, probably around three years old, with matching red hair and big, solemn eyes, clinging to her hand.

The woman looked up at Jim, and the relief faded from her face, replaced by shuttered reservation. She was clutching a brown paper shopping bag filled with clothing and baby toys. A dingy yellow Big Bird doll peeked out of the top.

"Sorry," she muttered. "You got company, don't you?"

"Jewel," Emily said. "What happened? Who hit you? Please, come in."

Jim stepped back as Emily took the younger woman by the elbow and pulled her gently into the apartment. The redheaded woman was younger than he'd first thought, no more than a girl, really. She was pretty in an old-fashioned, Victorian way—or at least she would be if she washed off the layer of dust and grime that covered her, and maybe smiled a little. She had aristocratic features—a long, elegant nose, delicate lips, a graceful, if dirty, neck. She was eyeing him with distrust, and he smiled at her. Her expression didn't change.

"Jewel, this is...my brother, Dan," Emily said, her eyes meeting Jim's briefly in acknowledgment of her lie. "Dan, this is Jewel Hays. She's a former student of mine." She ruffled the hair of the little boy who still clutched Jewel's hand. "And this is her son, Billy." She turned her full attention to the girl. "Are you all right?"

Jewel shook her head no. "I'm in big trouble," she said, her gaze skittering toward Jim and then back to Emily. "Can we talk...in private?"

Emily nodded. "Why don't you come into the bathroom? We can get you cleaned up," she said. She looked at Jim. "Will you keep an eye on Billy?"

"He's hungry," Jewel said, looking down at the little boy. "He hasn't had nothing to eat since night before last."

"I'll get him some food," Jim said.

"Thanks," Emily said. "I'm not sure what I have that he'd like..."

"I'll improvise," Jim said. "We'll be fine."

As she led Jewel toward the bathroom, Emily glanced back to see the tiny little boy tipping his head to look way, way up at Jim.

Emily came into the living room to find Billy, perched atop several telephone books, sitting at her dining table, finishing up a sandwich—peanut butter and jelly on pita bread, the only bread she'd had in the house. Jim was sitting across from him, and Felipe Salazar was in the kitchen, leaning against the counter.

"Hey, guys, how's it going in here?" Emily said, smiling brightly for Billy's benefit.

"He's eating his second sandwich," Jim said. He smiled, too, but his eyes were full of questions. What was going on? Why the hell hadn't this kid been fed before this?

"I need your help," Emily said, looking from Jim to Felipe and back again.

Jim stood up. "Why don't we go out onto the deck and talk?" he said. He looked at Salazar. "Stay with the kid, okay?"

"No!" Billy looked up at Jim, his eyes wide. "Don't go!"

To Emily's surprise, Jim crouched down next to Billy's chair, so that he was at eye level with the child. "Hey, Bill," he said, "I'm just gonna be out there on the deck. You'll be able to see me through the window, okay?"

The little boy was not convinced.

"And your mom's in the shower," Jim continued. "She'll be out soon, and then maybe you can take a bath. In the meantime, what do ya say you and my friend Felipe here go into the living room and see if you can find a good cartoon to watch on TV?"

Billy looked at Salazar. "He's your friend?" he asked.

"My *best* friend," Jim said. "So be nice to him, okay?"

Billy nodded.

"Great," Jim said. "I'll be right outside, Bill, if you need me."

He opened the sliding glass door, and Emily followed him out onto the deck. She'd thought Jim would be absolutely lost when it came to taking care of Billy. But he knew just the right way to talk to the little boy. He spoke to him as if he were an equal. He didn't talk down to the child at all.

"Do you deal with children very often?" she asked, closing the door behind her so that Billy couldn't hear their conversation.

Jim leaned his elbows against the wooden railing, looking out over the courtyard. "Not so much these days, no," he said.

"You were great with him," Emily said. "You know, I've never even heard Billy speak before. I didn't know he could."

"He told me someone named Uncle Hank hit his mother," Jim said, turning to look at her.

Emily swore softly.

"What's going on?" Jim asked.

"I don't know what to do," she admitted. "This is way out of my league."

"Tell me what's going on."

Emily took a deep breath. "Okay. When Jewel got pregnant, her parents sent her here, from their farm in Alabama. She was supposed to live with her aunt until she came to term, and then give the baby up for adoption. When the time came and the baby was born, she refused. Her parents wouldn't let her come home, so she and the baby—Billy— ended up staying on with the aunt, who isn't exactly a pillar of the community. Jewel picked up some nasty habits from the woman. She got addicted to crack, and started hooking to support her addiction. Apparently—and this is something I didn't know before today—her good old uncle Hank is quite the little pimp."

"Damn . . ." Jim breathed.

"Exactly," Emily said, anger making her eyes seem an even darker shade of blue. "Jewel's been in and out of rehab at least three times in the past two years. She just got out, again, a few days ago. Guess what Uncle Hank gave her as a homecoming present?''

"You mean, besides the black eye?''

"Yes,'' she said. "Besides the black eye.''

She reached into the pocket of her shorts and took out three little glass vials. Crack. It was crack.

Jim swore. "That son of a bitch—''

"He wanted her to start walking the streets again,'' Emily said. "I guess he figured the easiest way to get her to do that was to make sure she stayed dependent on the drugs.'' Her fingers clenched tightly around the vials. "Do you know how hard it is for an addict to stay clean? Especially right out of rehab? Jewel couldn't bring herself to throw this stuff away, she just couldn't do it. She wanted it. But she was strong enough to come here and ask for help.''

She sagged, sitting down on one of the deck chairs. "I've been trying to help this girl for years,'' she said. "I knew her home situation was bad, but this is…awful. She's got to get out of there. Permanently. But she says she's got nowhere else to go. She refuses to press charges—she thinks that she'll lose Billy if the police and the social services department get involved. I honestly don't know what to do.'' She stared down at the vials in her hand. "I don't even know how to dispose of this. Do I flush it down the toilet, or will it contaminate the water? What do I do?''

Jim held out his hand. "I'll take care of it,'' he said.

With relief, Emily gave him the drugs. "Thanks.''

He sat down on the chair, next to her. "Em, you can't let her stay here. You can't take on that responsibility.''

Her eyes flashed. "I certainly can't send her home.''

"I'm not telling you to do that,'' Jim said quietly. "Maybe there's some kind of halfway house or shelter—''

"She's tried that,'' Emily said. "All the places she's contacted won't let her bring Billy along. She'd have to have him placed in foster care. And that's unacceptable to her.''

Jim nodded, looking out at the crystal blueness of the apartment complex's swimming pool. "He's a sweet kid," he said.

"What am I going to do, Jim?"

Jim. She'd called him Jim. Not Detective. *Jim.* He took a deep breath, letting it slowly out. "Let me talk to Phil, okay?" he said. "Maybe he's got some ideas. He grew up in this city, he's got all kinds of connections. We'll try to find a place for her to go, Emily."

She was looking at him, looking searchingly into his eyes, with the oddest expression on her face.

"What?" he said.

She shook her head and stood up. "You're not supposed to be so nice," she said as she opened the sliding door and went back into the apartment.

Not supposed to—? What the hell did *that* mean?

When Emily went into the living room, Jewel and Felipe Salazar were sitting on the couch, with Billy between them.

Jewel's hair was still wet from her shower, and she was wearing Emily's spare bathrobe—a white terry-cloth robe that enveloped her slight frame and went all the way down to the floor.

Felipe was smiling, and Jewel's cheeks were slightly flushed as she smiled shyly back and answered the detective's gentle questions. It was heartrending to see that this girl, who was so experienced in many ways, was socially inexperienced, even shy.

"Phil, got a minute?" Jim called from the door to the deck.

With one last smile at Jewel and a murmured request to be excused, Felipe joined Jim outside.

Jewel looked up at Emily and smiled.

"Feeling better?" Emily asked, sitting down across from her in the rocking chair.

Jewel nodded. "Yeah. Thanks."

"Do you have any clean clothes?"

The girl's smile faded. "No. I only had time to grab some of Billy's things before we left."

"I'll lend you something of mine," Emily said. "And I think I've got some things that shrank in the dryer. A couple of T-shirts, some sweatpants, stuff like that. They're too small for me now. You can have them."

"Thanks." Jewel looked toward the big glass door that led onto the deck. The two men were standing out there, talking seriously. "Felipe says he's a friend of yours," she said.

Emily smiled, thinking *Your friend, the neighborhood police officer.* "Sure," she said. "I guess you could say he's a friend."

Jewel glanced back at the men on the deck. "He's cute," she said.

Emily looked out at Felipe Salazar. He *was* good-looking, with his easy smile, his exotic high cheekbones and his dark, chocolate-brown eyes. He was, as usual, impeccably dressed in a dark suit. His shirt and tie were the same color as his suit, and the effect was striking.

"He told me Billy was such a nice little boy, I must be a real good mother," Jewel said, and blushed.

Felipe had managed to totally captivate Jewel Hays, Emily realized with a smile. He *was* charismatic and handsome. And his kindness seemed genuine. Emily might have been attracted to him herself, if . . .

If what? If she didn't already have a boyfriend? She didn't have a boyfriend. She'd stopped thinking of Alex in those terms the night she overheard his conversation with Vincent Marino.

So how come she *didn't* find Felipe Salazar attractive? Her gaze moved almost involuntarily from Felipe to Jim. She could still feel the way Jim's arms had felt around her when he held her on the beach. She could still see that look in his eyes as he'd bent his head to kiss her. . . .

Jim looked up and through the glass of the door into the living room, directly at Emily. Their eyes met.

The connection was instantaneous, and so strong Emily almost gasped out loud.

Instead, she looked away.

But she'd answered her question. The reason she didn't find Felipe Salazar attractive—or any other man, for that matter—was that she was still tied to the past. To James Keegan, to be exact.

He was an insensitive, selfish, uncaring man...who had a special way with little kids. He was a heartbreaker...who sometimes seemed to have a heart of gold.

Emily had opened her house to Jim, thinking his presence would give her a clear view of the awful person he really was. And, sure, he'd given her instances of imperfect behavior to focus on. But he'd also shown her that he could be alarmingly kind, which left his bad-guy image extremely obscure and undefined.

The sliding glass door opened, and the two men came inside.

Jim sat down on the couch next to Jewel. "Emily told me about the trouble you're in," he said, coming straight to the point. "She says you need a place to stay."

Jewel nodded silently.

Felipe came farther into the room. "I know of a place in my neighborhood, a kind of a shelter, that might have room for you and Billy," he said. "I have time to take you over there now, if you would like."

The wariness was back in Jewel's eyes. "What if they don't?" she asked. "Have room for us, I mean."

Felipe smiled gently. "Then I will find you someplace else to stay," he said. He glanced at Jim. "I have a friend whose apartment is empty right now—but that would be a last resort, of course."

"Come on, Jewel," Emily said, heading toward the bedroom. "I'll find you something to wear."

But Jewel didn't move. "Why are you helping me?" she asked the two men. "What do you want in return? 'Cause I know nothin's free," she added flatly.

"Jewel—" Emily started to protest.

Jim stopped her. "No, she's right," he said. "Nothing comes for free." He turned to Jewel. "You've got to stay clean—no drugs, no alcohol. And *that's* the easy part. You live in the shelter, you don't just sit around, watching TV, sponging off the state. You either enter a program to get your GED, or you take vocational classes, learn a trade."

"What I *meant* was, what do you get?" Jewel said.

"Jewel, I am a police detective," Felipe said. "I will get the satisfaction of knowing that I will not have to bust you someday."

The girl's eyes were wide. "You're the *man?*"

Felipe nodded. "Yes."

"Come on, Jewel," Emily said gently. "Let's find you some clothes, and get Billy into the tub."

At six o'clock, Emily returned from Carly's apartment with the dress she had borrowed for tonight's date with Alex. The dress was blue, scattered with sequins, way too tight and much too short. But, it had the distinct advantage of not being the same dress she'd worn to the last country club function to which Alex had taken her. Holding it up on the hanger, it looked more like a blue tube of crinkly material with spaghetti straps than a dress.

"Do you and your friend borrow clothes from each other all the time?" Jim asked when she came back inside.

He was sitting on the sofa, reading the newspaper, with his feet up on the coffee table. He'd changed back into his shorts, and his feet were bare. He looked entirely too comfortable sitting there. He was far too at home.

"I only have two formal dresses," Emily said. "I wore them both last week, and I can't afford to buy another. My budget's strained as it is." She made a face as she looked at the dress she'd borrowed from Carly. "Unfortunately, Carly's tastes aren't very conservative. On top of that, she's shorter than me."

Jim pulled his feet off the table, folded the newspaper and put it down. "Won't Delmore buy you clothes? He's got more money than God."

Emily crossed her arms. "I'm not Alex's mistress, Detective."

Jim looked up at her. "I know," he said. "Actually, my sources tell me that you were on track to become Mrs. Delmore. The whole town is predicting a Christmas wedding."

Emily laughed. "Then they're going to be disappointed, aren't they?"

She turned to go down the hall toward her bedroom, but his words stopped her.

"You could've looked the other way, and half of everything Delmore has could've been yours," Jim said. "You never would've had to borrow someone else's dress, ever again."

He was serious. He was sitting there, looking up at her, his eyes intense and devoid of any humor or teasing.

Emily laughed again. It was a small, mirthless sound. "You never did get to know me very well, did you?"

It was meant to be a rhetorical question, but he answered it anyway. "I thought I did," he said. "But I guess I didn't really know how tough you could be."

Jim had always thought of her as someone fragile, someone to be protected from the harshness and unfairness of life. But here she was, taking a stand for something she believed in. For Emily, there was no gray to the black-and-white issue of drug trafficking. She believed that it was wrong, and that it had to be stopped. End of discussion. The fact that the leading suspect in the case was her almost-fiancé made no difference to the overall picture.

"I hate drugs," she said, her words somehow more emphatic for the lack of emotion in her voice. "I hate crack. It kills my kids. Or, worse, it turns them into animals."

"Your kids?" Jim said.

"My students," Emily said. "For every kid like Jewel who makes it into rehab, there are plenty of others who don't. They wind up on the street. They steal or turn tricks to support their habits. If they don't end up in jail, they usually end up dead." Her voice shook slightly, and she stopped and took a deep breath. When she spoke again, she was back in absolute control. "You're a cop. You know the story."

"Yeah," Jim said. "I do."

"If Alex Delmore *is* bringing drugs into the country," she said, "then he's made a fortune from other people's misery." She disappeared down the hall. "And I'm going to make *damn* sure he goes to jail."

Chapter 7

"They are sitting at a table with four other couples," Felipe Salazar's voice reported over the telephone. "Everything is—"

Jim interrupted him. "What about Emily?"

He was pacing the length of the living room, carrying the phone with him as he impatiently walked back and forth, back and forth.

"Emily looks enchanting," his partner told him from the telephone at the country club's bar. "She is wearing a very... beautiful dress..."

"I *know* how she looks," Jim said, fuming. God, he couldn't *believe* how Emily looked in that blue dress. He'd known that she had gorgeous legs, but in that short, sexy dress, with black high heels, her shapely legs looked five miles long. And the way that dress clung to her slender curves should be illegal. She was wearing her hair up, off her smooth, bare shoulders, in some kind of elegant twist thing that emphasized her long, graceful neck.

In that dress, with her sweet girl-next-door face, Emily was an incredible combination of fresh innocence and pure, unadulterated sex. It was mind-blowing. When she first walked out into the living room, Jim's blood had run hot—and then cold, as he remembered she was going out to spend the evening with Alex Delmore.

So far, nothing about this evening had gone right.

Delmore's limo had arrived nearly twenty minutes early—without Delmore. The millionaire had been tied up at the office, and would meet Emily at the country club, or so the limo driver had informed them. So much for their plan to introduce Delmore to Emily's brother Dan. And so much for Jim's chance to finagle an invitation onto Delmore's yacht.

But worst of all was the fact that, with Delmore's limo driver standing sentinel in the living room while Emily put the finishing touches on her makeup, Jim hadn't gotten a chance to talk to her, to make sure she was okay, to make sure that she hadn't suddenly gotten cold feet. He hadn't had the chance to give her any advice, any warnings—or any reassurances.

Then she had come walking out of the bathroom, wearing that amazing blue dress with her amazingly long legs, and Jim's heart had nearly stopped beating. But he'd barely had enough time to focus his eyes before she was gone.

After an hour and a half of pacing the floor, he'd given in, called the country club and paged Salazar.

"Emily is eating the veal Oscar," Salazar told him. "It's very tasty. I was eating it myself, before I was called away to the telephone—"

"Phil."

"Diego. She is fine. I am here—"

"And I'm not," Jim muttered.

"You care for this girl more than just a little, don't you, man?" his partner asked.

Jim evaded the question. "Nothing's gone right tonight, Felipe. Make sure Emily knows where you are at all times, in case she needs assistance. God knows what else will go wrong."

"She knows where I am," Salazar told him. "She is doing fine. She's quite good at pretending that she is enjoying herself."

"And Delmore?" Jim asked.

Salazar laughed. "Mr. Delmore does not have to pretend that he is enjoying himself. Ah, I see them now, out on the dance floor. You tell me—what man wouldn't be pleased to hold a woman as beautiful as Emily Marshall in his arms?"

Jim briefly closed his eyes, trying to banish the sudden, vivid picture of Emily dancing with Delmore's arms around her, swaying in time to some old romantic song. "Damn," he said.

"Excuse me?" Salazar said.

"Stay accessible," Jim ordered him. "And call me when they leave."

Emily made her way slowly to the ladies' room, taking her time and stopping to chat with a group of Alex's friends who greeted her. In between the small talk, she glanced toward the bar, where she'd last spotted Detective Salazar, hoping that he was still there. She was in luck—he was. And he was watching her. She caught his eye, hoping he would be able to read her mind. She needed to talk to him. To her relief, he nodded, almost imperceptibly.

She went out into the lobby where the ladies' room was located, to find that it wasn't deserted as she had hoped. Instead, groups of men and woman were standing and talking, away from the noise of the dance band. Emily hesitated, unsure of what to do. A soft touch on her arm made her spin around.

"I'm sorry," Felipe Salazar said. "I didn't mean to startle you."

Emily stared at him. Were they simply going to stand here, in full view of everyone, and carry on a conversation, as if nothing were wrong?

"Ms. Marshall, is it not?" the detective said, and suddenly she understood.

"Yes," she said. Of course they could stand here and talk. As long as they appeared to be making party chatter, talking here, out in the open, would look far less suspicious than whispering together in some dark, secluded corner.

"Felipe Salazar," he said, holding out his hand to her and smiling charmingly. "We have a mutual friend, remember? A Ms. Hays."

"Yes, of course," Emily said. "How is Jewel?"

"She is doing as well as can be expected," he replied, then lowered his voice. "There was space for her and Billy in one of the mothers-and-toddlers dorms. I had her put on a waiting list for a semiprivate room. She was very frightened when I left. I'll go back tomorrow to see how she's doing."

"Don't go out of your way," Emily said. "She's a tough kid. She'll be fine."

"It's not out of my way," he said.

"Be careful that she doesn't get too dependent on you," she warned him.

"Better to be dependent on *me* than on crack," he said with a shrug. He lowered his voice even further. "Was there something you wished to tell me? And don't look so serious. This is a party. You're supposed to be having fun."

Emily smiled at him brightly. "Right. Fun. Alex has to leave. He says it's business, but it seems odd to me. It's a little bit late at night for regular, legitimate business, don't you think?"

Felipe glanced at his watch. It was nearly ten-thirty.

"His driver is going to take me home," she said. "But I wanted to tell you, in case you wanted to follow Alex, see what he's up to."

He nodded. "Thanks."

"I'm sure I'll see you soon," Emily said, as if she were ending just another casual party conversation. "Take care."

"I will," Felipe said. "And say hello to your brother for me."

Her pretend brother. Jim. Who was waiting at home for her. Who had looked at her as if he wanted to devour her whole as she nearly ran out the door tonight...

Could this night get any worse?

Emily heard Carly's familiar husky laughter as she opened her apartment door.

Jim was sitting in the rocking chair, his feet still bare and his shirttail untucked from his shorts. He looked up at Emily with real surprise in his eyes. "Hey!" he said. "What are you doing back so early?"

"Wow!" Carly said from where she was sitting cross-legged on the couch. "My dress looks *great* on you."

"Alex had to cut our date short," Emily said, closing the door behind her. As she crossed toward the kitchen and put her purse on the little dining table, she could feel Jim's eyes on her. "He had his driver bring me home. Apparently he had some unscheduled business to attend to."

She turned toward Jim, to emphasize her words with a silent message, but his eyes weren't on her face. They were traveling slowly up her legs, then up her body. Finally he met her eyes and smiled. Emily felt herself flush. The nerve of the man! He was practically propositioning her with his eyes, yet not even five minutes ago he'd been getting cozy with Carly.

"Poor baby," Carly was saying. "So you didn't even get properly kissed good-night."

Jim was still watching her, and Emily felt his gaze intensify. She pointedly turned her back on him and looked into the oval mirror that was on the wall beside the front door. "I'll live," she said. She began unfastening the clips that held her hair in place.

Actually, she'd been relieved when Alex didn't give her more than a cursory peck on the cheek as he said goodbye. She'd been dreading the moment all evening long. It had been hard enough to dance with him, to have him hold her as close as he had.

Emily tossed her hair clips on the table next to her purse and ran her fingers through her hair.

"So," she said to Carly, "I go out for only a few hours, and when I get back I find you hitting on my brother." Her tone was light, teasing, but inside she was feeling oddly off balance. The thought of Jim and Carly together was disturbing. She glanced at Jim. "Or were *you* hitting on Carly?"

"Oh, I wish," Carly said, with a flirtatious smile at Jim. "No, I was working late, and got home about a half hour ago. I saw the light on, so I came over. Dan was telling me about how he used to chase you around the house, making monster faces at you, when you were kids. You know, *I* had an older sister, and I remember that she used to..."

Emily sank down next to Carly on the couch and put her head back. Brother, she was exhausted. And...relieved? Oh, shoot, was it possible that she was actually *relieved* that Jim hadn't invited Carly over here, that he hadn't been hanging out with her all evening long?

Jim met her eyes and smiled, and Emily realized that she'd been staring at him. She quickly looked away, hoping that he hadn't somehow managed to read her mind. Lord, if he got the idea that she still found him desirable, he would be all over her. Relentlessly. She closed her eyes, trying to banish the unbidden memory of Jim holding her on the beach.

"...she was *awful*," Carly was saying. "No redeeming qualities. Her one goal in life was to torture me. Was Dan like that, Em?"

Carly was talking to her. Emily opened her eyes. "Dan?" she said foggily. Dan who?

"I wasn't awful all the time." Jim jumped in and saved the day before she blew his cover. "I tried to take care of her—she was so little. Big brothers are supposed to do that, right? They protect you, keep you out of trouble, make sure you fly straight. They're always there for you, you know?"

Something about Jim's voice caught Emily's attention. He wasn't just making things up in order to keep Carly believing he was Emily's older brother. He was speaking from experience. But it sounded like it was the experience of a younger brother who had had an older brother to look up to and admire.

That was odd. Emily knew that Jim had several older sisters, but the only brother he'd ever mentioned was much younger than he was. She would've remembered him talking about a big brother, wouldn't she?

"Look, Carly," Jim said, standing up, "Emily looks beat, and—"

"We should let her go to sleep," Carly said, also getting to her feet. "So...do you want to come over to my place?"

Jim looked surprised, as if he hadn't expected Carly to issue such an invitation. And then he actually looked flustered. "Ah..." he said. "No. Thank you," he added quickly, "but...I don't think that would be a good idea. You see, I'm—"

"No need to explain," Carly said good-naturedly, handling the obvious rejection like a pro. "It was just a thought."

"I'm involved with someone," he said. "It's pretty serious."

"You are?" The words were out of Emily's mouth before she could stop them.

Carly laughed. "Uh-oh," she said, opening the door. "I think you just woke your sister up. Gee, maybe you two can have a double wedding, save your parents some bucks. See y'all tomorrow."

Emily could feel Jim watching her as he closed the door behind Carly.

"I'm sorry," she said, bending to pick her shoes up off the floor. "Whether or not you're involved with someone isn't my business."

"I'm involved with someone the same way you're involved with Delmore," Jim said quietly.

Emily looked up at him, not understanding.

He sat down next to her on the couch. "It's fictional, Em," he said. "See, I don't need Carly hanging around all the time, getting in the way of this investigation. So it's easier to tell her I'm involved. You hear what I'm saying?"

Emily nodded, looking down at the shoes she held on her lap.

She looked so tired, and so damned fragile. Jim wanted to touch her. He wanted to hold her close and—

"Tell me more about this unscheduled business of Delmore's," he said.

"He got a phone call," Emily said. "At about ten-fifteen. When he came back to the table, he apologized and said he had to leave, that some important business deal was finally going to go through." She glanced up at Jim. "I managed to tell Felipe, and he followed Alex."

"*That's* why Phil didn't call me when you left the country club," Jim said.

"Oh, *no!*" Emily said, sitting up straight.

"What?"

"I just realized..." She turned to Jim, her eyes wide with dismay. "Alex left so quickly, he didn't... we didn't make another date. As it stands now, I have no plans to see him again. What if he doesn't call me?"

Jim had to laugh.

"What's so funny?"

He was grinning with genuine amusement, his eyes sparkling and dancing with humor as he looked at her. "Trust me, Em," he said. "The guy is gonna call you."

"There's no way you can know that for sure," Emily argued.

Jim scratched his head, still smiling at her. "I'm as sure of this as I'm sure the sun's going to rise in the morning. Delmore will call."

"Suddenly you're a psychic?"

"No, just a man."

She still didn't understand.

"Come here," Jim said, standing up. She didn't move to follow him, so he reached down and took her hand and pulled her up off the couch.

"What are you doing?" Emily halfheartedly tried to pull her hand free, but he wouldn't let go.

"I want to show you something," he said, leading her down the hall.

Emily's bedroom was dimly lit by the streetlight that shone in through the open blinds. Jim tugged her gently into the room and pushed the door closed.

Her heart was pounding. What was he doing? What was he—?

He stood behind her, held her gently by the shoulders and pointed her toward the full-length mirror on the back of her bedroom door. "Look," he commanded.

He was standing so close behind her that she could feel his body heat. His grip on her shoulders tightened slightly as she met his eyes in the mirror.

"Look at *yourself*," he said.

Emily looked. She saw... herself. Sure, the dress was fancy, and its style flattered her trim body in a way that could be called sexy, but underneath it all she was still Emily. True, she rarely showed other people the side of her personality that liked wearing little blue sequined dresses, but it was part of her just the same.

Her legs were long and in good shape. In fact, her entire body was well toned. Her face— It was the same face she'd had all her life. It was pretty enough, she supposed. At least, taken all together, her features seemed to fit in the space provided for them. Separately, her nose was a little too big and slightly crooked, her mouth was a touch too wide, her chin a little too pointed.

She looked closer. She should have looked tired—jeez, she had been exhausted just a minute ago—but she couldn't see even a hint of fatigue in her eyes. No, they were bright with an odd mix of wariness, fear... and anticipation.

"Look at how beautiful you are," Jim murmured, and Emily looked up at him. "And that's just the wrapping on the package. There's no man on earth who wouldn't call you for another date."

He ran his rough fingers down the lengths of her arms, lightly caressing her bare skin, as Emily stared at him, frozen in place. In the mirror, his lean face looked mysterious, almost frighteningly intense. He'd long since stopped smiling, and his deep blue eyes glittered colorlessly in the darkness with unconcealed desire.

But then his eyes met hers.

Jim pulled his hands away and took a rapid step back, putting some space between them. She was still staring at him, and he knew from her expression that everything he'd been feeling and thinking had been clearly written on his face. "Sorry," he said. "I'm sorry."

He ran one shaking hand through his hair. Damn! What was he doing? Another minute and he might have started undressing her. God knows he wanted to. He couldn't remember when he'd last wanted a woman this badly—

Yes, he could. Seven years ago. Then, too, the woman he'd wanted so desperately had been Emily. He'd wanted her enough to throw away all his good intentions. He'd actually gone and made love to her, despite his resolve to stay away from her.

He still found her that irresistible. Only this time around, Emily wasn't going to come to him the way she had seven years ago. This time around, she knew better.

Jim took a deep breath. "You're tired," he said, forcing a smile. "I know. I know what it's like to be out there pretending to be someone you're not for hours. You can't relax, not even for a second, for fear you'll say something wrong or make a mistake."

"Excuse me," Emily said, and he realized that by standing there the way he was, he had penned her into the corner.

Jim moved aside, and she opened the bedroom door. He was in the middle of her bedroom now, not two feet away from the big double bed Emily would be sleeping in tonight. He could picture her lying there, and it didn't take much to go another step farther and picture himself there, too. And oh, baby, that was one dangerous thought. He yanked his eyes away from the miniature flowers on the print of her bedspread to find her watching him. Self-consciously he smiled and moved past her, out into the relative safety of the hall.

"I'm exhausted," Emily said, and her voice shook very slightly. "And you're right. It's not easy spending so much time with a man I despise."

That statement seemed to be loaded with hidden meanings, and Jim tried to look into Emily's eyes, to see exactly what she had meant. Was she talking about Delmore—or God, was she talking about *him?* But she didn't look up at him for longer than an instant as she murmured a good-night and closed the bedroom door.

Jim walked slowly back into the living room, forcing himself to face the facts. He was poised at the brink of an emotional avalanche. He wanted this woman physically, there was no denying that. But it also seemed that she'd awakened more in him than merely his libido. He felt all sorts of frightening sensations whenever she was around—hell, he felt them whenever he so much as thought about her. And he thought about her damn near one hundred percent of the time.

He felt protective. Possessive. He felt proud—God, she was undeniably her own person, standing up so firmly for the things she believed in. He respected her, he admired her, he liked her. Yeah, he definitely liked her.

But feeling those things didn't mean that he loved her, did it? No, even *he* wouldn't be stupid enough to fall back in love with a woman who disliked him—and probably even despised him.

Chapter 8

Emily's dream started the way it always did. It started the way that awful evening had started—with deceptive calm and normality.

This time, she was having dinner with Carly. They were at that new place on Venice Road, the restaurant with all the big-screen TVs. Country Music Television was playing, showing a Dwight Yoakam video.

Carly was telling her about the latest stud she was dating, but right in the middle of a description of the guy's peculiar eating habits, Carly turned into Michele Harris, Emily's college roommate from her freshman year.

Michele was talking about something just as important and gripping as Carly's latest conquest, but although her mouth moved, Emily couldn't hear the words. Yet she knew that whatever her old roommate was saying didn't matter. She knew as soon as she saw Michele's face that the nightmare had begun.

Sure enough, the restaurant on Venice Road disappeared, replaced by Emily's freshman dorm dining room.

She and Michele were sitting in the corner, at a round table near the television. They were sitting exactly where they'd been that awful night.

The television was set to a channel showing reruns of "M*A*S*H," exactly as it had been. And the show was interrupted by a late-breaking news story, exactly as it had been.

Emily had dreamed about it hundreds of times before. She'd even lived through it once. But the horror was no less intense as the television newsperson reported live from the scene of a recent downtown shoot-out between local police and an escaped convicted killer.

"The killer, Laurence Macy, has been declared dead at the scene," the reporter's dispassionate voice said as the camera panned across the area. "But he didn't go down without a fight."

Emily watched in disbelief as the news camera lingered on Jim Keegan's beat-up old car. A portable police light still flashed from the roof. The car had been riddled with bullets, its windshield shattered.

"Two police officers have been shot," the reporter continued as the camera cut back to him, "and one is in critical condition." He turned to look over his shoulder at an ambulance parked haphazardly in the middle of the street. A crew of paramedics came into sight, shouting as they ran toward the vehicle, pulling a stretcher with them.

"The unidentified policeman," the reporter said as the camera zoomed in tighter on the figure on the stretcher, "is being taken to University Hospital."

It was Jim. His eyes were closed, and his mouth and nose were covered by an oxygen mask, but Emily recognized him immediately. And—oh, God! His chest was covered with blood. The paramedics scrambled around him, pulling him up and into the ambulance and slamming the doors tightly shut.

"We'll report in later from the hospital when we have information on the police officer's identity and condition," the reporter said, but Emily was no longer watching. She was already halfway out of the dining room.

The taxi ride was interminable. The hospital was only a few blocks away, but it seemed to take forever to get there. Still, Emily managed to arrive before the ambulance.

The emergency room was bustling, preparing for the ambulance. Emily stood in the lobby and prayed. Please, God, let Jim live. Please, God, don't let him die.

The ambulance pulled up with a squeal of tires, its siren wailing. The doctors ran outside to meet it, opening the van's doors and taking over from the paramedics. And then Jim was inside. Emily followed as they wheeled him down the hall.

His eyes were open and glazed with shock and pain. He was laboring to breathe, every breath a rattling effort. Bright red blood was everywhere, seeping through the bandages and the blanket that covered him, even flecking his lips.

How could someone lose that much blood and still live?

"Jim, hang on!" Emily cried, but he didn't, couldn't, hear her.

"We're losing him," a nurse reported, her voice cutting through the noise.

The medical team moved faster, but not fast enough.

As Emily watched, her own heart hammering in her chest, the machine hooked up to monitor Jim's heart rate flatlined.

The doctors and nurses worked frantically to revive him. Emily stood there in the hallway, watching in horror.

She felt the last of her control slipping, sliding away, as the doctors attempted to start Jim's heart with a jolt of electricity.

He was dying. He was going to die.

"No!" she cried. "No! It's not supposed to end this way! Jim! *Jim!* No—" She threw back her head and screamed, a piercing, primitive, throat-burning cry of grief and rage.

The door to her bedroom burst open, and light from the hallway flooded into her room and yanked Emily out of her dream.

She sat up with a start as Jim made a quick circuit of her room, checking the window locks and glancing into the closet. He was wearing only a pair of running shorts, and his hair was disheveled from sleep. He held a gun with an easy familiarity, as if it were an attachment to his arm.

"Are you all right?" he asked, putting the gun's safety on as he came to stand next to the bed.

Emily nodded.

He was still breathing hard, his broad chest rising and falling. She could see the faint scars where the bullets had struck him and where the surgeons had operated. He *wasn't* dead. He *hadn't* died. He was standing right here, in front of her, living, breathing proof that her dream had been only that—a dream.

Still, she couldn't seem to stop the tears that were streaming down her face.

"Nightmare?" Jim asked gently.

She nodded again, still silent, hugging her knees tight to her chest and closing her eyes. She heard the clunk as he put his gun on her bedside table, then felt the mattress sink as he sat down next to her on the bed.

"It must've been a bad one," he said. "You called out for me, and then you screamed. You scared the hell out of me, 'Em."

Emily lifted her head, pushing her hair out of her face with a hand that was still shaking. "I'm sorry—"

"Hey, shh...no," Jim said. "That's not why I was— You don't need to apologize." He reached for her before he realized what he was doing. It wasn't until he had his arms around her, until he felt her body stiffen, that he remembered she didn't want him to touch her. But before he could pull away, she put her arms around his neck. She held him so tightly it nearly took his breath away.

This had nothing to do with him, Jim told himself. Right now Emily needed someone to hold her, someone to hold on to, and he happened to be here. That was all this was, nothing more.

Still, he closed his eyes, breathing in the sweet fragrance of her hair as he rocked her back and forth. He gently stroked her back, soothingly running his hand up and down the soft cotton of her T-shirt.

"It's all right," he murmured. "It was only a dream."

After a while, he could feel her start to relax. He felt her stop trembling and heard her ragged breathing return to normal.

"I won't let anything bad happen, Emily," Jim said. "I promise you. Whatever you were dreaming about, it's not gonna happen, I swear."

"But it already did happen," Emily said.

Jim pulled back to look searchingly into her eyes. "Has Delmore hurt you?" His jaw tightened. "Damn it, I'll kill him—"

"I wasn't dreaming about Alex. I was dreaming about you." Tiredly, she let go of him. She moved away from him on the bed so that her back was against the headboard—and so that she was out of his reach.

"Me?" he said.

She could see the surprise on his face. He was surprised that she'd been dreaming about him—and equally surprised that she would admit it.

Emily pulled her knees up and rested her elbows on them. She supported her forehead in the palm of one hand. "I was dreaming about the night you were shot," she said. "I don't know, I guess seeing you again brought back the old nightmares."

"Nightmares?" he asked. "Plural? You mean, you've had this kind of dream before?"

She nodded. "I guess having my boyfriend shot made kind of an impact on me."

"You never told me."

"I didn't have them until after you were out of the hospital for a few months."

Until after they had split up. Until after he had staged that ugly little scene in the University Boulevard bar. Emily hadn't mentioned that night, but Jim knew that she was thinking about it.

"In my nightmare," Emily said, pulling the sheet higher up the bed, as if she were suddenly cold, "you always die, right there in the hall near the emergency room lobby." She looked up and briefly met his eyes. "It's as if my mind is playing out the worst-case scenario. It's as if I get to experience what I was most afraid of when I saw them wheel you in." Emily shrugged, sweeping her hair back from her face. "I don't know. I had a roommate who was a psychology major, and she said—"

She looked up, startled, when Jim caught her wrist. He was watching her intently, questioningly. "You saw them wheel me in?" he asked. "You *were* there. I thought I'd only imagined hearing your voice."

She was staring down at the fingers encircling her wrist, but he didn't release her.

"I got to the hospital before you did," she said.

"But how?" he asked, realizing suddenly that he'd never asked her how she'd first heard that he'd been shot. They'd never talked about it. "Who called you?"

"No one," she said, looking up into the piercing blue of his eyes. "I saw you on the news, being put into the ambulance."

"Oh, God," Jim breathed. He could remember the sense of disbelief he'd felt when the bullets hit him. No way. No way could he have been shot. He was off duty, he wasn't wearing a vest, he wasn't ready for it. There must be some mistake. But the only mistake was his. There was so much blood. There was blood *everywhere*.

And Emily had seen him that way. On television. Without warning.

Emily's eyes filled with tears. "Then, when they brought you in, they wouldn't let me near you. They wouldn't even let me hold your hand."

"I thought I heard your voice," Jim said. "I tried to find you. I wanted to tell you..."

He'd been so sure he was going to die. In fact, he'd been damn near ready to give up the fight. He'd been so tired and... But he'd wanted to tell Emily that he loved her. He'd tried to tell the doctor to give Emily a message from him, but the man wouldn't listen. He'd kept telling Jim to save his strength.

And then Jim had heard Emily's voice again. He'd heard her tell him to hang on, to keep fighting.

So he had.

But he hadn't really believed that she was actually there, in the hospital. It was bad enough that she'd seen him in the hospital bed, with all those tubes and monitors hooked up to him, after he was moved out of ICU. But, God, down in the ER, when he'd first been brought in, he'd been a real mess. That was enough to give anyone nightmares for the rest of their life.

"Emily, I'm sorry," he whispered, blinking back the sudden sharp sting of tears in his own eyes.

She wiped at her eyes, at a tear that threatened to roll down her cheek. "I am, too," she said.

Jim wasn't holding her wrist anymore, she realized. He was holding her hand. And she was holding on to him just as tightly.

"Sorry," she said, releasing him. She managed a watery smile. "Usually when I have these dreams, I don't have access to such solid proof that you really *are* all right."

He was looking at her with such wistful sadness in his eyes that she didn't flinch or pull away when he reached out to push her hair back from her face.

"I really blew it, didn't I?" he asked quietly. "By getting shot that way. I knew it was rough on you, but I had no idea..."

"It wasn't as if you got shot on purpose," Emily said. "It wasn't much fun for you, either."

"I didn't want you to have to live through something like that ever again," Jim said, cupping her face with his hand. His fingers were so rough, but he touched her so gently. Emily felt her pulse kick crazily into double time. "I never thought you would have nightmares."

She was looking up at him, her eyes wide and her lips slightly parted. She was wearing a faded white oversize T-shirt that didn't quite succeed in hiding her body from his view. The cotton was thin, and it clung to the soft fullness of her breasts. He forced his eyes back to her face. Her skin was so soft, and her beautiful hair was tousled from sleep. She looked sweet, so sweet and so innocent, as if somehow the past seven years had never touched her, as if she were somehow still eighteen years old, even after all this time.

He ran his thumb lightly across her lips. "God, Em, you're so beautiful—"

Desire. It was suddenly so palpable, it might have been a living thing, swirling around them, surrounding them, connecting them.

Emily knew that the desire she could see in Jim's eyes was mirrored in her own. Like him, she was helpless to hide it, powerless to conceal it. She could see it on his face, hear it in the way he breathed, feel it in his touch, in the heat of his skin.

She wanted him to touch her. She wanted to touch him. She wanted—

He kissed her.

Gently his mouth met hers in a kiss so sweet Emily nearly cried out. It had always amazed her—it *still* amazed her— that a man who was so much larger than life, a man who lived his life so passionately, so intensely, could be so breathtakingly tender.

Even as he deepened the kiss, as his tongue sought entry into her mouth, even then he was unquestionably gentle. Emily felt herself melt. She felt her bones turn to liquid, felt her body molding to fit against his as he took her into his arms and kissed her again and again.

His touch and taste were so familiar, it seemed as if they'd last made love just yesterday. Her memories were incredibly vivid. They'd tumbled together on his bed, a double bed just like this one, kissing and touching, exploring....

Emily felt Jim yank the sheet out from between them. She gasped as he rolled over, pulling her on top of him. Their legs intertwined, the roughness of his against the soft smoothness of hers. She could feel the hard bulge of his sex pressing against her as he kissed her again. He wanted her— it was undeniable.

She knew she could tell him that she wanted him, too, without saying a single word. All she'd have to do was to keep responding to his kisses. Or maybe, more obviously, she could pull her T-shirt up and over her head. No doubt he'd catch on pretty quick if she was lying naked in his arms.

Emily could remember the way he had caressed every inch of her body as he made love to her. He had made her feel as if she were the most beautiful, most desirable, woman in the world. She could remember how he had somehow seemed to know when to unleash his passion, when to leave his sweet tenderness behind. She could remember how he'd let himself lose control, giving himself over to her completely, crying out her name as waves of intense pleasure exploded around them both.

She could remember how totally, how absolutely, how with all her heart, she had loved him.

Her memory of that love was so strong, she could almost feel it. It was as if she'd been thrown backward in time, back seven years, back before Jim had hurt her so badly, back before she had known the kind of man he really was.

She could make love to him again, as if it were seven years ago. She could pretend that she was eighteen again and in love for the first time.

But tomorrow morning, when they woke up, it wouldn't be seven years ago. It would be now, and they would be here, and it would be awful.

She wiggled free, escaping his arms. He sat up, as if to follow her, but stopped suddenly. She turned to look at him, and saw the expression on his face as he realized what they'd been doing—what they'd been about to do.

"Oh, *damn*," he said. "Emily, God, I don't know what happened. I didn't intend to—"

"I know," she said. "It's...all right. It wasn't your fault— I mean, it was my fault, too. I think talking about that night you were shot made it easy for us to...kind of...slip back into our old relationship. It was easy to pretend that we're still lovers." She looked down at her hands, clenched tightly in her lap. "But we're not."

"Em," Jim said.

She looked up at him. He was watching her intently. His lean face looked mysterious, and hauntingly handsome, in the shadows. He didn't smile as she met his eyes.

"We could be," he said softly, seriously.

Lovers. He was talking about them being lovers.

Emily swallowed, remembering his taste, his touch...

"No." She shook her head. "We couldn't." She turned away from him. "I need you to leave."

He left.

Wednesday, the phone rang only once. It was Felipe Salazar, calling to say that Delmore's odd business meeting on Tuesday night had been exactly what it appeared to be—a late-night meeting with a client. Nothing illegal had transpired.

Thursday, the phone rang twice, but neither time was it Alexander Delmore.

By Friday, Jim had had enough. He wasn't sleeping worth a damn, not with Emily in the other room. She was well within reach—or she would have been, if his hands hadn't been tied behind his back. He wanted her so badly he could barely remember his name, but every time he so much as said two words to her, she jumped a mile high, then thought up some phony excuse to get away from him. Time to do the laundry. Time to get groceries. Time to wash the deck furniture. Wash the *deck* furniture, for crying out loud...

Something had to happen soon, or he'd lose his mind.

At ten o'clock, he went out onto the deck, where Emily was repotting several of her houseplants. She only glanced up at him, but it was long enough for him to feel the now-familiar jolt of awareness. Still, she seemed determined to ignore the powerful chemistry between them.

"Can you be ready to go out in about an hour?" he asked. She was wearing a faded old pair of cutoff jeans that had ripped several inches up the outside seam of her right leg. The effect was outrageously sexy—and all the more so because she seemed so oblivious to it.

"Where are we going?" she asked, moving some kind of plant with lots of long, green-leafed vines into a larger pot. She packed potting soil loosely on top of its roots.

Her hands were covered with dark brown dirt, and she used the back of her arm to push her hair out of her face as she looked up at him, waiting for him to answer.

"Your 'brother' is going to take you someplace nice for lunch," Jim said. He smiled. "And—what a coincidence— it'll just happen to be the same restaurant where Delmore's having lunch. You'll introduce him to me, I'll get us invited out on his boat."

Emily raised a skeptical eyebrow. "Alex never goes to the same place twice in a row," she said. "And sometimes he doesn't decide where he's going until he's halfway there. There are about seventeen restaurants that he really likes. So we've got a one-in-seventeen chance of guessing where he's going. And that's assuming he doesn't try someplace new."

Jim shook his head. "We aren't going to do any guessing," he said. "We're going to be dressed and ready and sitting in a car downtown near Delmore's boat slip. Phil Salazar is going to follow Delmore to wherever he's having lunch, then call and tell us where to go."

"Then we walk in, sit down and pretend we're surprised to see Alex, right?" Emily laughed, her eyes flashing with amusement. "Nothing like having the police force on your side when you want to get a date." She rinsed her hands in a bucket of water, then dried them on a rag. "I need to take a shower, but I can be ready to go in about a half hour."

She opened the sliding glass door, but paused on the threshold, turning back to look at him. "Some of the places Alex likes to go for lunch require a jacket and tie. Do you have something to wear?"

Jim smiled. "I've got that under control."

Emily nodded. Under control. At least *something* here was under control.

"I'm ready."

Emily came out into the living room wearing a white denim skirt and a pale blue T-shirt and carrying a white sweater over her arm. The skirt went down to midcalf, and she wore flat leather sandals on her feet.

Jim shook his head. "No, you're not," he said.

"Sure I am," Emily said. "I even have a sweater in case the air-conditioning is up too high."

Jim went down the hall toward Emily's bedroom. "You look like a high school English teacher."

"I *am* a high school English teacher," Emily said, bristling slightly, as she followed him into her room.

"Right," Jim said, opening her closet door. "But today you've got to remind Delmore that you're also an incredible-looking babe."

Emily rolled her eyes.

"You've got to wear something more along the lines of that blue dress." He looked quickly through the clothes hanging in her closet and pulled out a long, flowing skirt with a bold floral print. "This is good," he said, tossing it onto the bed.

Emily crossed her arms. "You don't *really* think I'm going to let you pick out my clothes," she said. She looked at him pointedly. "Wearing *that* tie with *that* jacket isn't exactly going to get you on St. Simone's list of the best-dressed men of the year."

"My tie doesn't match?" he said, looking at himself in the mirror on the back of the bedroom door. He was wearing dark blue pants with a light, grayish-blue tweed sport jacket. His tie was a dull mix of drab green and yellow. He shrugged and pulled three other ties from the pockets of his sport jacket. "I hate these things. *You* pick, okay?"

Emily glanced at them. "The blue is the least awful," she said.

Jim laughed. "The least awful wins." He put the other ties back in his pockets.

Emily watched him as he took off the green tie and put on the blue. She was wrong. Jim Keegan would make anyone's best-dressed list—provided "anyone" was a woman. Jim could wear damn near anything, and *still* be better-looking than most of the rest of the male population.

His pants fit him sinfully well, hugging his long legs and stacking neatly around his boots. His jacket might well have been tailor-made for his broad shoulders. And the way he wore his tie with the top button of his shirt unfastened was charming, rather than sloppy.

He looked into the mirror to adjust the tie and caught her watching him.

The last time he had been in her room, he'd kissed her. Jim knew she was thinking about it, too—how could she not be? She'd spent most of the past few days avoiding any possibility of a repeat encounter. Yet here he was. Back at the scene of the crime.

As Jim watched, she smiled briefly at him and looked away, moving toward the bed and the skirt he'd thrown there. Okay, so she was going to play it cool. They'd come pretty damn close to making love right here on her bed a few nights ago, but she wanted to pretend it had never happened. It was not to be mentioned, not to be discussed. But, damn it, he *wanted* to discuss it.

"Emily—"

She knew what he was going to say, and she didn't want to hear it. She picked up the skirt and held it up to her waist, gesturing to indicate the blue T-shirt she was wearing. "Do you want me to wear this shirt with this skirt?"

As she met his steady gaze, she clenched the skirt's hanger tighter.

"Emily, I really think we should talk—"

"What's to talk about?" she said swiftly. Jim could hear a trace of desperation in her voice. "Either you want me to wear this shirt or you don't. A simple yes or no will do."

"That's not what I meant, and you know it."

As he watched, Emily took a deep breath, visibly calming herself. When she spoke, her voice was even. "Look, just tell me what to wear so that we can get this investigation over with."

"And me out of your house," Jim added flatly.

"Yes."

It couldn't get much clearer than that, could it? But what was he expecting? Did he really think that they could sit down, have a quick heart-to-heart, and become lovers again? Because that was what he wanted, wasn't it? He wanted back into her bed.

Except if it was just a physical thing, if it was mere lust, he'd be able to control it. The way he'd felt the other night had been beyond control—*way* beyond control.

"What do you want me to wear?" she asked again.

Jim made himself focus on the skirt.

The floral print was a mix of blue, black and off-white. Jim shook his head. "Don't wear a T-shirt," he said. "You got one of those— What are they called? You know, it ties at the back of your neck and behind your back, at your waist?"

"A halter top?" Emily said.

"Yeah." Jim nodded. "Something like that. Something you'd never wear to teach a class."

"I don't have anything like that."

"I'd bet Carly does," he said, glancing at his watch. "If we're lucky, she hasn't left for work yet."

"Oh, have you memorized Carly's work schedule?" Emily said, with a sudden flash of something that *couldn't* be jealousy. It didn't make sense for her to feel jealous.

She followed Jim out into the living room and watched him open the front door.

"She told me she works at the library afternoons and evenings," he said evenly. "Right now, it's still morning. Maybe she's home."

He was gone only a few minutes, and when he returned he was triumphantly waving something that looked an awful lot like a tiny black silk scarf.

"We're in luck," he said, handing it to Emily. "Carly had just what I was picturing."

"You want me to wear *this?*" Emily held the black silk up, and the sunlight streaming through the sliding glass doors made it seem almost translucent. "With *nothing* underneath?"

"Yeah. It'll look amazing with that skirt."

"Amazing," Emily echoed, nodding her head. "Right."
She looked up at Jim. "Why bother wearing anything at
all?" she said tartly. "Why don't I just go naked?"

He crossed his arms and leaned back against the wall,
giving her a long, appraising look. "That would be okay
with me, too."

She held the halter top out to him. "Thanks, but no
thanks."

He didn't take it. "I thought you wanted to get this investigation over with." She didn't move. "At least try it
on," he said, more gently.

Emily turned and went back into the bedroom to change.

Chapter 9

At one-fifteen, Jim's cellular phone chirped, and he flipped it open.

"Yeah." He held Emily's gaze as he listened to Felipe Salazar report which restaurant Delmore had gone to for lunch. "The Stone Wharf." He gave Emily a questioning look.

"I know where that is," she said with a nod. "I've been there with Alex several times. It's near those new condos, about three miles from here. It's part of that new development of expensive stores called the Quay."

Jim nodded, taking his sunglasses from his pocket. "Thanks, Phil," he said into the phone. "We're on our way."

He clicked off the telephone and put Emily's car into gear. They'd been sitting in it, with the motor running and the air-conditioning on full, for ages.

"About time," he said. "I'm starving. I was beginning to think Delmore was never going to eat lunch."

Emily looked over at him, startled. "We're not really going to eat there, are we?"

"We can't go in, sit down and only order a glass of water while we wait for Delmore to notice us," Jim said. "That would look a little suspicious, you know?"

"The Stone Wharf is really expensive," Emily said, gazing out the window at the posh hotels and high-class condos that lined the streets in this part of town. "Lunch for the two of us could easily cost eighty dollars. I can't afford that."

"It's covered by my expense account," Jim said. "You won't have to pay. You know, don't go crazy and order champagne or caviar or anything outrageous. But don't worry about getting stuck with the bill."

Emily nodded. "Thanks." She pointed out the window. "It's your next right. See the sign for the Quay?"

"I've driven past this place," Jim said, signaling to make a right turn into the upscale mall's driveway, "but I've never gone in. So far they've had no crimes committed on the premises, and as far as the restaurants go, an eighty-buck lunch date is a little out of my league."

Emily was silent as he found an empty space and parked the car. He turned off the motor and the air-conditioning, and the sudden lack of noise was deafening. But she didn't seem to notice. She stared out the front windshield, her eyes unfocused.

"Hey," Jim said, and she turned and looked at him. "You ready to go in?"

"Ready as I'll ever be," she said coolly, "considering that I feel half-naked wearing this ridiculous excuse for a top."

Jim's gaze dropped to the whisper-thin silk that covered Emily's full breasts. It was true—the halter top didn't leave a whole lot to the imagination. But it wasn't as blatantly revealing as she feared. The fabric was gathered, sort of like two large triangles of silk that were bunched together and attached to a wide band that went below her breasts and tied in the back. Sure, when she moved a certain way and the weight of her breasts strained against the silk, her nipples were clearly outlined. But that happened only infrequently—just enough for Jim to wish it would happen a little more often.

"You look great," he said. His voice was raspier than usual, so he cleared his throat. "You're really gonna turn heads when you walk into this place. You look sexy, but in a real classy way, you know?"

"And you're an expert on classy, right?" Emily said, suddenly wanting to lash out at him. His words, his voice, the soft look in his eyes, it suddenly all seemed too intimate, too personal. She didn't want him to look at her that way. She didn't want to care whether or not he thought she was sexy. She wanted to dislike him. Forget dislike—she wanted to *hate* him. At the very least, she wanted him to hate her. Either way, she wished he would stop being so damned *kind* all the time. "And how do you know whether or not I'm going to 'turn heads'? You've never been to this restaurant before. It's out of your league, right?"

Jim got quiet, very, very quiet, as he studied the front of the restaurant out the windshield of the car. But when he turned to look at Emily, she could see the flare of emotion in his eyes. She saw anger—and something else. She looked away quickly, praying that what she'd just seen in his eyes wasn't hurt.

"Just because I don't earn my money running illegal drugs," Jim said tightly, "just because I choose not to spend an amount that would feed an entire family of six for an entire week on one lousy meal, doesn't mean I don't know class when I see it. I don't pretend to have any class—I never have—but I'll tell you one thing I know for a fact, Emily. I've got a hell of a lot more of it than your boyfriend in there."

He got out of the car and slammed the door shut.

Emily couldn't breathe. She'd gotten him mad at her, all right, but she couldn't blame him for it at all. And he was right, he *did* have more class than Alex Delmore.

She got out of the car and closed the door behind her.

Jim was already halfway across the parking lot. Good. Let him go. She *wanted* him to be angry with her. She wanted him to hate her, remember?

Despite her intentions, she found herself running across the hot blacktop, chasing after him. "Jim!"

Jim stopped in his tracks. Damn it, every time she called him by his given name, his heart nearly stopped beating. It was as if he thought maybe this time she was ready to admit that the chemistry between them was undeniable. Of course, that was extremely unlikely right now, considering he'd just let her have a full dose of his notoriously hot temper. Still, he turned around to wait for her to catch up.

And then his heart nearly *did* stop beating. Emily was running. Toward him. Wearing that flimsy top. But what made him stand glued to the spot was the look in her eyes. She was scared. Unless he was reading her wrong, something had her really scared.

"Number one," he said gently when she reached him, "when we're out in public, you *have* to call me Dan. I'm your brother, remember? Don't forget it."

Emily nodded, out of breath.

"Number two," he deadpanned, "don't run in that halter top. This is Florida, remember? There're a lot of old guys around. You'll give 'em all heart attacks. I don't want to have to run you in for manslaughter."

That got a smile out of her. It was a rueful smile, but it was a smile just the same. "You'd be an accessory. It was your idea for me to wear this, remember?"

"Yeah, I remember," he said, walking backward toward the restaurant door, still watching her. "Come on. Let's go in there and wow Delmore, get invited onto his boat for a weekend cruise, and then have a great lunch, okay?"

"I'm not sure I'll be able to eat," Emily confessed.

"Sure you will," Jim said. His smile disappeared. "I'll be there with you, Em, the whole time. You're safe. You hear what I'm saying?"

He was dead serious, and Emily nodded slowly.

She was safe from Alex Delmore. But she didn't feel safe from Jim Keegan—because despite everything, even despite their wretched history, she was actually starting to like the man.

Emily sat back in her chair and calmly looked out at the magnificent view of the glistening Gulf waters. As she leaned forward to lift her ginger ale and take a sip, she looked at Jim.

"Has he seen us yet?" she asked quietly.

Alex Delmore was sitting slightly behind Emily and to her left. He was sitting with two other men in business suits. Jim glanced around the room again, not allowing his recognition of Delmore to show as he gave their table a cursory sweep with his eyes.

He smiled at Emily. "Yeah, I think maybe he has," he said. "Come on, smile. Remember, you're out to lunch with your favorite brother. Look happy, or Delmore's gonna think we come from a dysfunctional family."

Emily actually laughed.

Jim opened the menu. "What are you going to have?"

"A salad," Emily said.

"That's all?"

"Really," she said. "I'm not hungry."

"Well, I am," Jim said. "What do you suppose scallops meunière is?"

"Look, I'm sorry for what I said before," Emily said. Jim looked up from the menu, his eyes as vivid a blue as the water behind him. He almost looked surprised. "In the car," she explained. "I didn't mean what I said. And I can't believe you're not still mad at me."

He carefully closed his menu and glanced around the dining room to make sure Alex Delmore wasn't about to approach them. "We're both under a lot of stress right now," he said quietly. He took his time selecting a breadstick from the basket in the center of the table before he looked up at her again. "And you know, anyway, you were right. I don't know class from my—"

"Yes, you do."

Jim watched her across the table. His usually animated face was as serious as Emily had ever seen it. "Are you actually arguing in my defense?" he asked. "Correct me if I'm wrong, but it sounds like you're sticking up for me here."

"Yeah, I guess I am," Emily said.

Emily knew she'd set herself up. There were a thousand smartass quips Jim could make, and an equal number of possibilities for jokes, but he did neither.

"That's really nice," was all he said. He smiled at her, almost shyly, and Emily lowered her eyes, suddenly feeling self-conscious.

"Heads up," Jim said quietly. "Delmore's standing. He's going to come over here."

Emily closed her eyes briefly, but that was the only sign she gave that she was even slightly perturbed.

"Dan," Jim whispered. "Not Jim."

She smiled at him. "I know."

"Emily! What a surprise. No, please, stay in your seats." Delmore's smooth, refined voice made the hair on the back of Jim's neck stand up. God, two seconds into the game and he already hated the guy. No, not true. Jim had hated Alexander Delmore even before he set eyes on the millionaire. He'd hated him from the first moment he pictured Delmore making love to Emily.

Delmore was blond, with the kind of boyish good looks most often found at Ivy League colleges and in upscale fashion catalogs. Jim knew that the millionaire was probably nearing forty, but with a slight build on a six-foot frame he seemed much younger.

"I'm Alex," he said, offering his hand to Jim as he pulled over a chair from an empty table and sat down. "You must be Emily's brother." As he shook Jim's hand, he said in a loud aside to Emily, "Gee, I *hope* this guy's your brother," as if he were amused by the very idea that he might not be able to totally squash any kind of romantic competition.

The man positively reeked of confidence. Jim had to keep reminding himself to smile instead of snarl.

"This is my brother, Dan," Emily said. "Dan Marshall, Alex Delmore."

"Nice to meet you," Jim said, smiling broadly, thinking, *It'll be even nicer to throw your butt in jail, scumbag.*

"Likewise," Alex said. His attention swiveled over to Emily. "Don't *you* look terrific!"

"Thank you," Emily murmured.

Delmore launched into a description of the clients he was lunching with, filled with dropped names and six-digit figures with dollar signs in front of them. As the real estate mogul talked, his gaze traveled up and down Emily, settling more than once on the fullness of her breasts. Jim resisted the urge to grab the man by the neck and squeeze. And when Delmore reached out and lightly ran his fingers down Emily's arm from her shoulder to her hand, Jim made himself sit very still. He was afraid that if he moved even an inch, he would explode with jealousy.

Jealousy? No, please, not jealousy...

Emily sat and smiled at Delmore as he entwined his fingers with hers. There was nothing in her face or body language to give away her fear. Nothing that Jim noticed, anyway, except the pulse that beat at the base of her throat. He could see every beat of Emily's heart, and it was going way too fast.

Of course, Delmore, having an ego the size of a small planet, would merely assume that it was his touch that was making her heart pound.

Unless... Maybe Jim was wrong. Maybe Emily *was* turned on by this guy. After all, she'd been dating Alex for almost half a year. He had to assume they'd been lovers for nearly that long. It had been days since she'd seen Alex. And nearly a week since they would have had even a chance to make love...

"I've missed you," Alex said, in an intimate voice that was meant only for Emily's ears.

I'll bet, thought Jim. He watched Emily, waiting for her response.

But she said nothing. She only smiled as Delmore gazed into her eyes. What did it mean, that smile?

"I haven't called you in a few days," Delmore said, "because I wanted to give you some time alone with your brother." He smiled warmly at Jim.

This investigation wasn't set up to find out whether Emily still had a thing for Alex Delmore, Jim reminded himself. He had work to do here.

"Emily's told me about your yacht, the *Home Free*," Jim said. "When I lived up north, I used to sail all the time. I don't get out on the water much anymore."

Delmore took the hint. "Well, you'll have to come out for a sail while you're in town," he said. "I don't have my calendar with me now, but we'll set something up for one of these coming weekends."

"That'd be terrific," Jim said. "I'm going to hold you to that."

"How long are you going to be in town?" Delmore asked.

"I'm not exactly sure," Jim said. "I've got the whole summer off."

"You'll probably be going down to Sanibel Island," Delmore said. "Your family owns a condo on the beach there, right?"

"Yeah." Jim nodded. "And, of course, I'll be spending some time up in Connecticut, visiting the folks."

Emily stifled a nervous laugh. It was strange, hearing Jim talk about Sanibel and Connecticut as if he'd lived part of her life with her, as if he really *were* her brother.

"Do you two have plans for tonight?" Delmore asked.

Jim met Emily's eyes across the table. She hesitated, so he answered. "No, we don't."

He was hoping that Delmore would invite them to dinner, or even over to his house for a drink.

"Have dinner with me tonight," Delmore said.

Bingo, thought Jim. But then he realized the man was speaking only to Emily.

"You don't mind if I steal Emily away from you, do you?" Delmore said to Jim. "Do you? After all, you've had her to yourself all week long."

For the first time in a long time, Jim was speechless. He honestly didn't know what to say. If he objected, he might come across as being selfish and petty. What kind of brother would object to his sister dating a millionaire? But, damn it, he *wanted* to object. He didn't want Emily to have to deal with Delmore on her own. He didn't want Emily to go.

The silence was stretching on way too long, so Jim did the only thing he could. He passed the ball to Emily. As her brother's hostess, she could graciously refuse. "I guess that decision's up to Em," he said.

"How about it?" Delmore said, turning to Emily. "I'll pick you up around seven?"

Say no, Jim silently willed Emily with his eyes. Come on, Em, turn him down.

"Seven sounds fine," she finally said, smiling at Delmore.

What the *hell* was she doing? Why on earth would she agree to have dinner with this scumbag? Why would she do something she didn't want to do?

Unless she *did* want to...

Jim looked at Emily, sitting there with Delmore. The guy was holding her hand, and he had his other arm wrapped loosely around her shoulders.

"I'll see you later, then," Delmore said, kissing Emily on the lips. Jim's blood pressure rose another notch.

Delmore stood up, offering his hand to Jim. "Nice meeting you, Dan."

Jim kept his face carefully bland, concentrating on not letting himself break all of Delmore's fingers as they shook hands.

And then Alexander Delmore was gone, back to his own table.

Jim's hand was shaking as he picked up his glass of water and took a sip. Emily glanced up at him. He smiled at her, but his eyes were unmistakably icy.

"Why did you agree to have dinner with him?" His voice was low, but rough with emotion. And he was still smiling, as if they were having a pleasant conversation.

"I thought you wanted me to," Emily said. Was he actually *angry* at her? She was mystified. With his words, Jim had clearly left the decision about whether or not to have dinner with Alex up to her. But his eyes had told her an entirely different story. She had been so sure he wanted her to accept Alex's invitation. Apparently she'd been wrong.

"Why the *hell* would I want you to?" Jim shot back. "I can't protect you when you're off somewhere, alone with him."

With one last wave in Emily and Jim's direction, Alex and his clients went out of the restaurant. As the door closed tightly behind them, Jim's smile vanished.

"Now I've got to call Salazar, arrange for surveillance," Jim said tightly as he glared at her. "Damn it, we don't even know where Delmore'll be taking you, so we'll have to set up a tail and—"

Emily's temper flared. "Sorry to inconvenience you," she said. "Maybe next time you could manage to tell me what you would like me to do and say *in advance,* rather than assume I'll be able to read your mind."

"I thought your avoiding a one-on-one situation with Delmore was the obvious choice," he countered. "But it seems you don't find him as much of a threat as I do. God knows you'll get a better dinner by going out with him than you would staying home with me. What I can't figure out is what else you'll get."

Jim stared across the table at Emily. Her cheeks were flushed, but was it from anger or embarrassment? There was no reason for her to feel embarrassed, was there? Unless, of course, he'd hit upon her real reason for having accepted Delmore's dinner invitation. Maybe, despite everything, she was still in love with the guy.

Next to the table, their waiter cleared his throat. "Are you ready to order?"

Jim stood up, throwing his napkin, a twenty-dollar bill and Emily's car keys on the table. "I'm not hungry anymore," he said, and walked out of the restaurant.

Emily was dressed and ready for her date with Alex before Jim returned to the apartment.

As she let him in the door, she knew from his carefully neutral expression, and from the way he wouldn't hold her gaze, that he was still angry. What she couldn't figure out was why.

But why didn't matter, she tried to convince herself. What mattered was that he was giving her a healthy reminder of just how rude and childish he really was. This was a solid dose of reality. His kindness and concern were probably no more than an act. And his kisses... His kisses were pure fantasy, that was for sure. There was nothing even remotely permanent or real-life about them. Sure, they were nice while they lasted, but Emily wasn't interested in any kind of relationship that was based completely on sex.

Jim took a can of soda from the refrigerator and popped open the top. "Can you leave me your car keys, please?" he asked politely.

"They're on the table," Emily said, coolly but no less politely, checking her makeup in the front mirror.

"Phil's out in the parking lot right now," he told her, leaning against the wall and watching as she ran a brush through her hair. She was wearing it down tonight, and it hung in a full, rich sheet, ending just above her shoulders. "After Delmore picks you up, he's gonna follow you. When you get where you're going, he's gonna give me a call and tell me what restaurant you're at. I'm going to use your car to drive over and meet him. Then, together, we'll trail you for the rest of the evening."

Emily nodded and checked her watch. Ten minutes to seven. Alex would be here any second. Suddenly she was so nervous she could barely breathe. She sat down on the couch and closed her eyes, trying to regain her inner calm. What could happen? Nothing, really—right? The worst-case scenario was that Alex would have his hands all over her all night long, the way he had at lunch. And—oh, shoot, she was forgetting about having to kiss him good-night....

She was wearing one of her church dresses. It was a demure 1940s-retro thing in a tiny-flowered pink print. It had a sweetheart neckline, short capped sleeves and a long, sweeping skirt. It was a far cry from the blue sequined dress she'd worn the other night. It was also miles removed from the barely-there halter top she'd had on at lunch. Wearing this dress, she looked as if she could win the year's award for Miss Innocence. And that was the idea.

"Pretty dress," Jim said, and Emily opened her eyes.

He was sitting across from her in the rocking chair, watching her and drinking his soda.

"Thanks," she said. She closed her eyes again—and opened them quickly, sitting up as she suddenly imagined a new worst-case scenario. This one had Alex somehow finding out that she was working with the police. This one involved Alex turning her over to the organized-crime thugs that he worked alongside of. This one had Vincent Marino's boys disposing of her body in the darkest, densest part of the Everglades....

The doorbell rang, and Emily looked sharply over at Jim. The fear was back, screaming through her veins with every pounding beat of her heart.

But Jim wasn't looking at her. He'd already gotten to his feet and was opening the door.

"Hi, Dan, how are you?" Alex shook Jim's hand as he came into Emily's apartment.

Would they kill her quickly, or would she be alive when they took her into the alligator-infested swamp?

Emily took a deep breath, stood up and made herself smile at Alex.

"Ready to go?" he asked with an answering smile.

"Hey, you know, I intend to hold you to that offer to take me on a sail," Jim said. "Did you get a chance to check your calendar yet?"

It was amazing the way Jim sounded so easygoing. And with his wide, friendly smile, his reminder of Alex's invitation was not intrusive or at all offensive.

Alex shook his head. "Damn. No, I *knew* there was something I forgot to do when I left the yacht this afternoon." He shrugged sheepishly. "I'll have to get back to you with a date."

Would they put a bullet in her brain, or would they simply tie her up and leave her there—free lunch for the gators? She could imagine their yellow eyes, their razor-sharp teeth, the way their noses would break the water as they slowly swam toward her....

"I'm counting on it," Jim said.

"All right," Alex said. "Have a good evening."

"Don't keep Emily out too late," Jim said, his words softened by a smile. "We're planing to hit the beach pretty early in the morning." He turned to Emily. "See you later, Em."

She was smiling back at him, but as soon as she met his gaze, Jim saw that something was wrong. Was she *scared?* On impulse, he pulled her in for a quick hug that confirmed it for him. She *was* scared. She was actually shaking.

But Delmore took her by the hand and pulled her out the door before Jim could figure out what he could do to help her.

Then he saw it. Emily's purse. She'd forgotten it again. It was sitting on the table next to the front door.

Her bedroom looked out over the parking lot, and Jim dashed down the hall and quickly wound the casement window open. Delmore was just about to help Emily into his limousine.

"Yo, Em!" Jim shouted, and she looked up in surprise. "You forgot your purse!"

As he watched, Emily put her hand on Delmore's arm and shook her head, as if saying, *Stay here, I'll dash back to the apartment by myself.* Sure enough, she moved briskly away from the limo, while Alex leaned against it, waiting for her.

Jim met her at the door, but instead of handing her the purse, he took her by the arm and pulled her inside, shutting the door behind her.

"You okay?" he asked, looking down at her intently.

"Yeah."

"You're lying," he said, not unkindly. He held her shoulders to keep her from turning away. "This is scaring the hell out of you, isn't it?"

His eyes were so warm, and so full of concern. Emily couldn't seem to break free from his gaze. "Yes," she finally admitted in a whisper. "What if he finds out—?"

His grip on her shoulders tightened. "You don't have to do this," he said. "Em, you don't have to go—"

"Yes, I do," she said vehemently. "If Alex is running drugs, I want to see him rot in jail."

"There are other ways—"

"I can't wait for other ways!"

Her eyes were flashing with a passion she rarely let show. Jim had always known it was back there. Oh, yeah, he'd had the opportunity to see firsthand the power of the passion and spark she kept hidden behind her quiet calm. She'd looked at him with that same liquid fire in her eyes when they made love.

The memory rose with very little encouragement. She was naked, kneeling on his bed— Jim shook his head. This was *not* the time for erotic reminiscences. "Emily..." he said.

"I'll be okay," she said. "He's *not* going to find out, and besides, you're going to follow me, right?"

"Yeah, but—"

"Then I'll be fine," she said.

"God, I wasn't thinking," Jim said. "We should've had you wired for sound. Look, let me go down there and tell Delmore that you're sick, that you're not feeling well," he said, talking fast. Emily had already taken too much time. Delmore would be wondering what was keeping her. Soon he'd come to see what the problem was. "We can reschedule— Damn, this is making me *crazy*. I don't want you to do this if you're scared—"

Emily shook her head. "I'm okay. I've got to go—"

But he couldn't release her. Still holding her shoulders tightly, he stared down into the swirling blue of her eyes, feeling again the loss of gravity, the absence of any solid ground. "Please," he heard himself say, his voice no more than a hoarse whisper. But please *what?* Please don't go? Or please kiss me?

"Jim, I'll be okay," she said again.

Perfect. He'd meant to reassure her, but she was the one doing the reassuring here.

Jim did the only thing he could think to do under the circumstances. He kissed her.

It was remarkable. One moment he was gazing into Emily's beautiful eyes, and the next he was locked with her in an embrace that told the truth about the fire that still burned between them. It was an explosion of desire, a chemical reaction between two highly volatile substances kept too long apart.

Jim heard himself groan as he kissed her again. She tasted sweet, so sweet, and she clung to him, returning his kisses with an equal desperation. Her body was so soft against his. He could feel her heart pounding, every beat an echo of his own drumming pulse.

And then the doorbell rang.

Emily sprang away from him guiltily, her eyes wide and her cheeks flushed as she stared at him.

"Don't go," he said. It wasn't a request, it was a demand, only there was something wrong with his voice. The words came out a mere whisper that made them sound more like a plea.

Emily's eyes filled with tears. *Don't go.* But she had to. She bent down to pick up her purse from where it had fallen on the floor. She was afraid to go, but the truth was, she was more afraid to stay. She turned and opened the door.

Alex surely noticed the tears that were still brimming in her eyes, and Jim's tight-lipped expression. But he politely didn't comment, at least not until he was helping her into the back seat of his limo.

"Isn't it strange how you can be apart from someone like a brother or a sister for years, but then, when you see them again, nothing has changed?" Alex said, with unexpected sensitivity. "Everything's exactly the same. It's as if you pick up right where you left off, with all of the old issues and emotions and arguments suddenly alive again."

Emily murmured her agreement.

He reached over and squeezed her hand. "This evening is perfect for you," he said with a smile. "What you need is a little time away from him." *Him* being Dan, who was, in reality, Jim.

Alex had no idea just how right he was.

As Jim watched Delmore's limousine pull out of the driveway, he dialed the number of Felipe Salazar's car phone.

It rang once, twice, three times. Where the hell was he? God, was it possible that Salazar wasn't even in his car? And if he wasn't in his car, then he wasn't following Delmore and Emily—

Salazar didn't pick up the phone until after the fifth ring. *"Hola."*

"Answer the damn phone when it rings, damn it," Jim barked.

"Ah, Diego. I am fine, and how are you?" Salazar said, not one bit fazed.

"Are you following Delmore?"

"Yes, but it would be much easier if I were not distracted by the 'damn phone.' The limousine made a left turn across heavy traffic, and my choice was either to concentrate on following it or to lose them and answer the phone. I let it ring."

"I'm sorry. I'm just..." Jim took a deep breath, and let it out slowly. "Felipe, don't lose her," he said softly.

"You know I won't, man," Salazar said.

"When they get to their destination," Jim said, "go in, let Emily see that you're there. She was pretty nervous about being alone with Delmore."

"Got it," Salazar said. "I'll call you from inside."

"Thanks," Jim said.

"Later," Salazar said, and the line was cut.

Jim slowly hung up the phone. The silence in the apartment surrounded him, and he started to pace.

Emily was scared. He could still see the traces of fear in her eyes, could still feel her trembling as he held her in his arms. *What if he finds out—?* There was no doubt about it, she was scared. Of Delmore.

Jim stopped pacing. He stood in the middle of Emily's living room and stared sightlessly out the sliding glass door.

It was obvious now that Emily had dreaded this date with Delmore. Jim had been wrong, thinking that she might still be in love with the millionaire. No way could she be in love with a man she was so afraid of. Yeah, he'd been dead wrong about her reasons for accepting this dinner date with Delmore.

He couldn't remember the last time being wrong about something had made him feel so good.

Chapter 10

As Salazar cracked open another pistachio nut with his teeth, Jim glanced at his watch. Ten-thirty. Delmore and Emily had been inside Aquavia's restaurant for close to three hours now.

Salazar had been going inside every ten minutes to check on Emily. According to Jim's partner, Emily had ordered some kind of broiled whitefish for dinner, but she hadn't eaten much of the meal. She and Delmore had been sitting alone in a secluded corner of the harborside restaurant until about an hour ago, when another couple had motored up to the dock on their yacht. They were friends of Delmore's, and they'd joined him and Emily. Now they all sat at a bigger table, having dessert and drinks. Emily was drinking herbal tea, Salazar reported.

"This is driving me crazy," Jim muttered, staring at the back of Delmore's limousine. Salazar cracked open another nut, and Jim shot him a look. "And you're not helping any," he added.

"Sorry," Salazar said, crumpling up the paper bag that held the rest of the nuts and the discarded shells.

They sat for a moment in a silence broken only by the soft purr of the car's engine and air conditioner.

"Do you want to talk about it?" Salazar asked suddenly. "You know, about what's going on between you and Emily?"

Jim turned to find his partner watching him. *Talk* about it? What could he possibly say? "There's nothing going on," he said flatly.

Salazar nodded slowly. He obviously didn't buy it. "You trust me with your life, Diego," he said. "You can trust me with this, too."

Jim raked his fingers through his hair. There was no way he could talk about what he was feeling. Hell, in order to put his thoughts into words, he'd have to figure out exactly what he *was* feeling. And that was way too frightening. "I'm sorry, Phil," he said. "It's not that I don't trust you, but... I can't... talk about it."

Salazar looked out the windshield at Delmore's limousine. "Me, I'm in too deep with that girl, Jewel," he said, as easily as if he were telling Jim what he had had for lunch that day. "You know, that friend of Emily's?"

Jim couldn't hide his astonishment. "The redhead?"

"Yes." Salazar smiled. "Jewel Hays. I have been going to visit her every day." He laughed and tapped his fingers on the steering wheel as he shot Jim a sidelong glance that was a mix of humor and despair. "Can you believe it? Me, Mr. Clean, getting involved with a crack addict."

Jim found his voice. "But... she's been through rehab."

"Three times," Salazar said. "Which means she has already slipped back twice." He sighed. "She looks like an angel—but I know she's not one. Far from it, in fact. She was on the street, turning tricks, before she was fifteen. *Fifteen*." He broke off, muttering something in Spanish.

Jim caught enough of it to know his partner was damning to hell everyone responsible for leading a child so far astray.

Another minute ticked by on Jim's watch as he stared out at the brightly lit parking lot. He'd been just a little bit older than Felipe Salazar when he first met Emily....

"Still," Salazar said, breaking the silence, "when she looks at me and smiles..." He shrugged and smiled ruefully. "You know, I'm not in love with her. I'm not crazy enough to let it go that far. But I can't control what *she's* feeling. I know she's got a crush on me. I know this attraction thing is very mutual, and way too strong, you know?"

Jim nodded. He knew. "What are you going to do?"

"What can I do?" Salazar sighed. "I'm going to keep visiting her. She needs *someone* to care, man, and it looks like I'm it."

Jim nodded again. He knew how *that* felt, too.

"And I'm going to pray that she stays away from the drugs," Salazar continued. "I know enough about addicts to know that keeping her drug-free is not something I can do for her. She has to do that herself. She seems to be doing okay, but, you know, she's still in the honeymoon phase."

The alarm on Jim's wristwatch beeped. As he turned it off, Salazar climbed out of the car. Ten minutes had passed. It was time to check on Emily.

Emily. Beautiful Emily, who deep down inside was nowhere near as cool and serene as she pretended to be. Emily, who had kissed him back as though there were no tomorrow. Emily, who was sitting in that restaurant right now, with another man's arm around her shoulders...

Big deal, Jim told himself sternly. Compared to Felipe Salazar's, his problems were nothing. At least the woman *Jim* was attracted to wasn't a recovering drug addict. Sure, it was true that Felipe didn't want any kind of lasting relationship with Jewel. He wasn't in love with Jewel, the way Jim was in love with—

The way he was in— No. Jim felt himself start to sweat, and he pushed the air conditioner's fan up a notch higher. He *wasn't* falling in love with Emily again. No way. Only a fool would set himself up for such total and absolute failure. Sure, Emily was still physically attracted to him. That was clear from the way she'd returned his kisses. But she'd damn near run out of the apartment afterward. Jim shook his head. She couldn't wait to get away from him. She'd told him, in plain English, that she didn't like him. Yeah, he had a screw coming loose if he thought falling in love with Emily again would bring him anything but pain.

So he wouldn't let himself fall. Easier said than done. Jim felt like a man clinging to the side of a rocky cliff, hanging on with his fingernails and the sheer force of his willpower. Every thought of Emily—which was damn near every thought—was like a strong wind, buffeting him, straining his tentative hold.

Felipe Salazar climbed back into the car. "They are all still sitting at the table," he reported. "I made eye contact with Emily. She's doing fine. She even smiled at me. That is one tough lady."

Jim murmured his agreement, wishing Salazar would change the subject. He wanted to know that Emily was all right—period, the end. He didn't want to know if she was smiling or if Delmore was holding her hand. He didn't want to remember her short but well-manicured fingernails, or her long, slender, cool fingers, or that only one touch of her graceful hands could drive him damn near wild....

"Jewel told me Emily teaches both remedial English and honors AP English," Salazar went on. "Apparently remedial English is where they send the troublemakers in her school. According to Jewel, before Emily came along, that class was little more than baby-sitting the students the school's administration hoped would drop out when they reached age sixteen. But from the bits and pieces I've heard from Jewel, Emily wouldn't give up on those kids. She got them involved in creative writing. They published their own literary magazine—these kids who had never written anything that wasn't spray-painted on a wall. It was like magic. They were hooked. But from what I have heard from Jewel, I think it was more than the magazine that hooked the kids. I think it was Emily. I think she treats these kids like human beings. She respects them, and she gives them opportunities to gain her trust. And once she trusts them, she stands by them. She believes in them, so they can believe in themselves."

Jim knew what it felt like to have Emily believe in him. He could remember her eyes shining as she'd smiled up at him, back when they were dating. He could see her sitting by his bed in the hospital, believing that he would pull through, that his pain would soon ease, believing enough for both of them. He could remember her coming to his apartment, to his bed, giving herself to him, strong in her belief that he would not abuse her trust.

And then he had.

He'd destroyed everything between them.

And still she believed in him. He'd heard it in her voice, only a few hours ago. She'd said, "You're going to follow me, right? Then I'll be fine." She believed he would keep her safe.

As if his memory had been captured on film, lit by a strobe light, Jim saw Emily's face as she stared up at him, as he bent his head to kiss her. Contact. Heat. Soft, sweet mouth. Fingers in his hair. Pulling him closer. Closer. His tongue against hers. Her body molding to his. A flash of pleasure so intense it was nearly pain.

And then it *was* pain.

Who the hell was he kidding here? He wasn't going to fall in love with Emily again. It just wasn't possible.

He wasn't going to fall in love with her again—because, damn it, he'd never stopped loving her in the first place.

* * *

Emily heard the words, but they didn't register at first.

"It's still early," Alex's friend Marty was saying, swishing around the ice in her Long Island iced tea. "Why don't you and Emily sail back to the cottage with us?" She smiled. "I'm dying to show off the new pool we've just put in. What do you say? We can all go for a swim."

Sail? Across the harbor, to Marty and Ken's palatial "cottage"? Emily felt a flash of panic. If they sailed, if they didn't take the limo, Jim wouldn't be able to trail her. He'd have no idea where she'd gone, no way to find her.

"That sounds great," Alex said. He turned toward Emily. "I've been hearing about this new swimming pool for close to a year now."

"But . . . I didn't bring my bathing suit," Emily said.

Marty lit a cigarette and smiled at Emily from behind a cloud of smoke. "With a body like yours, you don't need one." She laughed, the lines around her eyes crinkling with genuine amusement. "On second thought, with a body like yours, we better keep you covered up. We don't want Ken's blood pressure to get *too* high. There're some extra suits in the boathouse. I'm sure there's something that would fit you."

"Great," Alex said again, as if it were settled. "Let me take care of this bill, and we'll get going."

"I should call . . . Dan," Emily said, "and tell him not to wait up for me."

"Emily's brother is in town," Alex explained to Ken and Marty, searching through his wallet for his credit card. "Use the phone at the bar," he said, glancing up at Emily. "Those public phones have lousy wiring."

Emily scooped her purse off the table, heading first toward the ladies' room. She had the phone number for Jim's cellular phone written on a piece of paper in her purse. But since she was supposedly calling her home, it would look strange for her to look up the phone number. She would quickly memorize it in the ladies' room.

But inside the ladies' room, in the privacy of one of the stalls, Emily realized that Jim's phone number was not in her purse. Too late, she remembered putting her wallet and her keys and the paper with Jim's phone number in her other purse, the white one—which was no doubt sitting on her dresser in her bedroom.

Silently she cursed her own stupidity. Jim was sitting in Felipe's car, not more than a few hundred yards away from her, yet he might as well be a thousand miles away.

She quickly searched through her purse. What did she have in here, anyway? A lipstick, an eyeliner pencil, a wide-toothed comb, a sticky pack of wildberry Lifesavers, about three dollars in change—mostly pennies—some gas receipts, last year's calendar datebook, a wrapped granola bar, a small packet of tissues, a tampon and an expired credit card.

She wasn't carrying a phone book. She didn't have any obvious solutions. She didn't even have a pencil so that she could scribble a note to Jim telling him where they were going.

Come to think of it, even if she had Jim's phone number, she couldn't tell him where they were going. She had no idea what Marty and Ken's street address was. Shoot, she didn't even know their last name!

Emily closed her eyes, trying to imagine what would happen after she and Alex left the restaurant on Marty and Ken's yacht.

The limo driver would leave his seat at the bar, where he was drinking glass after glass of ginger ale. He would go out to the limo, get in and drive away.

Jim and Felipe would watch in astonishment. Felipe would come into the restaurant to find their table empty and Alex and Emily gone. It wouldn't take him long to figure out that they'd left by boat.

Jim would be mad as hell. And worried, too. Emily could still see the look in his eyes when she'd admitted that, yes, she was afraid to go to dinner with Alex. Jim had looked almost desperate. And then he'd kissed her...

Emily shook her head. She couldn't think about that kiss right now. She didn't *want* to think about it now. Or ever, for that matter. But it was hard not to. She could still feel the rough stubble of his beard against her face. She could still taste the too-familiar sweetness of his mouth. She could feel his arms around her, pulling her against the hard, lean length of his body....

Emily heard the water running in the sink, and smelled the unmistakable aroma of cigarette smoke that followed Marty around. She took a deep breath and left the illusion of safety and privacy that the bathroom stall had given her.

Marty was touching up her lipstick, looking into the long mirror that was on the wall above a line of sinks. She met Emily's eyes in the mirror and smiled.

Emily washed her hands. "Marty," she said, "I realized suddenly that I don't even know your last name."

This was normal, polite conversation. There was no reason Marty would suspect that Emily wanted to know her last name in order to inform the police of Alex Delmore's whereabouts....

Marty put her lipstick back in her purse and closed it with a snap. "Bevin," she said. "Martina Bevin. Your last name's Marshfield, right?"

"Marshall," Emily told the older woman, drying her hands on a paper towel.

Marty shrugged. "Oh, well," she said. "I'm lousy with names. But I won't need to remember Marshall much longer, right?" She smile slyly. "I've heard rumors you'll be changing your name to Delmore soon."

The woman was obviously fishing for gossip. If she only knew what Emily knew... Of course, maybe she did. Maybe Marty and Ken were as involved with running drugs as Alex was. The thought was chilling. They seemed so nice. Of course, before overhearing his conversation with Vincent Marino, Emily had considered Alex nice, too.

Emily murmured something polite, yet vague enough to neither confirm nor deny Marty's hint about wedding plans, and fled back into the restaurant. The day she married Alex would be the day the world stopped turning, that was for sure.

Once outside the ladies' room, she took a deep breath. Now what?

Ken and Marty *Bevin*. At least she had something to tell Jim. But short of writing him a message on the ladies' room mirror in lipstick, she really had only one alternative.

She had to leave a message on her own answering machine. With any luck, Jim would think to call and check for messages. No, he'd get the message, and it wouldn't be because of luck. Jim was good at what he did. He was thorough. Checking her answering machine would be one of the first things he did after he realized he and Felipe had lost her.

The bartender already had the telephone out and waiting for her on the bar. "Just dial nine to get an outside line," he told her with a friendly smile. He was a big man with long hair pulled back into a ponytail. Something about the way he moved reminded her of Jim. Inwardly she made a face. It didn't take much these days for her to be reminded of Jim.

She quickly dialed her number. The telephone rang four times before the machine picked up.

"Hi, Dan," she said, in case anyone was listening in, "it's Emily. I wanted to let you know that I'm going to be back later than I thought. Alex and I are going over to Ken and Marty Bevin's house—I'm not sure of the address, but it's somewhere down here on the water." She lowered her voice. "Don't worry about me. Everything's fine. I'm okay. I'll see you later."

She pushed down the hook with one finger, cutting the connection. Taking one more deep breath, she plastered a smile on her face and went to the table where Alex was waiting for her.

"Ready?" he asked.

She nodded. She was as ready as she'd ever be.

Damn it, this was hell.

Jim slammed down the telephone for the tenth time in the past half hour. Where was she? Where the hell *was* she?

All his efforts at tracking down Ken and Marty Bevin had failed miserably. No such people existed. They didn't own property, they had no criminal records, no priors—not even a single parking ticket. They didn't have a telephone—listed or unlisted—they didn't file state income tax, they weren't even registered to vote, for crying out loud!

Each time a potential lead came up blank, Jim got more worried. Who were these people? Their name was obviously an alias. Damn it, it scared him that Emily was with them. It scared him that he didn't know where she was. She could be *anywhere*. She could be on a plane to God knows where. She could be handcuffed and unconscious, lying belowdecks on some boat, heading for South America. She could be dead—

With a growl, he pushed himself up and off the couch and started pacing again.

How could he have lost her? Why hadn't he been prepared for something like this to happen? He should have arranged for her to wear a listening device. He should have considered the fact that Aquavia's was on the waterfront. He should have realized that there would be nautical traffic to and from the wharf. He should have been prepared to follow Emily by boat.

Jim looked at his watch and cursed. It was nearly quarter to two in the morning. Where the *hell* was she?

Shortly after midnight, he and Salazar had split up. They had come back to Emily's apartment to see if maybe she'd returned. That was when Jim had found her other purse, the one that held her wallet, his cellular phone number—and her keys. That was perfect, just perfect. Now he had to wonder if maybe she'd tried to come home but had been locked out.

Felipe had gone back to Delmore's house to watch for any sign of either him or Emily. Jim had stayed behind, hoping that she would call again, hoping that she would come home, praying that she was safe.

Praying. Jesus, when was the last time he'd actually prayed? He couldn't remember. But, God, he was making up for it now.

At one-fifty, the telephone rang.

Jim picked it up before it completed its first ring. But it wasn't Emily. It was Frank Gale, from the police station downtown. He had been searching computer files, trying to find any mention at all of Ken and Marty Bevin.

"I figured it out," he said. "Bevin's a stage name. Martina Bevin, remember? She used to have bit parts in those really cheap horror flicks back in the early seventies? She was always the girl with the big chest who took off her shirt and got killed early on in the movie. She keeps a low profile these days. Apparently some nutball fan stalked her, and she dropped out of the business. Back in '82, she married a local man—Ken Trudeau. Rich guy. He owns that resort out on the point."

Jim scribbled the name in his notebook. "You got an address on him?"

"Yeah—211 Flamingo Lane," Frank said. "It's off Ocean Avenue."

"Thanks, Frank."

"My pleasure, pal."

Jim hung up, then turned as the apartment door opened and Emily slipped inside.

Emily.

She closed the door, locked the dead bolt and leaned back as if she were exhausted.

Relief hit Jim like a punch in the stomach. She was alive. She was all right. She was... The relief soured instantly, turning to a rapidly growing disbelief.

Her hair was a mess, as if it had been wet, or windblown, or as if someone—Delmore—had touched it, run his fingers through it over and over. She was holding her high-heeled pumps in one hand, and he could see that she'd taken her panty hose off and stuck them into the toe of one shoe. Her legs were bare, and her dress looked rumpled, as if she'd taken it off and thrown it casually over a chair—

Jealousy knifed through him, hot and sharp and painful as hell.

"I'm sorry I couldn't call you," she said. "I didn't bring your phone number...."

"I know." He made an effort to keep his voice from shaking. "Are you all right?" What he really wanted to know was what she'd been doing all this time. Had she slept with Delmore? Had she made love to him? But he couldn't bring himself to ask.

Emily nodded. "I'm fine." She smiled, but it was tight, unnatural. "Better than fine. I got Alex to invite you to a party on his yacht. Next Saturday—a week from tomorrow. He's having a cocktail cruise on the *Home Free* from five-thirty until nine. We're both invited. He wanted to take the two of us out alone, another time, but I thought it would be better if there was a crowd. That way, you can sneak down to his office and not be missed."

"Yeah," Jim said. "That's good." Outwardly, he was calm. Inwardly, he was dying. She'd gotten Delmore to give him an invitation. He couldn't shake the picture of Emily doing her persuading in Delmore's bed.

"You'll need a tux," she said, meeting his eyes only briefly before she looked away.

What Jim was thinking was too terrible. Emily was afraid of Delmore. If she didn't want to go to dinner with him, she certainly wouldn't be eager to have sex with the man. But would she do it anyway? In an effort to hurry along the investigation, in an effort to find the information they needed to put Delmore in jail—and get Jim out of her life—would she force herself to make love to Alexander Delmore one more time?

Jim hated the fact that he didn't know. He hated the fact that he suspected not only that she would, but that she had. He wanted desperately to believe that she wouldn't prostitute herself that way, but he couldn't get past the obvious evidence. At some point during the evening, she'd taken off her clothes. He couldn't ignore that, and it was killing him. Despite all the danger and jeopardy he'd imagined her to be in over the past few hours, he hadn't let himself think about the possibility of Delmore making love to her. But he couldn't stop thinking about it now, and it made him feel sick.

"I need to take a shower," she said, and he realized he was blocking the hallway that led to the bathroom.

But he didn't want her to go. He knew that unless he stood and waited outside the bathroom door, she would slip quietly into her bedroom after her shower and he wouldn't see her again until morning. Then he'd be alone with his suspicions and his jealousy all night long.

He took a step toward her and motioned toward the couch. "Sit down and . . . tell me what happened," he said.

She glanced at the couch and shook her head. "Nothing suspicious happened." She looked down at the shoes she was holding in her hand. "We sailed out to Ken and Marty Bevin's—"

"Trudeau," Jim said, interrupting her, and she looked up at him, frowning slightly. "It's Ken and Marty *Trudeau*. It took my investigator until just a few minutes ago to figure out that Bevin is Marty's stage name. She used to be an actress."

Emily understood instantly. "Oh, shoot," she exclaimed. She dropped one of her shoes, but didn't bother to pick it up. She stared up at Jim, concern darkening her eyes. "So, all that time, you had no idea where I was or who I was with. Jim, I'm sorry—"

"No," he said, taking another step toward her and grasping her by the shoulders. "No, Emily, don't. I should be the one apologizing here. I told you I'd stay with you. I promised I'd follow you. Damn it, I should have made sure you were wired for sound—"

"Good thing you didn't," Emily said, then blushed. Jim froze.

She gently pulled free and stepped around him, heading toward the bathroom. He turned and caught her arm, stopping her.

"Why?" he asked. His voice was low, and Emily caught her breath when she saw the tension around his mouth and the dangerous light in his eyes. "What happened that you didn't want me to hear?"

She didn't answer, and his fingers tightened around her arm. "What did you do, Emily?" he asked. His voice got steadily louder. "Where did you go after you left the Trudeaus'? I know you didn't go back to Delmore's house. Salazar was staked out there all night. So where did you go? To Delmore's boat, right?"

Emily stared up at him. What was he implying? Oh, God, was he implying—? He thought she'd slept with Alex. He actually thought she'd stoop that low. Angry tears burned her eyelids as she tried to wrench herself free. But his fingers tightened on her arm.

To her horror, she burst into tears.

He pulled her into his arms, instantly contrite. "God, I'm sorry," he said as he held her tightly. "I'm so sorry. I shouldn't have yelled at you. I...I lost it, and I shouldn't have, but I was so worried about you, and then... But what's important now is that you're here and you're safe. That's what I've got to focus on. You don't know how glad I was to see you walk in that door. God, I was so scared, and so damned helpless. But you're okay now. You're okay. That's what matters. That's all that matters."

Emily felt more than heard the catch in Jim's voice, and the sudden unevenness of his breathing. Jim was crying. He was actually crying, too.

She could feel his cheek pressed against the side of her head. She could feel his ragged breathing, warm against her ear. He was so solid as she leaned against him, enveloped by his powerful arms. For the first time all evening, she felt protected and safe.

And needed, she realized suddenly. He was clinging to her as tightly as she was holding him. This embrace was not one-sided. She was comforting him, too.

And that scared her to death.

She did the only thing she could. She let go of Jim and fled into the bathroom.

Chapter 11

Jim sat in Emily's living room, trying not to think about Emily and Delmore, alone on Delmore's yacht last night.

But, God, it was hard.

He tried to distract himself by watching the sun rise. The dawn sky was hazy and red. What was that old saying? Red sky at morning, sailors take warning. It was going to be another scorcher of a day—hot as hell, and muggy to boot, building up to violent late-afternoon thunderstorms. The storm would rid the air of this sticky humidity for only a few short moments. Before it even stopped raining, the puddles on the ground would begin to evaporate, creating more haze.

But hey—he shouldn't complain. This was Florida. It was summer. Heat and humidity came with the package. And he'd chosen to be here, right? He'd made a decision to leave the New York Police Department. He could have stayed up north. His boss had wanted him to stay. Even as a rookie detective, Jim had been good at what he did.

But he had had to leave. New York had already taken a solid chunk of his soul. His only hope of getting any of it back had been to get the hell out of there.

So then what had happened? He had moved to Tampa, not quite whole emotionally, but able to function, able to get the work done. But only a few months into the new job, he'd woken up to find he was missing a piece of his heart.

A piece? No. The whole damned thing. Emily had stolen the whole damned thing. He'd thought he'd gotten it back, but he'd realized last night that he was mistaken. Emily had possessed his heart all these long years. Nothing had changed. He loved her. He probably always would.

She was older now—they both were. God knows *he'd* grown up a hell of a lot in the past seven years. He'd come to terms with who he was and what he'd done. Yeah, he'd gotten at least some of his ravaged soul back. It was patched and uneven—not a pretty sight—but he'd come to realize that he wasn't as bad a person as he'd thought he was.

No, he wasn't that bad. But was he good enough for Emily?

He was a cop. He knew the risks he took every day when he went to work. His world and the people in it were brutal and ugly. And sometimes, in order to catch the bad guys, he had to be just as brutal and just as ugly. More than once, he'd pointed his gun at another human being and pulled the trigger. More than once he'd taken another's life. And in doing so he'd been dragged down to their despicable level.

No, he wasn't the kind of monster he'd imagined himself to be, but he was no golden prize, either.

As the sun gathered its strength and climbed higher in the sky, Jim pushed himself off the couch and went into the kitchen to brew another pot of coffee.

Whether or not Emily deserved a man better than him was a moot point. She didn't like him. There wasn't much he could do to make her like him—much less to make her *love*

him again. He wasn't even sure he *wanted* her to love him
again.

But he knew one thing that he had to do. He had to tell
her the truth. He had to tell her why he'd hurt her, why he'd
left her all those years ago. Maybe she wouldn't believe him.
But maybe she would. Maybe at least she'd understand and
forgive him.

And maybe that would be enough.

Emily woke up at ten-thirty, still exhausted.

She lay in bed, listening for the sounds from the living
room that would let her know Jim was awake. She heard
nothing. But she doubted he was sleeping. He never slept
past eight.

She shivered, remembering the way he'd held her last
night, remembering how he'd cried.

Having her disappear from the restaurant must have been
a major shock for him. It certainly had had more of an impact on him than she would have imagined. But as she
thought about it, his emotional reaction, his anger and upset, made sense. He had been assigned to protect her. He
was responsible for her safety. Through no fault of his own,
he'd found himself in a situation in which he was unable to
do that. Added to that had been the stress of having failed.
He was not a man who failed often—or took failure lightly.

She wouldn't allow herself to consider that his emotional
upset had anything to do with her on a personal level.
Thinking that way was dangerous.

Emily sighed. It had been one hell of an awful night.

Alex had asked her to marry him.

She'd been dreading that, and when he finally asked it
had been both better and worse than she'd anticipated.
Better because he hadn't seemed at all surprised when she
told him she'd need some time to think it over before she
gave him an answer. And worse because, throughout the
course of their entire discussion, not even once had Alex

mentioned love. He wanted to marry her not because he loved her, but because he thought she would make the perfect little wife.

In a way, it was good. She would feel no guilt about betraying a man who didn't love her. But, despite that, she felt oddly depressed. She wanted to be loved. Jim hadn't loved her, either, and she was starting to wonder if anyone ever would.

She'd been *really* glad that she wasn't wearing some kind of bug that would have let Jim listen in on her conversation with Alex. *That* would have been too hard to take. It was going to be difficult enough to *tell* him about Alex's loveless marriage proposal.

Emily climbed out of bed and took her beach bag from the closet. She and Alex had purposely made no plans to see each other before next Saturday. That was a relief. She needed some time away. She needed it desperately.

All she really needed to pack was her bathing suit, a couple pairs of underwear, an extra pair of shorts and a T-shirt. She threw the clothes into the bag and hurriedly got dressed.

Carrying her bag with her, she went into the bathroom, washed her face, brushed her hair and teeth and packed up everything else she'd need for a few days away.

Taking a deep breath, she opened the bathroom door and went out into the living room.

Jim was sitting on the couch, staring down into a cup of coffee. He looked awful. Emily was willing to bet that he'd been awake all night, no doubt still kicking himself for failing to be a perfect cop. Still, when he glanced up at her, he forced a smile.

"Hey," he said. "Good morning. There's a fresh pot of coffee on."

Emily set her beach bag by the door and went into the kitchen. She poured herself a mug.

"Emily," Jim said, and she jumped, sloshing the hot coffee onto her hand.

He swore softly and put his own mug down on the counter. Moving toward the sink, he turned on the cold water.

"You startled me," Emily said. "I didn't hear you follow me."

"I'm sorry," Jim said. He reached for her hand, to pull it under the stream of cool water, but she shook her head.

"I'm all right."

He took her hand anyway. "Humor me."

The water was cold, and it contrasted oddly with the warmth of Jim's hand. She glanced up to find him watching her, and she quickly looked away. But he was standing way too close. She could smell traces of his shampoo in his still-damp hair. She could smell the fresh, tangy soap he'd used when he showered. He'd shaved this morning, too, and his lean face was smooth and seemingly vulnerable without his tough-guy stubble. Emily resisted the sudden urge to reach out and touch his cheek.

As he reached across the sink to turn off the tap, she risked another glance at him. He seemed preoccupied now, and his eyes were unfocused as he tore a paper towel from the roll and handed it to her.

"I need to tell you what happened last night," she said as she dried her hands.

Jim looked at her then, his gaze suddenly sharp and very, very blue. "No, you don't," he said quietly. He smiled then. It came out forced and a little shaky, but it was sweet just the same. His eyes held a glimmer of pain as he reached forward to push her hair back from her face. His fingers lingered briefly on the curve of her cheek. "Whatever happened last night is all right," he said. "It's over and done with, anyway."

Emily stood frozen by an icy wave of disbelief. "You still think I... You still think Alex and I..."

"Didn't you?" Jim shook his head, catching himself. "No, don't answer that. It doesn't matter."

But it did matter. "You think I let Alex have sex with me last night," Emily said. The icy cold turned suddenly to red-hot anger. "You think that's how I got that invitation onto his boat, don't you?"

Jim was looking away from her, down at the floor. He didn't answer, so Emily shoved him, hard. "You *do* think that, don't you?" she said.

He looked up at her in surprise. Her eyes were flashing, and she looked mad enough to spit. After the way she'd shoved him, he wouldn't be surprised if she did. Spit, that is. And right at him.

"Listen up, Detective," Emily said hotly, "because I'm only going to say this one more time. My relationship with Alex Delmore is *not,* nor has it *ever been,* nor will it *ever be,* sexual. I have never slept with the man. Not last night, not any night. Can you get that through your thick skull? Last night Alex and I went to Marty and Ken's house, we swam in their new pool and tried out their new hot tub. Then we went back to the *Home Free,* and Alex checked his calendar to see when he was available to take you for a sail. Then I came home."

Swam in their pool. Emily had gone swimming. That was why she'd looked so disheveled. She *hadn't* slept with Delmore. Jim started to laugh with relief. God, had he gotten it all wrong!

"What, you think this is funny?" Emily said. "You can go to hell, Keegan. I hear it's really funny there, too."

She was so mad, tears of anger blurred her vision as she spun toward the front door. How *dare* he think she would sleep with Alex, particularly now, when she suspected that the man was a criminal! How *dare* Jim assume such things!

Jim caught her arm as she bent down to pick up her beach bag. "Em, wait! Please—"

She pulled hard to get away from him and caught her foot in one of the large loop handles of the bag. She went down hard, with Jim following close behind. He twisted to avoid landing directly on top of her.

With the air knocked out of her, Emily couldn't protest as Jim pulled her onto his lap.

"Listen to me," he said, holding her tightly to keep her from squirming away. "Just listen, damn it! I thought you and Alex already were...you know...involved, because I couldn't...I *still* can't believe there's a man alive who could spend any time at all with you without falling in love with you—without wanting to make love to you."

Emily felt the fight drain from her. She felt her anger dissolve, leaving only hurt. No one loved her. *No one.* "You're wrong," she whispered.

"I spent half of last night trying not to imagine you making love to him," he said huskily, as if he hadn't heard her protest. Emily sat quietly now, listening to his soft voice, too worn-out to protest. "And I spent the other half trying to talk myself into believing that if you *had* made love to Delmore, it didn't matter. But it did matter. It *does* matter. I don't want him touching you."

Jim touched her bare arm, sliding his fingers along her smooth skin from her shoulder to her hand, much the same way Alex had done at lunch the other day. But while Alex's touch had repulsed her, Jim's sent arrows of sensation shooting through her body. Emily shivered as he gently entangled his fingers in her hair.

"I don't want him kissing you, either," Jim murmured, pulling her head back so that she was looking directly up at him through a shimmer of tears. The heat in his eyes was unmistakable, but Emily couldn't move, couldn't run away. He moistened his lips, and she closed her eyes as he lowered his mouth to hers in a tender kiss.

She heard his sudden intake of breath as she opened her mouth to him and willingly deepened the kiss. He tasted of coffee and desire, sweet and hot. His tongue filled her mouth, and she angled her head, wanting more, *more*.

Maybe this was just a lie. Maybe she was only fooling herself, maybe this was make-believe, but damn it, when he kissed her, when he touched her, she felt loved. And she needed that right now. She needed him.

He shifted her weight on his lap, turning her so that she was facing him, and he kissed her again, even harder this time.

"I don't want him making love to you," Jim breathed as he trailed hot kisses down her throat.

He lowered her onto the floor, and she welcomed the weight of his muscular body on top of hers. She pulled him even closer, drawing him between her legs and pressing herself upward to meet the hard evidence of his arousal.

He groaned—it was a low, guttural sound, born half of ecstasy, half of despair. Emily gasped as his hand covered her breast, as he caught her hardened nipple between his thumb and forefinger. She clung to him, hot with desire and dizzy from a barrage of emotions so intense she could barely breathe. This game of make-believe they were playing wasn't all pretend. She loved him. After all this time, after all he'd done, after the way he'd hurt her, Emily had fallen in love with Jim Keegan all over again.

He pushed her T-shirt up and unfastened the front clasp of her bra. He caressed her breasts first with his hands, then with his mouth.

"So beautiful," he murmured. "You're so beautiful."

Emily was lost. As she ran her fingers through the silky dark waves of his hair, she knew that she was making a colossal mistake, but she was past caring. She needed him, here and now, and here and now was what James Keegan was best at.

She tugged at his T-shirt, and he pulled it off as she slipped her own shirt over her head.

Then Jim did the unexpected. He hesitated. Kneeling there between her legs, the heat in his eyes strong enough to burn her, a sheen of perspiration making his tanned chest glisten, the corded muscles standing out in his strong arms as he supported his weight above her, he actually hesitated. "Em, do you think—"

She reached up for him, answering him with the blazing heat of a kiss, with the shockingly intimate sensation of skin against skin, soft breasts against hard muscle. No, she didn't want to think. She wanted to feel, only to *feel*.

Jim was lost. Caught in the explosive passion of her embrace, he didn't stand a chance. Something had happened to make Emily give in to the desire that sprang to life whenever they exchanged even a glance, but he didn't know what or why that something was. Finding out what had changed her mind mattered to him, and he knew he should stop kissing her, stop touching her, pull free from her arms. But her lips were so sweet, her body so soft, and God, it had been so long. His body was weak, and his heart was on fire. After seven years of the occasional poor substitute, and days and nights filled with a desperate loneliness he hadn't even recognized, he couldn't stop.

Her long, slender fingers were in his hair, touching him, stroking his back, his arms. Jim caught his breath as she reached between them and unfastened the top button of his shorts. The zipper stuck, and her touch was excruciatingly light as she attempted to pull it down. He took her hand and pressed it against him, against the hard bulge of his sex.

She gazed up at him, her beautiful eyes luminous, the rose-colored tips of her full breasts taut with desire. Her chest rose and fell with each ragged breath she took as she touched him.

"I need you," she whispered, and Jim felt a surge of heat so strong he had to close his eyes and pull back slightly to keep from losing his control.

And then he kissed her, returning her words with the urgency of his mouth against hers. He wished desperately that he could somehow make time stand still. He wanted this moment to last forever, this hot anticipation of knowing, of actually *knowing,* that he was going to make love to Emily. He wanted to be able to carry it with him always. He wanted to be able to look across a crowded room to meet Emily's eyes, and see a hint of this same liquid fire, to see this promise of paradise. He wanted to wear it like a bullet-proof vest, protecting him from the pain and despair he was forced to face nearly every day out on the city's streets.

Except he wanted to know that there was something precious behind the desire in her eyes as she looked at him. He wanted more than lust to spark the flame of her need. He wanted Emily to love him.

He wanted more than he deserved.

She pulled again at his zipper, and this time it opened. And instead of time standing still, life went into fast-forward. Emily pushed him over onto his back, and together they pulled his shorts and his briefs down his legs. Her hand closed tightly around his shaft, and he reached for her. He pulled her onto his lap, burying his face in the exquisite softness of her breasts. His hands explored the smooth curve of her derriere as he noted with amazement that somehow, over the course of the past few seconds, the last of her clothes had disappeared.

Without a word of warning, she shifted her weight and, with one swift motion, ensheathed him with her smooth, moist heat.

Jim heard himself cry out as she set a rhythm that was too fast, too strong, a wild, furious, plunging movement that stripped him of the last of his control and drove him mercilessly to the edge.

But he wasn't wearing any protection. He was seconds from release, and he would have sold his soul to the devil for a chance to send his seed deep inside this woman he loved so fiercely. In less time than it took to blink an eye, Jim imagined Emily pregnant with his child. In less than a second, he saw a baby—*their* baby—growing into a child. He saw himself as he'd never imagined himself before—happy in a way he'd never known, happy with an inner peace, with a deep contentment, secure in his love for his family, secure in the warmth of their love for him.

He wanted that. Oh, how he wanted that.

But that was only a fantasy. Emily didn't love him. And he loved her way too much to risk burdening her with an unwanted pregnancy.

Jim took her by the hips and lifted her up and off him.

"No," she breathed, kissing his neck and his freshly shaven face. "I don't want to stop—"

"Let me get a condom, Em," Jim said hoarsely, straining to reach his shorts and the wallet that was still in his back pocket. His fingers fumbled, and his money spilled onto the floor, but even so, he doubted he'd ever put a condom on quite that quickly before.

Emily waited just long enough for him to finish covering himself before she straddled him again. But Jim picked her up and pressed her back against the floor.

"My turn," he whispered, gazing into her eyes as he entered her slowly.

He took his time. Each stroke lasted an eternity, filling her deeply and ending with a kiss that claimed her completely. It was exquisite torture, stripping her of the last of her defenses, leaving her vulnerable, all her feelings exposed.

Emily closed her eyes, afraid that if she continued to hold Jim's electric blue gaze, he'd see her for the fool that she was. He would know that she loved him.

She arched up toward him, pulling him down so that the full weight of his body was on top of her. She locked her legs around him, and he groaned, moving faster now, in sync with her every need.

"Em," he breathed, and she opened her eyes.

He was still watching her, his eyes bright, almost feverish, beneath his half-closed lids. His hair curled as it clung to his slick skin, and a bead of perspiration trailed down past his ear. Emily reached up to catch it with one finger, and he pressed his cheek into her palm.

"You're making me crazy," he said huskily. "We gotta slow down, or—"

But she didn't want to slow down. He might not love her, but she knew that when it came down to sex, she had power over him. Right now, as they made love, *she* was in control.

It was a sad consolation, an unfair trade-off, considering that the rest of the time Jim was running the show. He owned her heart, and Emily was forced to confront the truth: he'd probably own it for the rest of her life. She, on the other hand, owned only his body, and only for the next few minutes.

But if she had anything to say about it, it was going to be one hell of a next few minutes.

She pulled his mouth to hers and kissed him fiercely, increasing the slow rhythm of their bodies to a wild, primitive pace, each thrust harder and deeper than the last. She felt his arms tighten around her. She felt his body tense, then heard him cry out her name as he exploded inside of her.

And then she was no longer in control. Her body answered his, wave upon wave of exquisite pleasure surrounding her, lifting her, rocketing her to a height she'd only dreamed possible. She loved him. Absolutely. Completely. And unrequitedly.

It was over then, and tears stung Emily's eyes as she drifted back to earth.

Jim lifted his head, slowly becoming aware that he was still lying on top of Emily. She had her eyes tightly closed, and she only opened them very briefly as he rolled off her. He drew her into his arms, and she nestled against him, pressing her face into his neck, as if her body were cold, rather than slick with sweat and hot to the touch.

He kissed the top of her head, and slowly stroked her from her shoulder blades to her buttocks and up again.

Reality wormed its ugly way into the picture as Jim realized they were lying on the tan carpeting in front of the door. In front of the door, for crying out loud. He hadn't even had enough class to take her on the living room floor. He hadn't even taken the time to walk the few extra steps needed to make it to the couch. What a guy.

He sighed, wishing she would say something, *anything*. He wished she would tell him that she loved him. Of course, it was entirely possible that she was lying there next to him wishing the same damn wish, wasn't it?

Jim cleared his throat. "Hey, Em?"

She didn't move.

He cleared his throat again. "I gotta tell you, um..." This was a lot harder than he thought it would be. Come on, Keegan. Three words. Pronoun, verb, pronoun. Not that challenging. All he had to do was put them in the right order. Of course, he knew damn well it was what those three little words meant that made them so hard to say. But he meant it with all his heart. And he'd missed his chance to say it seven years ago. Besides, maybe, just maybe, she was wishing he'd say it....

"I, um..." Jim had to clear his throat one more time. Then he said it. He took a deep breath and just said it. "Emily, I love you."

Emily stiffened. Then she sat up, pulling away from him, and quickly gathered up her clothes. So much for thinking that she wanted to hear him say it... His heart sank, and he felt slightly sick. He had a bad feeling that things were going to start spiraling in a downward direction pretty damn fast.

But she didn't say a word to him. She simply pulled her shirt over her head, not bothering to take the time to put her bra on again, and quickly slipped into her underpants and shorts. She stood up then, without even giving him a second glance, and walked down the hall toward the bathroom.

''Hey!'' Jim sat up, a burst of anger replacing the heart-sick feeling. ''You're not going to say anything? You're just going to walk away? Thanks a lot, it was fun?''

She didn't turn around.

Jim stood up in one quick motion and followed her down the hall. He caught the bathroom door before she closed it, bracing one hand on the door, the other on the frame.

''I believe the correct response should be 'Thanks a lot, it was a blast,''' she said. Her voice was cool, but she didn't meet his eyes. ''So thanks a lot. It was a—''

Jim reeled. ''Oh, *perfect.*''

She started to close the bathroom door, and he spun back, again forcing it to remain open. He was standing there na-ked, but he didn't care.

''Damn it, I just told you that I love you.'' His voice cracked with emotion, but Emily didn't seem to notice.

She bristled with anger. ''Does it work better that way?'' she said. ''It probably does. Women probably like it better when you pretend to love them. It makes the sex seem less cheap, I bet.'' She pushed past him, out of the bathroom. ''Well, you blew it this time, Romeo. You forgot that I know you. I know how you operate. Love's not a part of your game. Don't insult my intelligence by pretending that it is.''

''Emily, damn it, give me a chance to—''

''You had your chance seven years ago, Detective.''

Emily scooped her beach bag from the floor, and her car keys from the table, and headed for the front door. But Jim got there first. He blocked it. It was clear he had no inten-tion of letting her leave.

He was still naked, and still oblivious to that fact. But Emily wasn't oblivious. He was much too gorgeous. Every last inch of him was lean, well-toned muscle—muscle that rippled beneath his skin as he moved. It was distracting. Distracting and disturbing, because it made her realize she still wanted him. Despite the fact that they'd made love not more than a few minutes ago, despite the fact that he was

making a mockery of her most treasured hope, despite the
fact that she'd made a first-class fool of herself by giving in
to his lust and her own wishful thinking... Despite all those
things, she knew that if she stayed here much longer she'd
end up back in his arms. Back down on the floor with him.
Or on the dining table. Or up on the kitchen counter. Or
wherever and whenever else he wanted her...

He gestured toward his clothes and his wallet, still scattered on the floor. "Then what just happened here?" he
asked hotly. "If you weren't giving me a second chance,
then what the hell were we just doing?"

Emily turned away, heading for the sliding glass doors
that led to her tiny deck.

Jim followed, only a step behind. "Explain it to me,
damn it!" he said, even louder. "What were we just doing?"

"We were having casual sex," Emily said, her voice
shaking. "All right? That's all it was."

Jim shook his head. "No. No way. I know you. You don't
have *casual* sex."

Emily laughed humorlessly as she slid open the glass door.
"I'm not an eighteen-year-old virgin anymore," she said,
going out onto the deck and looking over the rail. There was
about a twelve-foot drop to the ground. She wouldn't get
out of here *that* way.

She went back inside. Jim was frowning, staring at her as
if she'd just announced she would be taking a trip to the
moon.

"Wait a minute," he said. His voice was suddenly much
softer, but no less intense. "Are you telling me—? When we
first made love...you were a *virgin?*"

Emily stepped past him. He didn't block her route to the
door. He didn't even move. He just turned and watched her,
that incredulous look on his face, waiting for her to answer
him.

But she didn't. She didn't say a word. She hadn't meant for him to find out. She hadn't talked about it seven years ago, and she had no intention of discussing it now. Emily opened the door and went out onto the landing, heading for the stairs that led down to the parking lot.

Jim moved then, sprinting after her. "Emily, *wait!* God, I didn't know—"

But she didn't stop. She didn't even slow down.

Halfway to the stairs, Jim realized he wasn't wearing any clothes. He swore, and dashed back into Emily's apartment. He jumped into his shorts and ran after her, taking the stairs two at a time as he fastened the top button.

But when he reached the parking lot, Emily's car was already gone.

Thanks a lot. It was a blast.

For the first time, the impact of what he'd done to Emily seven years ago hit him square in the face.

Chapter 12

Sanibel Island was in an entirely different world, an entirely different Florida. Though it was only a few dozen miles down the Gulf Coast, it seemed to Emily as if it were a million light-years away. It was a tropical island, connected to the mainland by a toll bridge. Once over that bridge, everything moved more slowly, the air smelled mysterious and thick with tropical flowers, and the plants and underbrush seemed more green and lush, like a jungle on the verge of reclaiming the sidewalks and streets. Where the road wound between two particularly swampy areas, Alligator Crossing signs were posted.

When Emily first came to Sanibel, she had thought those signs were just a corny joke. But after seeing one or two of the giant reptiles at the side of the road, and after coming face-to-snout with one in her parents' backyard, she knew that Alligator Crossing *meant* Alligator Crossing.

The entire island was a throwback to Florida's past. Early in the island's development, rules had been set prohibiting the building of structures higher than a certain number of feet. The result was condos and hotels that were hidden from the beaches, instead of towering above the sand, blocking out the sun.

Emily sat in front of her parents' beach house, watching the sun set across the Gulf of Mexico. It was beautiful. The sky was a blaze of oranges and pinks and reds, the colors swirling together and reflecting off the water. The beach had been close to empty for most of the day, due to the heat, but now it was totally deserted, as the few people who had braved the burning sun had gone inside for dinner.

This was Emily's favorite time to be on the beach. She was alone, save for the birds that floated overhead and occasionally dived after the fish that swam in the crystal stillness of the water. Shadows were long, and the brilliant blues of the sky and the sea were muted, softened by the redorange shades of the sunset.

Emily sat there, on her favorite beach in the world, at her favorite time of day, and *still* she felt lousy.

And the depressing thing was, she didn't see herself feeling any better anytime in the near future.

She hadn't slept more than a few hours last night. Whenever she'd closed her eyes, she could feel Jim Keegan's touch, feel the heat of his mouth, the gentleness of his strong hands. When she finally fell asleep, she'd dreamed she was back in his arms, making love to him.

He'd hit the nail right on the head with his comment about casual sex. Emily *didn't* take sex lightly. She wouldn't make love to someone she didn't care deeply about. And she cared about Jim. Reprimanding herself and telling herself that she was a fool to be taken in by the same man twice was all well and good, but it didn't change the way she felt.

It had taken every ounce of her control not to cry yesterday morning after they made love, when Jim had told her so casually that he loved her. It had taken all her strength not to burst into tears at his words. How had he known to say that? Somehow he'd figured out the one thing to say that would hurt her the most. His lightly spoken words of love made a mockery of her own devastating feelings. She knew damn well that he didn't love her.

But she loved him. She really loved him. She'd set out to uncover the real James Keegan, hoping to find someone she would dislike, someone selfish and uncaring and cruel, someone more bad than good. Instead, she'd found this man. He wasn't the perfect superhero she'd thought him to be back when she was eighteen. He was human, with a whole array of human strengths and weaknesses, a curious mixture of good and bad, with the good often outweighing the bad. He was not perfect, and somehow his imperfections made her love him all the more.

If only he could mean it when he told her he loved her, too.

Emily pulled her knees in close to her chest, and rested her head on her arms, letting a tear escape. It trickled down her cheek to her chin, and plopped down into the sand between her feet. It was just one of a thousand tears she'd shed because of Jim Keegan. Emily sighed. One tear or an ocean of tears—it didn't matter. Crying wouldn't change the fact that she'd never have what she truly wanted. She'd never have Jim's love. She'd never have his real, true, honest love. Sure, she could have his automatic words, spoken in response to an intensely sensual physical joining, but those words were meaningless.

"Emily."

Startled, Emily lifted her head, then scrambled to her feet. Jim.

He was standing only a few feet away from her, his lean face shadowed in the soft light of dusk. He looked different somehow, and Emily realized he was wearing his hair pulled austerely back in a ponytail. His face seemed more angular, more rugged.

He was wearing a short-sleeved button-down shirt carefully tucked into a clean pair of jeans. It was obvious that he'd taken some pains with his appearance. But why? Because he was nervous about seeing her again? If he was that nervous, why would he even bother to come?

"What are you doing here?" she asked, keeping her voice even.

"It didn't take much to track you down, you know?" he said, his familiar, husky voice blending with the gentle hush of the surf. "I figured you'd either head down here or fly up to Connecticut." He pushed his hands into his front pockets, kicking at the sand with the toe of one boot. He glanced up at her, his eyes catching the last of the light from the fading sky. "You scared me when you didn't come home last night, Em."

Home. The way he said it made it sound as if it were *their* home, as if they shared it together.

Emily didn't answer. What could she say? She had no intention of apologizing.

He sighed and took a step toward her. "Look, Em—"

She took a step back, away from him, and he stopped.

"You've found me," she said. "I'm safe, you can stop worrying." She looked out at the glistening ocean. "Now, if you don't mind, I came here to be alone."

"I *do* mind," Jim said, taking another step forward. Again she stepped away from him, and he gritted his teeth to keep from cursing. "*I* came here because we need to talk."

She stood there, so cool and serene. He only caught the slightest trace of something flickering in her eyes when she turned to look back at him. But it might've only been his imagination, or maybe a reflection of the sunset.

"I have nothing to say," she told him.

He tried to keep his hurt from showing in his voice, and instead his words came out with a sarcastic-sounding edge. "You have nothing to say to me at all?" he said. "*Nothing?* Well, that's just great. You make love to me as if the world were coming to an end. And if *that's* not enough to totally blow my mind, as you're walking out the door, you let slip the fact that seven years ago, I took your virginity." He exhaled loudly in disbelief. "Honey, we got truckloads to talk about here."

Her expression didn't change. "You took something from me far more valuable than my virginity," Emily said in a low voice. "But what happened between us seven years ago is over and done. Talking about it won't change anything."

He took another step toward her. "I need you to know why I . . . split up with you the way I did," Jim said.

This time she stood her ground. But anger and hurt flared in her eyes, cracking her calm facade. "Believe me, you made that more than clear at the time." She turned and started toward the house. "I'd like you to leave now."

Jim caught her arm just as she went up the steps to the wide wooden porch. "I thought you deserved someone better than me," he said, determined to make her listen. "I thought if we stayed together, I thought if you married me, you'd end up hurt."

"Married?" Emily laughed, then wrenched her arm free, her smile quickly fading. "You had no intention of marrying me, and you know it."

"You're right," Jim said. "I had no intention of marrying you."

She turned away again, and he reached for her, to stop her, but she jerked her hand out of his grasp. "Don't *touch* me!"

Jim held up his hands, as if in surrender. "I won't," he said. "I won't, all right? But you've got to *listen,* Em. Give me a chance here—"

"Why should I?" Her calm coolness was gone at last. She stood there, trembling with anger and emotion.

"Because even though I didn't marry you, even though I didn't ask you—God, Emily, I wanted to. It was crazy, you were only eighteen, but I wanted to *marry* you. I wanted you."

"Yeah, well, you got me," Emily said hotly. "Twice. So now you can just leave me *alone.*"

She reached for the screen door, but Jim was ahead of her. He pressed one palm against it, keeping it tightly shut.

"I was in *love* with you, damn it," he said between clenched teeth.

Again, Emily laughed, but she had tears in her eyes, angry tears that threatened to overflow. "You were in love with me," she repeated. "And because you loved me, you broke my heart?" She shook her head. "You are *so* full of—"

"You gotta let me explain—"

"You keep saying that! 'Give me a chance, let me explain....' Well, why? Give me just *one* good reason—"

"Because, damn it, seven years ago, you loved me, too."

He was standing there, his features shadowy and mysterious in the rapidly fading dusk. His mouth was a grim line, his jaw was stiff and unyielding. And his eyes... More gray than blue in the growing darkness, his eyes were filled with tears.

"Please," he whispered. He didn't seem to notice as one tear escaped and made a gleaming trail down his face. "Just hear me out. That's all I'm asking, Emily. Just listen to what I have to say. Then ... I'll go."

She nodded, unable to speak.

Jim took a deep breath, relief making his knees suddenly feel weak. Emily was going to listen to him. She was giving him a chance to explain. He sat down on the porch, just sat right there on the wooden floor and leaned back against the house. He wiped his face in the crook of his arm, surprised to feel the moisture of his tears. God, had he actually been crying? Funny, he hadn't noticed. He must be in one hell of an emotional state, when the only way he could tell if he was crying or not was to check whether his face was wet.

He took another deep breath. "This story starts before I met you," he said, glancing up at Emily.

She was still standing, her arms crossed tightly in front of her.

"Are you just going to stand there?" he interrupted himself to ask.

"Yes."

He could barely make out her face in the darkness, but he knew enough not to argue. She was listening, and that was all he could ask for.

"Eight years ago," he said, trying to find the words that would explain, that would make her understand what he'd been carrying around all those years before—what he was *still* carrying around. "I was twenty-four years old, working for the New York Police Department. I'd just made detective, everything was perfect. I was living in Brooklyn, in an apartment in my brother Bob's house. Bob and Molly's house... He was, you know, married. They had a little baby, a little girl, Shannon. I was an uncle for the first time. Bob had a great job, and they really didn't need the rent from the apartment, but he was my big brother. Even though we were both grown-up, he was still looking out for me."

He was quiet for a moment. "Yeah, everything was perfect. The neighborhood wasn't the greatest, but that was okay, because, you know, I was a cop. Everyone knew I was with the twelfth precinct." He laughed. "I think everyone's property values went up just a little bit the minute I moved in. I'm not bragging—that's just the way those neighborhoods are." He laughed again. "Of course, Bob used to say that the property value would've gone up a whole lot higher if I'd been working for the mob."

Emily listened, staring out at where the ocean glimmered and gleamed, sparkling through the darkness like a living blanket of reflected light. Jim's husky New York accent seemed to thicken as he spoke, as if he had somehow been pulled back into the past.

"It was summer," he said, "and I was working with a team assigned to try to stop gang violence. Some of these kids were thirteen years old, walking around with automatic weapons, blowing away other kids because they were wearing the wrong colors. At the same time, there were members of the same gangs that were in their forties. I helped lock up some of the older members of this one gang, and they—"

Emily heard him shifting his position, and she glanced toward him. She could barely see him as he ran his hands up through his hair. He cleared his throat—a sudden loud noise in the darkness.

"The gang retaliated," he said. "They found out where I lived. They drove by my house as I was getting home from work, and they blew me away. Except they made a mistake. It wasn't me they killed. No, those sons of bitches didn't kill *me.*" His voice shook, but he didn't stop. "They killed Bob. They killed my brother. They gunned him down like a dog in the street."

Emily made a sound, a small sound from the shadows that told Jim he had her attention. She was listening. As he watched, she slowly sat down on the edge of a wooden lounge chair.

"Eight years, Em," he said quietly. "It happened eight years ago, and it still hurts as much as if it happened only yesterday."

Inside the beach house, an automatic light clicked on and shone out through the window, illuminating them. Emily was watching him, her eyes reflecting the pain that he knew was etched on his face.

"Molly never forgave me," he said. "She said she did, she said it wasn't my fault, but I knew she hated me for it. God, I hated myself. I couldn't look Molly—or my mother—in the eye. I still can't face my mother. I haven't talked to her in years. She calls me every few months, leaves a message on my answering machine, but I still can't bear to call her back."

Jim looked up, unable to hold Emily's gaze in the dim light. His eyes looked tortured, and his face was lined with despair. "I still sometimes hate myself," he whispered.

"I'm sorry," Emily murmured.

"There's more," Jim said, his voice harsh. "It gets worse."

Worse than his brother dying? Emily tried to imagine feeling responsible for her brother Danny's death, but she couldn't. She couldn't even imagine how awful that would be. The thought of Danny dead, his quick smile and his cheery "Hey, kiddo" gone forever, was awful enough.

"I wasn't assigned to the case," Jim said, "you know, to find Bob's killers. They wouldn't let me handle it, I was too involved. But I wanted to find those bastards. I wanted to find them and— So I kept on top of the investigation. There were witnesses who IDed the shooter and the driver of the car. We knew who they were, we just had to find them. But New York's a big city, and these guys didn't want to be found."

Jim fell silent, leaning his head back against the wall and closing his eyes.

"What happened?" Emily asked softly.

He looked directly at her. All the sparkle and life was gone from his eyes, leaving them flat, devoid of expression.

"I found them," he said. "I found them, and I killed them. I shot them dead, like they shot Bob."

Silence. It surrounded them as completely as the night had closed in around them. But the darkness had been interrupted by the light coming on inside the house. In the same way, Emily broke the silence.

"I can't believe that," she said.

"Believe it," he said. "It happened."

Emily leaned forward. "Are you telling me that you went out after these guys, intending to kill them?"

"No!" he said, but his conviction soon faltered. "I don't know." He swept his hands across his face. "Maybe, subconsciously, I did. After it was all over, everyone assumed I went out for revenge, and it made me wonder. You know, maybe I did plan to kill them. It all happened so fast...."

"How did you find them?"

"I was working the desk at the precinct," Jim said, "and a call came in. Everyone on the street knew we were looking for these guys, and one of our usual informers spotted them going into an apartment. While the lieutenant was organizing the raid, my partner and I went down to keep an eye on the place, make sure they didn't leave. We were supposed to sit outside in my car and just watch. But I went into the building. I couldn't just sit tight. I even went up the stairs— I don't know what I was thinking. I didn't have a warrant, I didn't have any backup, I only had this... this... *anger*. My partner was behind me and he kept telling me we had to go back to the car, that we were going to get in trouble doing this, but I didn't give a damn. And then it happened. The guys we were after came down the stairs. They recognized me, and they started shooting. When it was all over, two of them were dead, killed by bullets fired from my gun."

He was quiet for a moment, staring down at his boots. "They brought me down to their level, Emily," he said. "Killing them didn't bring Bob back. It only made me... a monster. By killing those bastards, I was no better than they were. It made me sick. I felt subhuman, I felt—" He took a deep breath. "It took me a long time to crawl out of that hell. I still don't know for sure if I went after those guys with the intent to kill, or if it just happened. But I *do* know now that I'm not a monster. I'm human. And, like all humans, I'm not perfect. I can forgive myself. Sometimes, on really good days, I can even forgive myself for Bob's death. Sometimes.

"But when I first met you, I couldn't forgive myself for anything. I knew I didn't deserve someone like you. And I couldn't believe I would bring you anything but unhappi-

ness." He looked up at her, meeting her eyes steadily for the
first time in many long minutes. "So I staged that scene at
the bar, to make you stop loving me. Everything I said, you
know, about other women, about not sleeping alone, it was
a lie. I loved you with all my heart, Em. There was never
anyone but you."

Emily's eyes filled with tears. "Why didn't you tell me?"
she whispered. "Why didn't you tell me about your brother,
about everything you'd been through? How could you make
a decision like that, about our future, without letting *me*
have a say? Oh, Jim, I would've helped you. Don't you
know I would've done *anything—*"

He shook his head. "I thought you'd be better off without me. And I thought—" His voice broke.

"What?" She moved toward him, kneeling next to him
on the dry wooden floor.

"How could I have the life I wanted with you, knowing
that Bob's life was over? He never got to watch his daughter grow up. He never got to hold his wife in his arms again.
He was dead, Emily, so how could I let myself have you?
How could I give myself that kind of happiness, when all he
had was...nothing?"

Emily couldn't answer. She couldn't say a word.

"I still don't deserve you," he said in a low voice. "But,
God help me, I want you." He didn't reach out toward her.
He didn't take her in his arms the way he wanted to. Instead, he let his eyes caress her face, memorizing every last
freckle, studying the way her eyelashes looked, matted with
her tears. She was so beautiful, it hurt. "I know I...I had
my chance with you, and I blew it seven years ago. I don't
blame you for not believing me or trusting me, or even
wanting me around. It's my own fault. That, and...bad
timing."

She didn't say a word. She just sat there, watching him,
her eyes luminous with unshed tears. Jim felt his own eyes
start to sting. He felt the thick sensation of deep emotion

tightening his chest. Another few minutes of this, and he was going to break down and cry like a baby....

"Em, I can't think straight anymore," he told her desperately. "I can't think at all, and it's driving me nuts. The way things are between us right now, I can't do my job. I can't take care of you the way I should, so unless you tell me otherwise, unless you want me to stick around, I'm going to have myself taken off this case. I just wanted you to know that I never meant to hurt you. I did what I did seven years ago only because I loved you."

There. He'd said it all. He'd gotten it all out in the open. He'd done everything he could, except maybe throwing himself on his knees and begging her to forgive him, to give him another chance.

But Emily still didn't speak. She didn't comment, didn't reply, didn't open her mouth.

Jim felt the tightness in his chest contract, making it hard for him to breathe. She didn't forgive him. She didn't want him to stay. In some ways, it made things easier. He knew he could live with the pain. He knew he could exist without her, doing the same kind of half living he'd been doing for the past seven years. And this way, he wouldn't have to wrestle with the daily knowledge that he had a life, while Bob's was gone.

Jim pulled himself to his feet, praying that the tears wouldn't come until he was in his car, until he'd had a chance to pull away from the front of the beach house. He moved toward the steps, his boots sounding too loud on the wooden planks.

Emily reached out and caught his hand.

Jim stopped, looking down first at their hands, their fingers intertwined, then at Emily.

"Don't go," she whispered. Her face was streaked with tears, and her eyes were so soft, so full of forgiveness. "Please?"

She scrambled to her feet and put her arms around him, holding him tight, giving him the comfort he'd denied himself for so long.

But the steel belt around Jim's chest didn't loosen. Instead, it got tighter. And, holding the woman he'd loved for so long in his arms, he wept.

Because, God help him, he still didn't deserve her.

Chapter 13

Emily woke up alone in the big double bed. She wrapped the top sheet around her, using it as a makeshift robe, and went down the stairs and into the living room.

There was no sign of Jim.

She finally found him, sitting out on the back porch, watching the rising sun set fire to the ocean. He looked up at her and smiled, his eyes warm and welcoming, and she felt her pulse rate increase. This all still seemed so strange, so bizarre, so much like a dream. She hoped that if it was one she wouldn't wake up too soon.

"Couldn't you sleep?" she asked.

He reached for her, pulling her down onto his lap. "No."

"You should've woken me," she said.

He kissed her, running his fingers through her thick chestnut hair, then gently massaging the back of her neck and her shoulders. "I kept you up all night. It didn't seem fair to wake you so early this morning."

Emily closed her eyes, wondering if he knew that the soft touch of his hands had the power to make her heart pound—even at five-thirty in the morning. "*I* was the one who kept *you* up all night," she said, feeling the sheet slip farther off her shoulders. "That gives you the right to wake me up whenever you want."

Jim laughed. He had a rich, husky, sexy-sounding laugh that sent shivers up and down her spine. Or maybe it was the way he was kissing the base of her throat that felt so good.

"I have to tell you something," Emily said softly, and Jim sat up. He wanted to hear her say that she loved him. She hadn't said it—at least not in words—and, God, he needed to hear it.

She smiled at him uncertainly. "This is kind of weird," she said. "I mean, my telling you this after...what we spent last night doing..." She held his gaze, but a delicate tinge of pink covered her cheeks. She was actually blushing.

Jim felt an overpowering rush of love for her, and he held her tighter, pulling her mouth down to his for a lingering kiss.

"You're not making this any easier," she said, nestling against his shoulder, brushing her lips lightly against his bare skin. She felt his arms tighten around her, felt the unmistakable evidence of his desire for her, and she knew it wouldn't take much to table this discussion—at least temporarily. But she had to tell him about Alex. If she didn't tell him, it would feel as if she were keeping secrets from him, and she didn't want that. She closed her eyes—it was easier that way—and said, "The other night, Alex Delmore proposed."

Jim froze. "Marriage?" He knew as soon as he asked that of *course* it was marriage that Delmore had proposed. But Emily didn't comment on the stupidity of his question. He looked down into the deep blue of her eyes as she nodded.

"I told him I needed time to think it over," she said.

What the hell was this that he was feeling? What *was* it? Jealousy? Outrage? Fear? Possessiveness? Hell, yes. All of it, yes. *You're mine,* he wanted to say. *You're mine now.*

He wanted her off the case, out of danger, away from Alexander Delmore. Fear that something would happen to Emily, some horrible, dangerous thing that he'd be powerless to prevent, lodged in his chest and made it hard for him to breathe.

"Em, let's not go back," he whispered.

"Not ever?" she said with a smile.

He shook his head and kissed her. *No, not ever.*

She didn't take him seriously. "Alex isn't expecting to see me until Saturday—until the party on his boat," Emily said. "We can stay here until then. If you want . . ."

Jim nodded. He wanted. "I have to call in, make sure it's all right," he said. His voice sounded huskier than usual, and he cleared his throat. "I think it will be—I'm supposed to be protecting you."

"*Protecting* me." Emily's smile nearly took his breath away. "Is that what you call this?"

He could see every one of last night's kisses, every one of last night's caresses, reflected on her face. The memory of making love to her was suddenly so strong, so vivid, that he ached, wanting to feel himself inside her again, surrounded by her, buried deep within her. God, would he never get enough of her?

From the slow burn of desire in her eyes, he knew she was remembering, too. Again the blush crept back on her cheeks. It was too charming, too sweet, too incredibly sexy.

"Are you real?" he murmured, his hands slipping down beneath the cotton sheet, stroking the satiny smoothness of her body. "Or have I died and gone to heaven?"

Emily answered him with a long, slow kiss.

She tasted so sweet, so warm, he could have gone on kissing her all morning long. But she pulled back to reposition herself on his lap, straddling him on the wooden lounge chair, so that they were face-to-face. The sheet fell away, and Jim caught his breath at the sight of her, naked in the silvery morning light.

She was beautiful. The creamy white of her full breasts contrasted with the rose-colored peaks of her nipples and the golden tan of the rest of her skin. Her stomach was flat, but wonderfully soft, flaring out into slender hips and strong thighs—thighs that gripped him in anticipation of pleasures to come.

Oh, yeah, she was beautiful. With her eyes half-closed, watching him watch her, with her hair mussed from sleep, with her lips slightly parted, the heat of her desire radiated from her. She wanted him. And it amazed him that she would sit here, out in the open like this, his shy, modest Emily, unmindful of the fact that she was naked for all the world to see. It was true that this house was secluded, and that this part of the beach was wide. But from time to time joggers *did* run past, and if they glanced up toward the house... Yeah, they'd certainly get an eyeful.

But it was one eyeful Jim didn't want to share with anyone. He sat up, sliding toward the end of the chair. As he stood up, he lifted Emily, too. She wrapped her arms around his neck and her long legs around his waist as he carried her into the house.

He didn't make it to the bedroom.

Jim swam in circles around Emily as she floated serenely in the warm ocean. He wondered how to bring up the subject of removing her from the investigation. The one time he'd brought it up over the past few days, she'd told him in no uncertain terms that she had absolutely no intention of quitting—not now that they were so close. The problem was, he had absolutely no intention of letting her put herself in further danger. But, short of flat-out forbidding her to continue with the investigation, he wasn't sure how to achieve his goal.

"Did you get in touch with Felipe?" Emily asked lazily, treading the water with the smallest of motions. She was wearing a high-waisted blue batik-print bikini that managed to be both modest and sexy as all hell. Just like Emily.

"Yeah," he said, standing up and shaking the water out of his ears. "He's been following Delmore all week. Nothing's out of the ordinary. According to Phil, the guy's been playing it clean. Hasn't even exceeded the speed limit."

"Did Felipe happen to mention Jewel Hays?" Emily asked, opening her eyes to look up at him. "He was visiting her regularly for a while there. Do you know if he's seen her lately?"

Jim squeezed the seawater out of his long hair. "Yeah," he said again.

Emily floated toward him. "Yeah what?" she asked, looping her arms around his neck and kissing his smoothly shaved chin. "Yeah, he mentioned her, or yeah, you know whether or not he's seen her lately?"

"Both," Jim said, smiling down into her sun-kissed face. She looked like some kind of wonderful sea creature, a mermaid or a sea sprite. "Jewel's doing really well. Her little boy, Billy, is, too. Phil was helping her study for her GED."

"But he's not anymore?" Emily asked.

Jim pulled her closer, fitting their bodies neatly together underneath the cover of the water. If only they weren't wearing these bathing suits...

"Mmm..." Emily said as he kissed her, but she was only temporarily distracted. "Something happened, didn't it? Jewel got too intense for Felipe, right?"

Jim sighed. "Felipe got too intense for Felipe," he said. "He's attracted to her, Em, but he says he's not ready for any kind of serious, strings-attached kind of relationship. And Jewel comes with all kinds of strings attached. He knows he's got a real weakness when it comes to women, and he also knows that a casual sexual relationship is *not* what Jewel needs right now. So he's keeping his distance."

"He's afraid he can't control himself, so Jewel loses a friend," Emily said.

"He's doing what he knows is best, Em."

"It still stinks," she said. "Jewel's got to be wondering what happened. She's probably hurt."

"This isn't easy for Felipe, either. What is he supposed to do?" Jim asked. "Whenever they're together, she starts coming on to him. He's a man, not a saint, Em."

"Maybe she's coming on to him because she doesn't know how to interact with a man in any other way," Emily said. "Maybe all she really wants is to be his friend."

Emily started wading to shore. "He could try talking to her," she said. "He could tell her what he's feeling, instead of leaving her completely in the dark." She stopped and turned to look back at him, hoping he'd realize that she was talking about more than Jewel and Felipe. "He could let her take part in the decision making."

Jim was looking down at the water, not meeting her eyes. He knew exactly what she was talking about. "Yeah, well..." he said. "That's not always easy, is it?"

He slipped underneath the water, ending the conversation. Emily went up to the beach alone.

"Excuse me?" Emily said, crossing her arms tightly in front of her and leaning back against the kitchen counter. "I must not have heard you right. It sounded to me like you just told me that you weren't going to *allow* me to help catch Alex."

"Yeah, that's what I said," Jim said. He gripped her shoulders, begging her with his eyes to listen to what he was saying. "Em, if you're out there, something could happen. Anything could go wrong. You could be hurt—or worse. I can't take that risk. It's killing me. The only obvious solution is to take you off the case, so that's what I'm gonna do. I promise you, I'll find another way to get this guy—"

"You have no right—"

"Yeah, actually, I do," he countered. "I have both the right *and* the authority."

"I'm not talking about police procedures," Emily said hotly. "I'm talking about your macho male-chauvinist Y-chromosome-loaded assumption that as my lover you have the right to tell me what I can and can not do. Didn't it occur to you to discuss this with me first, *master?*"

Well, no, actually, it hadn't. He went back to cutting vegetables for their salad. "Emily, stop. I'm not going to play games with your safety."

"I'm not talking about *games,* I'm talking about decision making. I'm talking about democracy, about a partnership, about equal give-and-take," she said, smacking the countertop with her hand to get his attention. "Don't I *matter* to you?"

He turned toward her, dropping the knife. "Of course—"

"Don't you respect my ability to come to my own conclusions, to make up my own mind?"

"Yeah, but—"

"I'm not quitting now," she said. "Not when we're so close. We're going to have a chance to get you onto Alex's boat *tomorrow,* Jim." She reached out to him, gripping the smooth muscles of his forearms, then letting her hands slide down to his wrists, to his hands. "It's not like I'll be alone with him. It's a society party. Dozens of people will be there. You'll be there, too."

Jim locked their fingers together to keep her from slipping away. He stared down at their intertwined hands.

"You'll be there, so I'll be safe," she said with total conviction.

Safe. Like the last time she'd gone out with Delmore, and he and Phil had lost her?

"What'll you do if he wants an answer to his marriage proposal?" he asked quietly.

She was ready for that. "I'll tell him I need more time."

No. Every nerve in his body was screaming no, he shouldn't let her talk him into this. But, damn it, she was making sense. They *were* so close. And what could Delmore do to Emily in the middle of a high-society cocktail party?

The problem was, with Jim's experience working on the streets, he could think of quite a few nasty things Delmore could do, party or no party. But Jim would be there, to watch over Emily, to protect her...

Emily slipped her arms around his waist, standing on her toes to kiss him lightly. Her breath was warm against his face, her body fitting his perfectly. "If we don't find the evidence we need to catch Alex tomorrow, then I'll think about quitting, okay?" She kissed him again, longer this time.

"You're trying to distract me," he said.

She smiled into his eyes, running her fingers through the soft curls of his hair. "Is it working?"

"Yeah," he said, kissing her full on the mouth, pulling her in closer to him. It was working.

Saturday dawned bright and sunny—the perfect kind of day for a sail on a millionaire drug runner's yacht.

Jim woke up early and lay quietly in bed, watching Emily sleep beside him.

Tangled in the sheets, damp with perspiration from the relentless summer heat which even the air conditioners and the permanently turning ceiling fans couldn't relieve, Emily lay in the bed, her dark hair spread across the pillow. Her eyes were closed, and her lashes were long and dark against the soft curve of her cheeks. She looked so young and innocent, so pure and perfect. He loved her so much, he ached inside.

Was this the way Bob had loved Molly?

They'd been childhood sweethearts, his brother Bob and his wife, Molly. Bob had never even dated anyone else. He'd sworn up and down that he'd been in love with Molly since fourth grade. He'd always looked at Molly with such feeling in his eyes, declaring that they were two of the lucky ones to have found the kind of love they shared.

Molly had spent the past eight years alone, with only her little daughter, Shannon, by her side.

Molly was alone.

Bob was forever alone.

So what gave Jim the right to have Emily?

He climbed out of bed, careful not to wake her, exiling himself to the solitude and heat of the back porch.

Chapter 14

Emily swirled the ice cubes around the bottom of her empty glass, aware of Jim's eyes on her from the other side of Alex's yacht.

Alex deftly took the glass from her hands and smoothed back her hair to place a well-aimed kiss underneath her ear. "I'll get you another drink," he said with a charming smile.

"Thanks." Emily made herself relax and return his smile. She glanced back across the deck as Alex walked toward the bar, but Jim wasn't there any longer.

"This is hell," a soft voice whispered in her ear, and she looked up to see him standing directly behind her.

Dressed the way he was, in a black tuxedo with a white shirt and black bow tie, with his hair pulled back into a ponytail at the nape of his neck, he looked incredible. His eyes glittered like blue ice—no, not ice, fire. As a matter of fact, she'd seen that same look in his eyes this morning, when they'd made love—after she'd woken up alone again, and gone out to find him sitting, again, on the back porch.

Something was wrong between them. But whenever she asked, he shrugged it off and wouldn't talk about it. It didn't have to do with the fact that he feared for her safety—he was more than willing to talk about *that*. No, there was something else bothering him, something eating away at him. But he wouldn't tell her what it was.

And that scared her.

Still, Emily had shut her eyes and played along this past week, pretending they were idyllic, blissful lovers, trying to believe Jim when he told her that he loved her. But the fact that he was holding something back kept her wary.

She hadn't told him that she loved him—at least not in words. She was afraid to. She was afraid saying it out loud would leave her vulnerable and unguarded. She was afraid of getting hurt again.

Emily knew Jim wanted to hear those words. She knew from the way he whispered of his own love for her, then watched her, waiting for some kind of response, some kind of reply. But she couldn't do it. Saying "I love you, too," would ring false. And to declare her emotions at any other time seemed too risky, too frightening.

But she *did* love him. Desperately. Just looking into his eyes like this could make her heart pound.

Emily quickly looked away, afraid that if she held his gaze too long people might notice the sensual flame that seemed to spark between them. Jim was playing the part of her brother, for crying out loud.

"Don't look at me like that," Emily murmured.

"I can't help it," he muttered. "You look too damn good. And it's driving me nuts, the way he's touching you all the time. Why'd I let you talk me into this?"

"Because stopping Alex is the right thing to do. When are you going to try to get into his office?" Emily asked quietly.

"I've already tried once," Jim answered. "There's too many people around. I need some kind of diversion."

"Like what?"

"I don't know—something big. A school of blue whales off the starboard bow," Jim said. "A meteor shower. A tidal wave. A falling UFO."

On the other side of the deck, Alex was talking to Marty Bevin and her husband.

"How about an engagement announcement?" Emily said.

"No," Jim said sharply. "Emily, don't do that."

If she went over to Alex now, in front of Marty, and told him she was accepting his marriage proposal, all hell would break loose. It wouldn't be quite as big as a falling UFO, but...

Jim caught her arm, trying hard to keep his voice low, glancing around to make sure they weren't being watched. "I don't want you even to pretend that you're gonna marry this guy."

"It would do the trick," she said. Emily forced herself to smile at a man and woman who were strolling a little too close to them.

Jim waited until the pair were out of earshot before he spoke. *"No."*

"Why *not?*"

"Because I want you to marry *me.*"

His words seemed to surprise himself as much as they surprised Emily. She stared at him staring back at her, both pairs of eyes widening in shock. Jim forced his face to relax and turned, leaning back on the railing with his elbows. To the casual observer, they were having a lighthearted chat.

Emily turned away, using the smooth wooden deck railing to support the weight that her knees suddenly couldn't hold. Jim wanted to *marry* her.

She looked out over the ocean. The water reflected the lights from the yacht. They sparkled and shimmered like diamonds in the darkness. He wanted to marry her. She felt tears sting her eyes, and she blinked hard to keep them back.

"Are you asking?" Emily finally said. Her voice was calm and cool, matching the poised set of her gaze. He would never know how she'd braced herself before looking up at him.

"No," he growled, his answer so abrupt and immediate that she actually flinched.

She started to turn away.

"Yes, damn it," he rasped. He turned his back on anyone who might have been watching them and closed his eyes briefly. "Yes, I'm asking."

A war of emotions was raging across his lean face. Terror fought exhilaration, shock went head-to-head with love and hope, as he pinned her to the spot with the intensity of his gaze.

"Say something," he breathed, then added, "No, don't. Em, you don't have to answer right away. You don't have to answer at all if you don't want—"

The battle was over—love had won, hands down. She could see it in the achingly desperate vulnerability in his eyes. He loved her. Whatever problems he was having, whatever it was that was tormenting him, whatever he was holding back from her, it wasn't that he didn't love her.

Jim forced himself to take a step back, to loosen the tightness in his shoulders. Damn it, this wasn't the time or the place to be having this conversation.

"Why wait to give you an answer," Emily said then, her voice shaking, "when I know I'd marry you in a split second?"

"You would?" he whispered, searching her face for the reasons, for the declaration he needed to hear.

On the off chance that he couldn't read it on her face, that he couldn't see it in the sheen of tears that glimmered in her eyes, Emily said it. Out loud. "I love you."

Jim turned away, afraid that if he didn't he'd give in to the temptation to take Emily into his arms. He gripped the deck railing so hard his knuckles turned white. He cleared his throat, glancing around to be sure he wouldn't be overheard. "What do you say we jump overboard, swim to land, and I make love to you for the next two weeks straight?"

He looked at her with such fire in his eyes that Emily nearly felt burned.

She took a deep breath. "What do you say I go create a diversion?" she whispered. "You go play James Bond and find the evidence we need to put Alex behind bars, and *then* we'll go home and make love for the next two weeks straight?"

Jim glanced over his shoulder at Alex Delmore, who was still deep in conversation with his friends. "I'm going to have to smile when I congratulate Delmore on catching you as his bride," he said, his mouth tight. He met Emily's eyes. "Later, you can give me an Oscar for my award-winning acting performance."

She smiled. "I'll give you *something* later," she said, almost inaudibly, "but it won't be an Oscar."

Jim smiled then, too—a quick flash of white teeth in the shadows. "Oh, baby."

"You better believe it," Emily said. "Now *go*. But be careful."

"You too, Em."

With one more look deep into her eyes, Jim disappeared toward the stern of the yacht. Emily took a steadying breath, plastered a smile on her face and headed toward Alex.

He looked up and smiled apologetically as she approached. "I'm sorry, were you getting thirsty?" Alex asked, handing her the drink he was holding in his left hand.

"You look radiant tonight, Emily," Marty commented, taking a long drag on her cigarette. "Who's the hunk you were talking to before?"

"Um..." Emily said. Dan, not Jim. God, she had to remember that. She'd almost called him Jim.

Marty's eyes narrowed, as if she'd somehow picked up on Emily's apprehension. "You're not playing around on our little Alex now, are you?" she said with mock outrage.

"That was my brother," Emily said, keeping her voice light. "Dan. He's here visiting for a few weeks. I told you about him, remember?"

"*That* was big brother Dan?" Marty said. "My, my... Good looks run in the family, don't they?"

Emily frowned at her drink, knowing with certainty that Alex, in his role as the impeccable host, would notice.

"Is there something wrong with your drink?" he asked.

Emily took a deep breath. Here goes. "Actually," she said with a smile, "I was thinking champagne might be more appropriate tonight."

Alex understood instantly—she could tell from the sudden smug satisfaction in his eyes. "I've got enough champagne on board to go around," he said. "How about I tell my crew to start opening it?"

"Are we celebrating something?" Marty asked eagerly.

"Emily's just agreed—" Alex broke off and turned back to Emily. "That *was* a yes, wasn't it?"

She forced herself to smile brightly. "Yes, it was."

Comprehension dawned in Marty's eyes. She screamed, loud and shrill and long, causing heads to turn. "Oh, my God! Oh, my God!" she shrieked. "Alex is getting *married!*"

Marty engulfed Emily in a smoky embrace as a crowd gathered around them. Partygoers came running from all ends of the yacht as the first bottle of champagne was popped open. Jim had his diversion.

"Congratulations," someone said, pumping her hand. "You must be very happy."

"Yes, thank you," Emily replied, able to say with heartfelt honesty, "I am."

Because she *was* getting married.

But not to Alex.

* * *

"I think," Alex said, trailing one finger along the line of the sapphire necklace that Emily had finally accepted, "now that you've consented to be my wife, we should celebrate."

Alex's pale eyes were heavy and reddened from wine and cigarette smoke. He'd finally taken his contact lenses out, and his nearsightedness made him squint at her slightly. Emily tried not to visibly back away, but she wanted to. Boy, she wanted to. And wearing this necklace was giving her the creeps. She couldn't wait to take it off. But after she agreed to marry Alex, there had been no way she could refuse it. The sapphire necklace had finally become an appropriate gift. At least she could be grateful Alex didn't have some enormous, even more expensive diamond ring ready to slip onto her finger.

She looked around the yacht. Most of the party guests were gone. The *Home Free* had been docked at the pier for close to two hours now, and only a few of Alex's friends lay sprawled on the lounge chairs that peppered the deck. Emily was well aware of Jim, not more than a few yards away, leaning against the wooden railing, grimly watching Alex touch her.

"We just had a party," Emily said lightly. "That was a great way to celebrate."

"I was thinking of something a little more...private," Alex said with a lopsided grin.

He was drunk. He kissed her—or he tried to, anyway. Emily moved her head so that his mouth landed on her cheek. Her eyes met Jim's. She could see the muscles working in his jaw. He stood up and walked toward them.

"It's late," he said. "Time to go."

Alex threw his arm around Emily's shoulders. "Well, hey, Dan," he said. "You heading out?"

"*We're* heading out," Jim said. "Emily and I."

"We were just discussing that," Alex said. "Emily's going to stay here tonight, so you can run on along home."

Jim shook his head. "Call me old-fashioned," he said, "but Emily's *not* staying with you. You're not married yet."

Alex laughed. "Is this guy for real?" he asked Emily.

She slipped free from his grip. "Oh, yeah," she said, with a smile at Jim—her first real smile in hours. "He's real."

Jim was silent in the car on the way home.

"Did you find out anything?" Emily finally asked.

He glanced up from the road and over at her. His face was lit in a pattern of darkness and then light as they passed under the streetlights.

"Yeah," he said.

Silence.

"Aren't you going to tell me?"

He glanced at her again, his eyes colorless in the darkness. "I hated him kissing you," he said tightly.

"I'm sorry," Emily said softly.

"It's not your fault."

"It's over now," she said. She took off the sapphire necklace and dropped it into the bottom of her bag. She was going to donate it to the high school's drug education program as soon as this charade was over.

Jim laughed in exasperation. "Oh, yeah?" he said. "Wait'll you see what happens tomorrow. Your engagement to Delmore will make the morning society news, and by eleven-thirty every high-class department store in the state will be calling you, trying to get you signed up with their bridal whatchamacallit. You know, register you for wedding presents." He braked as they approached a red light. He put the car into first gear and turned to look at Emily as they waited for the light to change to green. "It'll be a different world if you marry me, you know? Hell, the way *my* friends buy presents, it'll be safest to register down at Wal-Mart."

"Do you really think I care?"

There were no other cars on the road, behind them or even in front of them. Jim ignored the light as it turned green. He touched Emily's face, gently skimming her lips with his thumb. "I want to give you all that stuff, Em," he said quietly. "I want to give you fancy jewelry, too, but I can't. Do you hear what I'm saying? There's a lot I can't give you, a lot you'll be missing."

"I don't care."

Right now, she didn't care. But how about in a year or two? How about in ten years? How about when they scraped and struggled to put their kids through college—if he even lived that long.

This was definitely a mistake. Emily didn't deserve this kind of future. And as far as what *he* deserved ...

The light was red again. He went through it anyway, hoping that if they were moving, Emily would stop watching him that way, with her eyes so soft and gentle, as if she could see down deep within him. He didn't have to wonder if she saw all his scars and all the permanently torn and tattered places in his soul. He knew she did. And despite that, she still loved him. It was too damn amazing.

It made his chest feel tight and his eyes burn, and he changed the subject. He had to. If he continued even just *thinking* about the love in Emily's eyes, he'd lose control.

In another five minutes, they'd be back at Emily's apartment. Once they were inside, he *could* lose control. And he would. He'd do more than lose control—he'd lose himself, he'd bury himself deep inside Emily. He could let all these intense, crazy feelings loose when they made love. He could give in to his emotions, he could let himself be overwhelmed. And he'd be able to tell Emily all about the way he was feeling. He'd tell her with his mouth and his hands and his body. He'd tell her far more eloquently than he ever could with words.

But right now, he had to make it through the next five minutes. "Delmore's office was clean," he said, roughly clearing the thickness from his throat, "so I logged on to his computer."

"You're kidding." Emily was appalled. "Jim, what if someone had come in while you were on-line?"

"They didn't," Jim said shortly.

"But what if—"

"Em, it was cool. Nothing happened. No big deal."

"No big deal? If Alex had found you down there, with his computer on—"

"Look, you want to know what I found out?"

"*Yes*. But . . . I can't believe you."

"His records all looked perfect," Jim said, interrupting her. "At first. See, Delmore has all of his business transactions and records on his hard disk, and everything was very tidy. But I started thinking. If an honest, upstanding, tax-paying millionaire uses some of his millions to buy illegal drugs and sell them at an enormous profit, how's he gonna explain this enormous profit to Uncle Sam?"

He glanced at Emily. He knew she hadn't forgotten about being upset that he'd taken such a big risk by prying in Delmore's personal computer. He was going to hear about it, but not until later. Right now, she was listening intently, her eyes glued to his face.

"Good question," she said. "How *does* he explain it?"

"I figured he's got to have some sort of money-laundering operation," Jim said, "some way to report all that additional income. Because, you know, he can only keep so many millions in small bills under his mattress, right?"

"How does he do it? And how did you figure it out?"

"I didn't exactly figure it out," Jim admitted. "It was more like I stumbled onto it. See, one of Delmore's real estate transactions listed for last month was a condo at the same complex where I'm living. According to Delmore's records, he sold a one-bedroom unit for a hundred and twenty thousand dollars. On the surface, that's not so strange. There're plenty of condos around here that go for much more than that. But, see, I tried to sell *my* two-bedroom a few months ago, but I took it off the market when the agent told me I'd be lucky to get a whopping ninety-five thousand for it. Yet Delmore managed to make the sale of a *one*-bedroom for twenty-five thousand more? Either I want him to be *my* agent, too, or something pretty fishy's going on here. I bet my money on fishy, and dug deeper and found out that on top of the high price, Delmore's records show he's working for a twelve percent commission—almost twice as much as the fee other agents take. My guess is he's boosting both the sale price and his commission percentage on all his records—not by enough to make anyone notice, but enough to provide a supposedly legal source for all his extracurricular income."

"So now what?" Emily said. "Can you arrest him?"

Jim shook his head. "No. We can't bust him for accounting errors. We still need some hard evidence that proves he's bringing drugs into the country." He sighed in frustration. "It would be nice if we could catch him red-handed. I spent most of my time down in Delmore's office searching for some kind of sailing schedule or calendar—anything that would tell me the next time he plans to be out on his boat overnight."

"Monday night," Emily said. "Alex is going out late Monday afternoon, and he won't be back until Tuesday." At Jim's look of surprise, she explained. "He handed me his personal calendar and told me to pick a wedding date. He told me that anything he had written in pencil could be changed, but I'd have to work around the dates written in pen. I noticed that he had his sailing schedule marked off in pen, and that struck me as odd."

Jim was deep in thought as he pulled Emily's car into the parking lot of her apartment building. "I need to figure out a way to get onto Delmore's boat, to be there Monday night, when the shipment comes in."

"I can get us on board," Emily said.

He pulled up the parking brake and cut the engine, turning to give her an exasperated look. "What are you, nuts? No way am I going to let you near Delmore again—and especially not in a situation where you could be face-to-face with the people who are selling the stuff to him."

There was a dangerous glint in Emily's eyes. "That's strange. I *know* you wouldn't *dare* order me around, but that sure sounded more like an imperial command than a request to my ears."

"Emily—"

She leaned forward and kissed him. "Let's not argue about this now. Please? I'm exhausted. And I need a shower."

"I want you to catch a morning flight up to Connecticut," he said. "I want you to stay with your folks for a week or so, until we nail this guy."

"Jim—"

"Emily. You've got to let me keep you safe."

She kept her voice light. "I'm safe. After all, I'm living with a cop."

Jim didn't smile, the way she expected him to. Instead, his face became closed, shuttered. "Hell of a lot of good that did my brother," he said tightly, getting out of the car.

He came around and opened her door, standing stiffly, his anger evident in the set of his shoulders. All of a sudden, he seemed almost determined to fight with her. But Emily was just as determined *not* to argue. Not tonight.

She took his hand and pulled him gently toward the stairs that led up to the second-floor apartments.

"I'm serious about you going to your parents' house," he said as Emily unlocked her door. "I'm going to buy you a ticket tonight."

It was cool and dark inside Emily's apartment. She closed the door behind them and took off her high heels. The little red message light on her answering machine was flashing. But it was nearly 2:00 a.m. Whoever had called surely wouldn't mind if she waited until morning to listen to her messages. She went down the hall toward her bathroom without turning on a light.

"In fact, I'm going to call the airline right now," Jim said, switching on the lamp next to the couch, "and make a reservation."

Oh, no, you're not, Emily thought, turning on the shower. She took off her earrings and her necklace and put them in the jewelry box in the bedroom before going back down the hall to the living room.

Jim glanced up at her, the phone to his ear. He was obviously on hold. As she smiled at him, the muscle in his jaw jumped. He was more tense than she'd ever seen him before.

"Can you help me with my zipper?" she asked, turning around and pulling her hair up and off her neck.

She heard him stand up and move behind her, and felt his fingers fumble as he searched for the tiny zipper pull. He found it, and unzipped her dress slowly, careful not to catch the zipper's teeth in the delicate fabric.

Emily closed her eyes, allowing herself the luxury of remembering the way the world had seemed to tilt several hours earlier, when Jim had asked her to marry him. He wanted to marry her. As in forever. As in happily ever after.

They were finally alone together, after a grueling evening spent pretending they were something they weren't. She should be in his arms, he should be kissing her, loving her—they should be getting a head start on that happily ever after.

But Jim was still so stiff, so tense, so seemingly intentionally unhappy. It was as if he were making himself focus on all his fears about her safety, as if he didn't want to let himself be happy.

His hands fell away from her without touching her, without even the slightest caress. He was not going to be easily distracted—not this time. But Emily wouldn't accept defeat. She knew that he loved her. She *knew* that. And she was determined to see him smile again before the hour was out.

Turning, she reached for the base of the telephone, pushed the little buttons and cut Jim off.

"Damn it, Emily—"

With first a quick glance at the sliding glass door to be sure the curtains were closed, Emily pushed her dress off her shoulders. It pooled in a silky green pile at her feet. The sudden flare of heat in Jim's eyes was unmistakable as he took in her lacy black bra and matching panties, and all the smooth, tanned skin in between. But he stepped back, away from her, as if he were afraid to let her get too close.

He might be afraid, but she wasn't. She stepped out of her dress, toward him.

"Take a shower with me," she said, feeling her face heat slightly at the brazenness of her suggestion. "Please?" she added softly.

Jim's stomach twisted. She wanted to make love to him— she couldn't have made that any more obvious—and yet he was just standing here, staring at her like an idiot.

What was wrong with him?

Ten minutes ago, back in the car, all he could think about was when would they get here, how many minutes would it be until they closed the door to her apartment behind them, and how many seconds after that would it take him to pull her into his arms? Damn, he'd wanted her so badly, he'd imagined himself unable to wait even the short amount of time it would take to walk down the hallway to her bedroom. He'd imagined picking her up, wrapping her incredible legs around his waist and taking her, right there, standing up in the middle of the hall.

But that had been before she reminded him of Bob.

Now he still wanted her that badly, but his desire was covered by a sticky blanket of guilt. What gave him the right to spend the rest of the night in Emily's sweet arms? What gave him the right to have the kind of nearly hedonistic pleasure that awaited him if he took her outstretched hand and let her lead him toward the bathroom, toward the sound of that steamy shower? What gave him the right to *marry* her, for God's sake, to spend the rest of his life surrounded by her beautiful smile and her generous, warm, wonderful love?

The fact that he loved her more than he loved life itself wasn't enough. And wanting her as badly as he did wasn't enough, either. Even the answering light of love and desire he could see in Emily's eyes didn't erase the guilt he felt deep in his soul.

But, God help him, if she so much as touched him, he'd surrender completely to the need to lose himself, to bury himself, within her passion. For a while, he'd forget. But the guilt and pain would return. It always did, sooner or later.

She took another step toward him, and again he backed away, afraid of the power she had over him.

"Emily, we need to talk," he said huskily.

"We can talk later, can't we?" she said, unhooking the front clasp of her bra and stepping out of her panties. "After we make love?"

She held out her hands to him, and he was rocked by how vulnerable she was, standing there totally naked, wonderfully, gorgeously naked, with him still fully clothed.

She was vulnerable, yet she didn't seem to care as she gave him the ultimate gift of her love. She was offering him her body, and he was well aware it was part of a package deal, tightly tied to the even more awesome gifts of her heart and soul.

He might have been able to resist the sexual temptation—although where Emily was concerned, he wasn't totally convinced of that—but the promise of such intense physical pleasure, combined with the pure strength of her love and trust, well, that was something he had no defenses against.

He couldn't have backed away from her again if his life had depended on it.

So he reached for her, *lunged* for her, and the universe exploded as he met her sweet lips in a piercing, soul-shattering kiss. Her skin was so soft, her body so supple beneath his hands. He heard himself cry out—all his anguish and frustration and pain drawn out in one long, wordless sound.

Help me, he wanted to say. *Save me.* But even Emily, with her pure, sweet, nonjudgmental love, couldn't rescue him.

He knew he was touching her too roughly, kissing her too hard, and he tried to pull back, afraid that he would hurt her. But she kissed him just as savagely, welcoming the crushing strength of his arms and the fierce urgency of his hands.

Breaking free, she took his hand and pulled him toward the bathroom, toward the sound of the shower. The tiny room was thick with steam, and she pushed aside the shower curtain, then reached for Jim's bow tie.

One swift yank pulled it free, and as he reached for her again, as he kissed her, she peeled his jacket from his wide shoulders. The sleeves were inside out, but he didn't seem to notice or care as he threw it back behind him, out of the bathroom, onto the floor of the hall.

Emily unfastened the back catch of his cummerbund as he pressed his thigh between her legs, opening her to his searching fingers. *Yes.* She clung weakly to him as he explored her most intimate place, as he found her heat. This was what she wanted. This, and more, forever, for the rest of their lives. Her own fingers fumbled as she unfastened the button of his pants, as she pulled down his zipper and—

With a desperate-sounding groan, Jim picked her up and, stepping over the side of the tub and directly under the pounding stream of warm water, drove himself deep inside her.

The sensations were incredible—the cold tile at her back, the warm water pouring over them, and Jim plunging harder and deeper within her with each rhythmic thrust. Emily clutched the wet cotton of his shirt— He was still wearing his shirt and all the rest of his clothes, even his socks and shoes!

He didn't seem to notice that he was soaked. He didn't seem aware of anything but this incredible pleasure he was giving and taking. His eyes were tightly shut, and his face was a picture of intensity and emotion, made to seem even more so by the water dripping from his wet hair and running down his cheeks like tears.

"I love you," he whispered, his soft voice a gentle contrast to the physical onslaught of his body. "Emily, I love you so much...."

His words pushed her over the edge. True, the physical sensations were incredible, but it was hearing his confession of love that sent her rocketing toward a climax so exquisite it seemed otherworldly.

Waves of pleasure racked her body, and Emily cried out, in an explosion of sound that made Jim's eyes fly open. For several long seconds, he stared into her eyes, and time seemed to stand perfectly still as she felt a connection that was so much more than physical. They were one, two halves of a whole, made complete only by each other's love.

Unguarded, his dark blue eyes held such emotion, such love, such endless joy. All the dark clouds of worry, and all the sadness that had shadowed him were gone. He loved her, and nothing else mattered. Nothing else even existed.

She felt the tightening of his body as he was catapulted over the cliff of his own release. But still he looked into her eyes, holding her gaze as if he, too, wanted to share more than just his body with her, willingly letting her see that she had the power to touch his very soul.

He loved her. Endlessly, perfectly, truly.

Jim slowly became aware of the water running down past the collar of his shirt, soaking through the legs of his pants, dripping into his socks, making his shoes a sodden mess. He was still holding Emily. Her legs were still locked around him. Her head was resting on his shoulder, and he could feel the warmth of her breath against his neck as she clung to him.

He felt more than heard her laugh softly, felt her mouth curve up into a smile, felt her sigh with satisfaction. Then she lifted her head, and he helped her slide down.

Together, silently, they unbuttoned his tuxedo shirt and peeled it off him. Jim braced himself against the tile wall with one hand as he kicked off his shoes. His knees were wobbly, and from more than just the physical workout of their lovemaking. It was the emotion that made his legs feel weak, and he smiled wryly, thinking this was why so many men proposed marriage on their knees—their emotions were probably running so high, they couldn't have stood up if they'd wanted to. God knows right now it was taking all of his strength to stay vertical. Of course, he'd already done his proposing. He already knew that she wanted him forever, though what he'd done to deserve her love was beyond his knowledge.

A flicker of fear snuck through his sense of contentment, like the cold blade of a tiny knife, small but deadly. He shook his head, pushing it away, refusing it access. Don't think, he ordered himself. Just feel. Just *be*.

Emily threw his socks and his pants in the sink, and he gathered her into his arms, holding her under the stream of water, feeling her heart beating in sync with his own. Here, with the shower curtain drawn, the rest of the world seemed so far away, so remote. Here, in this dim, wet, tiny paradise, there was room only for two.

It was a crying shame they couldn't stay here forever.

Chapter 15

Reality stepped in and, with a swift left hook, knocked Jim out of the warmth of the safe, make-believe world he had allowed himself to be lost in for a while.

"What's wrong?" Emily asked softly, using her fingers to comb through his wet hair as he rubbed her dry with a towel.

"I didn't use a condom, Em," he said. A muscle jumped in his cheek as he looked up at her from where he was sitting on her bed.

That glimmer of darkness, of sorrow or pain or whatever it was, was back in his eyes. But Emily pretended she hadn't seen it. "You're only realizing that now?" she teased. "And here I thought it was some kind of macho-male possessive thing. I thought you figured as long as we're getting married, it was worth the risk."

Jim shook his head. "No," he said. "I was... We... It was too intense. I wasn't thinking about birth control, and I should have been. I'm sorry. It's my fault."

Emily leaned forward and kissed him. "I'd love to have a baby with you," she said simply, then smiled. "Preferably not for a few years, but it wouldn't be the end of the world, would it? Provided the baby has your smile, of course."

But he didn't give her one of those smiles. Instead, he pulled back, out of her arms. "Yeah, well," he said, clearing his throat. "I'm not ready for kids myself, you know? I think it would be a bad mistake right now."

That was a bald-faced lie, and Jim looked away, sure that if he met Emily's crystal-blue gaze she'd see through him to the truth. And the truth was, he would've killed for a chance to make a baby with her. Ever since Bob and Molly had had their baby, ever since he had watched Bob holding his tiny daughter in his arms, Jim had wanted a piece of that kind of happiness. And he wanted to share it with Emily. God, he wanted that more than he'd ever wanted anything.

"I mean, we should wait," he said. "You know, make sure we're right for each other, make sure it's going to work out. You hear what I'm saying?"

Emily's eyes dropped, and he knew his words had hurt her. She wanted words of love, promises of forever and happily ever after, not down-to-earth real-life warnings and cautions. But this *was* real life. And real life only rarely worked out. Real life usually sucker punched you, then kicked you when you were down and out. Real life was full of flat tires and broken dreams and forgotten promises. Real life meant getting gunned down in the street by punks out for revenge. Real life was Bob, bleeding to death, gasping his last words of love to Molly, without a prayer of survival.

Jim stood up, suddenly desperate for some fresh air.

He pulled on a pair of shorts and went out into the living room, pushing aside the curtains to open the sliding glass door to the deck.

The night air was humid, hot and thick. He closed the door behind him and sat down heavily on one of the lounge chairs, raking his still-wet hair back out of his face. Damn it, it was impossible to breathe, even out here.

The door slid open, and Emily slipped out onto the deck. She'd put on a sleeveless white cotton nightgown that made her look both impossibly innocent and gut-wrenchingly sexy. He wanted her again, Jim realized. He'd just had the most intense sexual experience of his life and yet, already, he wanted more.

He clenched his teeth and looked away from her, afraid to give himself away, afraid to let her see the power she had over him. Still, he heard her nightgown rustle softly as she sat down in the other chair. He felt her watching him.

"Do you want to talk about it?" she asked softly.

"Talk about what?" he asked huskily, not daring to meet her eyes.

"Whatever it is that's bothering you."

What was he supposed to say? I'm scared? Scared of what? He didn't know. Scared of being too happy, a small voice said, taunting him. Scared of having something you don't deserve, something you took away from Bob.

Jim stood up suddenly, gripping the wooden rail of the deck. "I've been trying to figure out a way to be on Delmore's boat when he sails on Monday night."

"I can get us there—"

"Me," he said, turning to face her. "Not you. You're done. I'm not letting you get within a hundred yards of Delmore again."

"Jim—"

"No." It came out too sharply, too harshly, and she flinched. But then she lifted her chin.

"If you're going to shout at me, we should go inside," she said.

"If you think that was shouting, you don't know what shouting is."

"I'm not fragile," Emily said evenly. "I *do* know what shouting is. Maybe you don't know this, but I've had kids pull knives on me—"

"Great. That's supposed to make me feel better?"

"Jim, I can get us onto that yacht," Emily said, leaning forward, as if maybe if she got close enough he'd start to understand.

"And I'm not letting you do it."

"Why not?"

"Why not doesn't matter," he said tightly. "This time I'm not going to let you talk me into—"

"You won't even discuss it?"

"There's nothing to discuss here. I've made up my mind."

A spark of real anger lit Emily's eyes. "Oh, you've made up your mind, have you? What about *my* mind? Or am I just supposed to bow to you?"

"This time, yes."

"What about next time?" Her voice was deceptively calm, deceptively cool. But her eyes couldn't hide her feelings.

Jim pushed himself out of the chair. "Look, if you want to marry me, then you gotta get used to me protecting you."

He pushed open the glass door and went into the living room. Emily followed. She was no longer trying to hide the anger in her eyes, and she closed the door with a little too much force. "*If* I want to marry you—? You're just going to say something like *that* and then walk away?"

"The conversation is over," Jim said. "I know what you're trying to do, and I'm not going to let you do it."

"Right now I'm trying to determine the bounds of this relationship," Emily said hotly. "I was under the impression that 'love, honor and *obey*' went out of style with... with... beehive hairdos. I thought our relationship was equal, that it was give-and-take. And by that I *don't* mean you give the orders and I take them."

"No way in *hell* am I letting you risk your life," he retorted. "And if you don't like it..."

He looked away, unable to meet her eyes.

"What?" she whispered, suddenly terribly afraid. "If I don't like it, what then?"

He was staring down at the floor, down at his bare feet. He wore only a pair of gray running shorts. They accentuated his tan and emphasized the long, muscular lengths of his legs. His hair was nearly dry now. It curled around his shoulders, thick and shiny and soft as silk. It was beautiful. *He* was beautiful. But when he finally looked up at her, his eyes were dull, almost lifeless, and pain was etched into the lines on his face.

"This isn't going to work," he said quietly. "You know. You and me."

With sudden clarity, like illumination from a tremendous lightning bolt out of the darkness of a storm, Emily understood. This argument they were having wasn't about whether or not Emily should risk putting herself in danger again to help catch Alex. Jim was an expert at subtly manipulating people. And it wouldn't have taken too much manipulation to make her give in. All he'd really have had to say was "I love you, and I don't want you to get hurt. Please, it's extremely important to me that you stay away from Alex Delmore," and she would have backed down. No, there was another reason he was arguing with her this way. There was another reason he'd picked a fight.

He didn't want to marry her. He was afraid.

"Oh, God," Emily said, as the realization hit her squarely in the stomach.

"I'm sorry," he said. "Em, I swear, I never meant to hurt you, but I can't... I... have to figure this all out."

Emily could feel the tears brimming in her eyes, but she followed him as he picked up his duffel bag and backpack and crossed toward the door. "Whatever the problem is, we can work it out," she said, and her voice shook with conviction. "You love me. I *know* you love me. And I love you."

"You shouldn't," he told her, his voice raspy. "I don't deserve it."

He opened the door.

"Jim, wait. Please. Talk to me."

He stopped and stood there, just outside her door, his head bowed.

"I need some time to think," he said, without turning around. His voice was so low Emily had to strain to hear his words. "I can't think at all when I'm around you, Em."

Emily held on to the doorframe, clinging to the memory of the joy she'd seen in Jim's eyes not more than an hour ago, when he made love to her. He hadn't been thinking then—only feeling. It hadn't been until later that the shadows and pain returned to cloud his view. It hadn't been until later that he tried to deny that their love for each other was enough to let them work through any problem.

But before she could tell him that, before she could beg him not to go, he had disappeared, fading into the darkness of the predawn.

The phone rang.

Emily leapt up from the couch, praying it was Jim. He'd only been gone a half hour—one long, endless half hour—but maybe he was calling to tell her he'd been wrong. Maybe he was calling to say that he *did* want to spend the rest of his life with her, that he *did* love her, that he was coming back, that everything was going to be okay.

Who else could possibly be calling at four-thirty in the morning?

"Jim?"

"No, I'm sorry, Emily. It's Felipe Salazar," came Felipe's familiar voice. He sounded different—tighter, strained, his words almost clipped. "Are you awake? Take a minute to wake up, okay?"

Emily pushed her hair out of her face. "I'm awake," she said. "I was awake before you called. Is something wrong?"

Fear flickered in the pit of her stomach. Jim had only been gone thirty minutes. There wasn't possibly enough time for something bad to have happened to him. Was there?

"Yes," Felipe said. "I'm at the hospital—"

"No," Emily said, the fear freezing her in place. "Not Jim—"

"Diego is fine," Felipe said, and relief washed over her, making her legs weak. She carried the phone over and sat down on the couch. "It's..." He cleared his throat. "It's Jewel. She is here in surgery. They don't know, uh..." He cleared his throat again. "They don't know if she will... survive."

The relief was gone, replaced by new horror. "Oh, God," Emily said. "Felipe, how? What happened?"

"She was hit by a car—" His voice broke. "She was walking out on the exit ramp of the highway. She was higher than a kite. The doctor told me there are traces of both crack and LSD in her blood."

"Oh, no," Emily breathed. "Oh, Jewel. I thought she was doing so well. What happened?"

"I happened," Felipe said harshly. "I let her down. She needed me, and, damn it, I wasn't there for her."

He was silent then, but Emily knew from the sound of his ragged breathing how upset he was.

"Felipe, she's an addict," she said. "You know you can't hold yourself responsible."

"No," he said, interrupting her. "You don't understand."

"Where are you?" Emily asked. "I'm coming over."

Felipe Salazar looked a wreck. His suit was creased and rumpled. His tie was long gone, and his usually pristine white shirt was wrinkled and partially unbuttoned. His gleaming black hair, usually neatly combed with not a lock out of place, was a wild jumble of curls.

He was sitting in the hospital waiting room, slumped over, elbows resting on his knees, head down, with his hands locked together on the back of his neck.

At the soft sound of Emily's sneakers on the tile floor, he looked up. His eyes were red and his face was tired, but he forced a smile and rose to his feet.

"Thanks for coming down here," he said.

Emily put her arms around him. "I'm so sorry," she said. "Is there anything I can do to help?"

Felipe pulled back. "You can help me pray," he said. "Man, I haven't prayed this hard since I was eight years old and my little brother had appendicitis." He shook his head. "It was the middle of the night, we were forty miles from the hospital, in the middle of nowhere, and my father's car broke down."

"What happened?" Emily asked softly.

"I prayed with all my heart for a miracle," he said. "Then a car came by, and the people stopped. They were college kids—hippies, you know, with long hair and headbands and everything. They'd gotten lost. They were looking for the highway. I remember they were happy to drive us to the hospital—one of them kept saying that their getting lost was a really groovy coincidence." He laughed softly. "But I knew it was no coincidence. It was my miracle. God had answered my prayers." He shook his head, and tears sprang into his eyes as he looked at Emily. "It has been at least fifteen years. Do you think I have a chance for another miracle today?"

Emily nodded, squeezing Felipe's hands, unable to speak.

"Phil, I got here as soon as I heard."

Jim.

Emily turned around to see Jim standing behind her. He met her eyes only very briefly before he returned his attention to his friend. She might as well have been a stranger or a mere acquaintance, for all the warmth—or lack of it—in his gaze. Could this possibly be the same man who had made love to her so passionately just a short time ago? Her stomach hurt, and she tried to convince herself that it was the gravity of the situation that was making him seem so cold. As soon as she had a chance to talk to him, she'd convince him that whatever problems he had could be worked out....

"What happened?" he asked Felipe.

"Jewel's aunt and uncle tracked her down, man," Felipe said. "They came to the shelter, insisted she was a runaway, proved she was underage. Did you know she was only seventeen?" he asked Emily.

Emily nodded her head. She hadn't realized that Felipe didn't know how young Jewel was.

"The aunt and uncle said that they were Billy's legal guardians, too," Felipe said. "They demanded she and Billy be returned to them. They told Jewel if she made a fuss, Billy would get taken away by the state."

He took several steps back, and sat down tiredly on the hard plastic bench. "She called me, Diego," he said, looking up at Jim. "She called me, man, yesterday, asking me to come to the shelter, telling me she needed me. I was home. I heard the answering machine take her message, but I didn't pick up. I didn't take the call, because I've been trying to keep my distance, you know? I've been staying away. I don't go and visit her every day like before. I figured that way it can't get out of hand. But she calls me all the time. I thought this was just another one of those calls. I thought she was trying to be dramatic, trying to get my attention. So I ignored her. *Madre de Dios,* she was in trouble, and I ignored her."

Jim didn't hesitate. He sat down next to Felipe and touched his shoulder. "You couldn't have known," he said softly. "Phil, you can't blame yourself for doing something you thought was best."

"She called me, too," Emily said, sitting down on Felipe's other side. "She left a message on my answering machine. I didn't call her back in time, either."

Felipe straightened up, trying hard to compose himself. Jim left his hand on his friend's shoulder, unembarrassed about offering what little warmth and comfort he could.

"How'd she get the drugs?" Jim asked.

"Her uncle made her take them," Felipe said. "He threatened Billy and forced her to shoot up. He wanted her hooked again, and back under his control." His face hardened, and his eyes glinted with a hatred so strong that Emily was taken aback. He turned to Jim. "Diego, I need you to help me, man. I need you to find that bastard and bring him in. So help me God, if I have to do it, I am afraid I will kill him. Please don't let me do that."

"I'll take care of it. Consider Hank Abbott already behind bars," Jim said, with a certainty in his voice that made Felipe relax slightly. "Where's Billy now?"

"With my mother," Felipe said. "I talked to Jewel before they took her into surgery. She was really out of it, but she was crazy with worry about Billy. She told me where he was hiding and asked me to get to him, to make sure he was safe—" His voice broke again. "She was bleeding internally, man, and her hip is fractured, both legs are broken, but all she could think about was her little boy." He closed his eyes. "God, please, give me another miracle. Give Jewel another chance— No, I was the one who let her down. Give *me* another chance. I know I don't deserve it...."

"You deserve it, Phil," Jim said softly. "You do deserve another chance, do you hear me? Everything's going to work out. Everything's going to be okay."

Emily looked up through the tears that were gathering in her eyes to find Jim watching her. But the instant their eyes met, he turned away and stood up.

"I'll call you from the station after I nail Uncle Hank," Jim told Felipe.

Felipe nodded. "Thanks, Diego."

"Be careful, Jim," Emily said.

He actually looked surprised at her words. How could he be surprised that she wanted him to take care? How could he not know that his safety was of the utmost importance to her?

He moved down the hall, and she stood up quickly, following him. "Jim, wait."

He stopped, turning slowly to face her.

"I love you," she said. "Will you come over later, so that we can talk?"

He jammed his hands into his pockets and looked down at the tile floor. "Nothing's changed, Em," he said softly.

"It can't hurt to talk," she said desperately.

He looked up at her then, his eyes dark with misery. "Yes, it can," he said. "It hurts like hell."

"Please—"

"I'm sorry."

He turned and walked away. Emily watched him go, too numb to move.

Everything's going to work out. You deserve another chance.

Deserve another chance.

I love you, Emily had told Jim before he walked out the door of her apartment.

You shouldn't, he'd said, his voice thick with emotion. *I don't deserve it.*

He didn't deserve her love. But why not?

Bob. It had to have something to do with Jim's brother, Bob.

He still felt responsible for Bob's death—so much so that he was determined to deny himself the chance to be happy. In a moment of weakness, he'd let his true hopes and desires come through, and he'd asked her to marry him. But long ago he'd painted himself into a guilt-ridden emotional corner, and he was trapped there, unable to break free. He couldn't marry her, because he didn't think he deserved more than the miserable, lonely life he'd purposely made for himself.

God, it was all so clear now.

Jim didn't think he deserved a chance to be happy, and Emily knew with stomach-wrenching certainty that talk alone wouldn't be enough to convince him that he was wrong. And if she couldn't convince him of that, everything was *not* going to work out.

At least not for her and Jim.

Chapter 16

The telephone was ringing when Emily opened the door to her apartment. But once again it wasn't Jim on the other end. It was Alex Delmore.

"Hey," he said, "you have plans for the next few days?"

"Um," Emily said, "I don't think so. Why?"

"I'm taking a few days off, sailing down the coast to Fort Myers," Alex told her. "We're lifting anchor in a few hours. Grab a bathing suit and your toothbrush and come along."

"I thought you weren't leaving until tomorrow," she said, her head awhirl. Alex wasn't supposed to go out sailing until tomorrow evening. What had made him change his plans?

There was sudden silence on the other end of the phone.

"You knew I was going sailing?" Alex finally said. "I don't remember mentioning it to you."

"I saw it in your calendar book last night," Emily said, the palms of her hands sweating. God, did he suspect her of spying on him?

But he laughed, and it seemed genuine. She felt a flood of relief. "Yeah, that's right," he said. "Of course. Well, my plans changed suddenly. I have to leave this afternoon."

Have to. Why else would he *have to,* unless he were meeting a shipment of drugs? Emily started sweating again.

She kept her voice light as she asked, "Going fishing again?"

"Fishing?" He was confused.

"Like you did last time," Emily said, trying hard to sound as if she didn't suspect him of being a drug smuggler. "In your dinghy, remember?"

"Oh, right, right," Alex said. "Fishing. Right. Yeah, I definitely will do some fishing."

Definitely.

The shipment must be coming in tonight.

"How about I have my driver pick you up in about two hours?" he asked.

What should she do? God, the police had wanted to plant a homing device that would help them track the *Home Free* by sending out a steady stream of beeps and blips over the radio waves. And Jim had talked about having a bug—a voice microphone—hidden on board the yacht. How were they going to do that in the next two hours, especially with Alex's crew preparing the ship for departure?

"Um..." she said, thinking hard and fast. "Dan's still in town, and I feel badly about going off without him."

Alex gave an exaggerated sigh. "He doesn't want us sleeping together, darling," he said. "I was hoping we could leave him home."

"He's very...protective," Emily said. "Please, may I ask him to join us?"

"Sure, why not?" Alex said, with a good-natured chuckle. "Bring him along. It'll be good practice for my self-control. Shall I have my driver get you?"

"No," Emily said. "No, I have . . . some errands to run. We'll meet you over at the *Home Free* by . . . what? Two o'clock?"

"Sounds good to me," Alex said. "See you then."

Emily slowly hung up the phone.

Jim was going to be mad as hell.

"I'm sorry, Detective Keegan isn't here. He hasn't been in since early this morning." The large, unhappy-looking uniformed policeman behind the front desk barely even looked up at Emily as he answered her question.

She felt a rising wave of impatience—and fear. What if she couldn't find Jim? What if he wasn't available to come on the *Home Free* with her? Would she have to go by herself?

"Please, can you tell me when he'll be back," she said, "or how I can get in touch with him?"

"Nope. Sorry." The beefy man with the dour expression didn't sound one bit sorry. He turned away from the counter with his pile of papers and files.

"All right, then," Emily said evenly, "I'll talk to Lieutenant Bell instead."

That got him at least to focus his eyes in Emily's direction.

"The lieutenant's tied up at the moment," he said, and turned to walk out of the room.

"Excuse me," Emily said loudly, feeling her blood pressure shoot upward from frustration. "I'd like you to tell Lieutenant Bell that Emily Marshall is here to see her, and I'd like you to tell her that *now,* please."

"Sarge, Ms. Marshall is helping us with an important case," a familiar voice said. "I am sure the lieutenant will wish to be interrupted."

Emily turned around to see Felipe Salazar standing behind her. He'd buttoned his shirt and fixed his tie, but he still looked rumpled and weary.

"What are you doing here?" he said to Emily.

"How's Jewel?" Emily asked, searching his eyes, hoping he was bringing good news. "Is she out of danger?"

Felipe shook his head tiredly. "No." He took a deep breath. "They wouldn't let me near her. I was going crazy, sitting there in the waiting room. I had to do *something*, so... here I am. Has Diego brought that bastard in yet?"

That bastard—? He meant Jewel's uncle Hank. "I don't think so," she said.

"Lieutenant Bell will see you," the burly sergeant said, without a trace of apology in his voice. "Do you know where to go?"

"I'll walk her back," Felipe told the man, taking her elbow and steering her down the corridor.

Lieutenant Bell greeted Emily at the door to her office. "This morning Detective Keegan told me you wanted off this case," the older woman said, wasting no time on pleasantries, peering over the tops of her glasses at Emily.

"Well, Detective Keegan was wrong," Emily replied, unable to keep exasperation from showing in her voice. She could feel Felipe Salazar watching her curiously.

"Sit down." The lieutenant waved toward a pair of hard wooden chairs placed across from her desk. "I'd like you to come in, too, Detective."

As Emily and Felipe went into the room, Lieutenant Bell sat behind her desk. She was wearing pants today—loose-fitting khaki-colored slacks that had been tailored to fit her shorter-than-average height. "Keegan seemed to think that the situation had become too dangerous to allow a civilian—"

"Excuse me, Lieutenant," Emily said, leaning forward in her chair, "but a young girl I know is in the hospital, in intensive care, because of a nasty combination of crack and greed. I can't sit by and let Alex get away with bringing more cocaine into this city—especially not now. As dangerous as continuing with the investigation might be—and, to be perfectly honest, I believe this sudden higher level of danger is all in Jim Keegan's mind—I consider it *much* more dangerous to let Alex go on distributing illegal drugs."

Bell's pale eyes studied Emily steadily. Finally she shifted her position, crossing her legs and leaning back in her seat. "Okay, Ms. Marshall," she said coolly. "Tell me why you're here."

Quickly Emily told the lieutenant about Alex's phone call, and about his invitation for her to join him on the *Home Free*—and the implication that the drug shipment would be arriving sooner than they all had expected.

"Alex invited Jim along, too," Emily said. "You know, as Dan, my brother..." She glanced at her watch. It was already quarter past one. She took a deep breath, calming herself. "But I haven't been able to find Jim, and the ship's scheduled to sail in forty-five minutes."

Bell tapped a pencil on her desk. "There's no way I can get a court order to plant any kind of listening device on Delmore's yacht before two o'clock," she said. "But a signal transmitter, or homing device, is a different story. Emily, do you think you can get on the boat, plant the homing device and get off before Delmore sails?"

Get off—?

"I can do it," Felipe said. "Let me."

Emily glanced at him. "Alex's crew double as bodyguards," she said. "You won't get within ten yards of the yacht."

"And if you get on," Felipe said, "how will you get off?"

"Feigning a stomachache might do the trick," Bell suggested. "I can't think of anyone in their right mind who'd want to risk getting seasick on top of some kind of stomach virus. It shouldn't be too difficult."

"This is not a good idea, Lieutenant," Felipe said. "Jim wanted to keep Emily far away from Alexander Delmore."

"Do you have any alternative suggestions, Detective?" Bell asked acerbically.

"Yes," he said. "Wait until next time."

Emily turned to look at him. "And how many more young girls like Jewel will be hurt or—God help us—killed because of the drugs that'll be on the streets if we don't stop Alex today?"

She was playing hardball, and, as she'd known they would, her words hit him deeply.

"Wouldn't even just one be too many?" she added softly.

She knew from the look on his face that she'd won.

"I want her to wear a wire," he said tersely to Bell. "And I want to stay close by. I want to listen in. And I want Diego updated on the situation the moment he comes in or calls."

"Fine," Bell said shortly. "We don't have a whole lot of time. Take Ms. Marshall downstairs and get her set up."

Jim couldn't stop thinking of Emily. He thought about her as he tracked down Jewel's scumbag of an uncle. He thought about her as he cuffed and Mirandaed the guy and stuffed him into the back seat of his car. He thought about her at every single traffic light. He thought about her as he drove, as he accelerated, as he braked, as he signaled for the turn into the precinct parking lot.

As he opened the back door of his car and motioned for Jewel's uncle to get out of the car, he thought about the welcoming warmth of Emily's smile. As he led Jewel's uncle up the steps and into the police station, he thought about the incredible blue of her eyes, and how with just one look she could make him forget everything and anything but the here and now.

And as he brought his prisoner to the desk to be booked, he thought of the way she had stood watching him in the waiting room at the hospital. He couldn't keep from thinking about the hurt in her eyes—hurt he alone was responsible for putting there. And that hurt wasn't going to disappear just because *he* disappeared.

He should have stayed away from her.

He should have, but he hadn't.

As Uncle Hank was led away to be fingerprinted and photographed, Jim closed his eyes, resting his head on his folded arms on top of the counter, for the first time all day allowing himself the luxury of imagining what it would be like to spend the rest of his life with Emily. Each night he'd sleep with her in his arms. Each morning he'd awaken to her soft smile. He'd never spend another moment alone, because even when she wasn't with him he'd carry her in his heart.

But that was only wishful thinking. Because no matter how much he wanted to turn that pipe dream into reality, the fact was, he couldn't escape the guilt and the blame.

All he could do now was stay the hell away from Emily, and hope to God that this time he hadn't hurt her beyond repair.

"Keegan."

Jim looked up to see Sergeant Curt Wolaski glaring at him from the other side of the counter. The big man tossed a folded piece of paper down in front of Jim. "Message from your pal Salazar," he said.

"Thanks," Jim said, but the sergeant had already turned away.

He unfolded the note and read it. And let out a stream of curses so pungent that heads turned in his direction from all over the room. Damn it, was Emily crazy? Did she *want* to get herself killed?

Fear hit him deep in his gut, and he turned and ran for the parking lot and his car.

His boots pounded the hot pavement, and his lungs strained as he pushed himself to the limit. He opened the car door and jumped in behind the wheel. He started the car with a roar, and threw it into gear before the engine had even finished turning over.

With a squeal of tires, Jim pulled out of the parking lot and onto the main road, heading toward the harbor—and Emily.

All his good intentions, all his plans to stay away from her, went right out the window. He wanted nothing more than to hold her in his arms and convince himself that she was safe.

Emily hadn't been free from Alex's company since she'd come on board the *Home Free*. She was carrying the homing device in her purse, but she hadn't had even the smallest opportunity to plant it somewhere on the yacht.

"Are you *sure* your brother said he'd meet you here at the harbor?" Alex asked again, scanning the crowded docks impatiently.

"He *said* he'd be here," Emily lied, hoping against hope that Jim would suddenly appear. He still hadn't checked in at the precinct when Felipe dropped her off here, so there was no way he could have known to come down to the marina. Still, she couldn't help hoping.

"We really have to get going," Alex said.

Emily glanced at her watch—it was five after two. "Can't you give him another ten minutes?" she asked.

He didn't look happy. "Emily, to be perfectly honest, I've got a deadline. . . ." His voice trailed off, and he looked uncomfortable, as if he were aware he'd said too much.

"Five minutes?" she said. "Please?"

She knew what she had to do. She had to go down to the head and use the privacy the tiny bathroom provided to hide the homing device in there. Then she'd come back on deck, the five minutes would have passed, Jim *still* wouldn't have appeared, and she'd regretfully tell Alex she couldn't desert her brother—she'd have to stay behind. She'd sadly wave goodbye as Alex sailed off down the coast, toward his illegal rendezvous, with the homing device signaling his every move to the police and the Coast Guard.

It just might work.

Alex cursed under his breath, and Emily looked up at him, surprised. She followed his line of vision to the end of the dock, where a familiar-looking dark-haired man, followed by several large men who looked like bodyguards, was walking toward them.

Emily felt a wave of panic, and she took a steadying breath. "Isn't that Vincent Marino?" she asked for Felipe's benefit, knowing he was listening in via the tiny radio microphone that was hidden in the delicate metal petals of the rose-shaped silver pin he'd given her to wear.

"Yeah," Alex said shortly. "It sure is."

"Were you expecting him?" Emily asked.

"Nope," Alex said. He looked scared. He looked the way she felt—like he wanted nothing more than to start running and not look back.

For one brief, crazy moment, Emily actually considered leaping over the side of the boat into the murky waters of the harbor. But before she could move, Marino was climbing on board the *Home Free* to stand right beside her, and her opportunity was gone.

"Mr. Delmore," Marino said with feigned politeness. He turned to look at Emily. "And Miss Marshall. A pleasure, as always. News of your upcoming nuptials was in the morning paper. May I offer my congratulations?"

"Get the hell off my yacht," Alex snarled. His hands were shaking, and he didn't look half as confident as he sounded.

Marino shook his head, making soft *tsk*ing sounds. "Such manners," he said. "It's a wonder you got anywhere in the business world."

"Get off," Alex said again, "or I'll have you thrown off." There was sweat on his upper lip.

Emily was in way over her head. Jim had been right. She was foolish to have tried this.

Marino laughed at Alex. It was a harsh, ugly sound.

"Cast off," he ordered Alex's crew. "We're going for a little sail. A little pleasure cruise. That all right with you, Delmore?"

It was not all right. Alex snapped his fingers. "Throw them over the side," he ordered his crew. But no one came to his aid. They all just continued preparing the yacht for departure. His voice rose with outrage and fear. "I said, get them out of here. Protect me. Do your jobs!"

Marino just kept laughing. "They *are* doing their jobs," he said. "They work for me now. You really should pay higher wages, Delmore. Didn't you know loyalty is directly related to the size of a paycheck?"

The sky was a hazy blue, and the sun glared off the gleaming wooden deck. The harbor was bustling with activity—there were people walking not five yards from the *Home Free*. It was the middle of the day, in a public place. It didn't seem possible that they were being kidnapped or hijacked or yacht-jacked, or whatever this was. But the hard-edged glint in Vincent Marino's eyes was frightening. Emily had an awful feeling that if she didn't get off here and now, she wasn't ever going to get off the yacht—at least not alive.

She walked calmly toward the gangplank. "Alex, it looks like Dan isn't going to make it," she said, unable to hide the breathlessness of fear in her voice, "so I better stay home. Call me when you get back—"

Marino grabbed her by the arm and pushed her none too gently toward one of the lounge chairs that were open on the deck. He shoved her down into it.

"Sorry, babe," he said. "But you're coming along for the ride."

Emily opened her mouth and screamed, but Marino was next to her in a flash, silencing her by covering her mouth with his beefy hand. He pressed a deadly-looking knife against her side, down where no one on the dock or the other ships could see it, and she felt the tip prick her.

"Next time you scream," he told her, almost matter-of-factly, "I'll give you something to scream about, you understand?"

Emily nodded slowly.

Felipe Salazar shouted into the radio.

"I *know* we didn't think we'd need the boat until later, but we need it *now,* damn it," he said. "I called three hours ago, and you said you had a powerboat. You didn't say anything about the fact that its engine was lying in pieces on the dock—"

"We've got the Coast Guard and the harbormaster ready to move in and intercept at the edge of the breakwater," the dispatcher told him.

"No!" Felipe said, adding several choice comments about *that* suggestion in Spanish. "Marino's got a small army of men on that ship. We have to assume they're armed with semiautomatics. And what do the Coast Guard have? Small handguns, and maybe a tranquilizer rifle? No way do I want to see the outcome of *that* gun battle, *muchas gracias.* Besides, we've got a civilian on board the *Home Free.* We don't want to risk a potential hostage situation."

"We can get you one of the Coast Guard's speedboats," the dispatcher suggested.

Felipe gritted his teeth. "Oh, that would be most inconspicuous," he said. "No, I need an *unmarked* boat, and I need it thirty minutes ago!"

Jim recognized the nondescript olive-green police surveillance van on the far side of the parking lot, and he pulled up to it, his tires sending a spray of little pebbles into the air as he stopped.

Leaping from his car, he hammered on the back door of the van until it opened.

The interior was dimly lit and crowded. Two other detectives sat with Phil Salazar in the glow from the high-tech equipment. The tape deck was whirring, and the receive signal lights were lit. Emily wasn't there, and Jim felt a stab of panic.

"Where is she?" he demanded harshly. "Delmore's boat isn't at its mooring, and it's not at the dock, and I *know* you'd never let her sail with that son of a bitch so where is she— Oh God."

The look on Salazar's face said everything Jim didn't want to hear.

"Jim, you have got to stay calm," Felipe said. "Going ballistic on me will not help this situation."

Jim took a deep breath. "Situation," he repeated. "So. We have a situation, do we?" He could feel his blood pounding angrily through his veins. So help him God, if anything happened to Emily...

"She was going to plant the homing device and get off the ship," Felipe said. "But then... Marino came on board."

Vincent Marino. The organized-crime boss who was nicknamed the Shark, due to his lack of mercy. Oh, God, no.

"From the conversations that we've overheard, Marino and Delmore are not on friendly terms," Felipe said. His jaw tightened. "It's my guess that Marino means to abscond with Delmore's arriving shipment of drugs. And it would not surprise me if Marino also intends to use the opportunity to remove Delmore from the crack market—permanently."

Jim felt dizzy. Jesus, this was worse than he'd imagined. "Get me a helicopter," he ordered huskily. "I've gotta get her out of there."

But Salazar was shaking his head. "*Think*, Diego," he said emphatically. "If you go after the *Home Free* in a police helicopter, what do you think is going to happen? You're gonna get her killed, man, and yourself, too."

Jim took a deep breath. Phil was right. He was right. Going after Emily, guns blazing, wasn't the solution. He had to slow down for a minute. He had to *think*.

"Where are we going?" Emily's voice said clearly via the surveillance microphone she was wearing. "Where are you taking us?"

She sounded so cool, so in control, but Jim knew better. He knew she was scared to death. God, he was scared to death for her. His throat tightened.

"We're gonna have a little party with a few of your fiancé's buddies," Marino answered. "I hate to break it to you, but you may not want to marry your little Alex after you meet these guys."

Emily didn't answer. Jim closed his eyes, wishing the microphone she was wearing could receive, as well as send. He wanted to talk to her, to tell her to play along with Marino, to tell her not to antagonize him.

Listening in like this was torture. If he'd ever experienced payback for what he'd done to Bob, this had to be it. God, if something happened to Emily, if Marino killed her... He loved her with his life, and without her his life would be over. Just like Bob's.

Except not more than a few hours ago, Jim had been willing to spend the rest of his life without Emily—a life that would have been cold and lonely and bleak as hell. He had been willing to do voluntarily what Marino could do permanently with a single bullet. He'd assumed that life without Emily was what he deserved.

"Oh, and if you're thinking about jumping overboard," Marino said, his voice getting louder as he leaned closer to Emily, "it's nearly two miles to shore. *And* I hear there're sharks in these waters."

"Apparently there are sharks out of the water, too," Emily said quietly. Jim held his breath. Was Marino going to get angry? But he only laughed, and Jim exhaled noisily.

"Ever hear of survival of the fittest, sweetheart?" Marino said. "I'd much rather be a shark than a blowfish like little Alex. You, you're more like a flounder—soft and delicious, and totally defenseless. One bite and you're history, you read me?"

"Yes," Emily said softly.

Jim read him, too, loud and clear. He swallowed, listening intently to the silence. Then Emily spoke again, almost inaudibly, and one of the detectives leapt forward to turn up the volume on the receiver.

"He's gone," she breathed. "Felipe, I'm not sure what to do. The homing device is still in my purse. I never had a chance to plant it anywhere. It's turned on, though, and you should be receiving its signal." She took a long, shaky breath.

"I'm not sure if I should try to jump overboard, or if I should just wait and see what's going to happen," she continued. "They have Alex down below. I think Marino's men beat him up." She was quiet for a moment. "I honestly can't imagine that Marino's going let me stay alive after everything I've seen and heard here."

Another pause. "Felipe, I need you to tell Jim that I love him. And make sure he doesn't come out here and get himself killed because of me. This was my mistake— Please, I don't want him to die because I made a bad decision."

"Hold on, Em," Jim whispered, even though Emily couldn't possibly hear him. "Don't give up. I'm on my way." He turned to Felipe. "We need a boat. Something big enough to hide all this stuff down below," he said, gesturing at the equipment that was receiving the signals from both Emily's surveillance microphone and the homing device.

"We're working on that," Felipe told him.

Jim's eyes flashed, and his voice rose dangerously. "What, am I hearing you tell me that Lieutenant Bell set this thing up and she didn't make damn sure you had a *boat?*"

"I'm sorry, man. There was a snafu and—"

"Get this equipment ready to travel and meet me down at the dock," Jim snapped, pushing his way out of the van.

Felipe jumped to work. The other two detectives exchanged a long look, glad as hell that *they* weren't wearing Lieutenant Bell's shoes.

It took Emily several moments to understand what the commotion was about. She sidled closer to the navigator's station, trying to eavesdrop.

Marino was arguing with one of his crew about some problem they were having with the ship's radio.

The vessel they were to rendezvous with had contacted them via radio. But they were having some difficulty communicating. They were picking up strange interference.

It was the transmission from the homing device that was in her purse, Emily realized with a wave of fear. The scratchy interference faded in and out with the same pulsating beat as the homing device's signal.

How soon would it be before Vincent Marino figured that out? How soon until he searched the ship and found the homing device in her handbag?

The handbag, Emily realized with dread, that she had unwittingly left over on the other side of the deck, next to the lounge chairs...

"Turn that damn thing off," she heard Marino say. "It's annoying the hell out of me."

The static was shut off, and Marino came out on deck, followed by one of his body guards.

"Could be the result of another radio signal," Emily heard the bodyguard say.

Marino stopped and turned toward the man, his foot mere inches from her handbag. Emily felt the palms of her hands start to sweat.

"Bring Delmore up here," Marino commanded. "We'll find out soon enough if he's got another radio on board."

He stepped back, and his foot bumped the handbag.

Emily could feel her heart pounding.

He looked down and noticed it.

Kick it to the side, she silently implored him. Don't pick it up....

He bent over and picked it up.

"Whoa, this weighs a ton. What do you have in here?" he said to Emily. "Your bowling ball?"

Her throat was so dry, she couldn't speak. She shook her head no. Please, God, don't let him look inside....

"Your nose is getting sunburned," he said. It was obvious from his mocking tone that he was toying with her. He was trying to make her squirm, and getting pleasure from it. "You might want to put some sunblock on."

Emily couldn't answer. She couldn't move.

"You got some sunblock in here?" he asked, opening her bag. "Jeez, you got everything else, don't you?"

This was it. It was all over. He was going to find the homing device, and he was going to kill her.

"Yep, here it is, right on top," Marino said, pulling out a bottle of number fifteen sunblock and waving it at her. He put it back inside, closed the zipper and tossed the bag to her.

Instinctively Emily reached for it, to catch it. But she didn't want to catch it. She didn't want it on this ship. So, when the canvas fabric hit her fingers, she fumbled.

The handbag—and the homing device—went over the side of the *Home Free*, and into the dark blue Gulf waters.

"Damn," Marino said with disgust. "Didn't anyone ever teach you to catch?"

Emily stared down into the water. Her handbag had already disappeared from view.

Vincent Marino would never find the homing device now.

Of course, it was also true that without that homing device, Jim and Felipe would probably never find *her*.

"Come on, come on," Jim said, taking an armload of equipment from Felipe and hurrying his partner and the other two detectives onto a sleek white powerboat.

He opened the throttle and headed away from the dock at a speed that made the other boat owners shake their fists.

"Where did you get this thing?" Felipe shouted over the roar of the powerful engine.

Jim slipped his sunglasses over his eyes as he rounded the buoy that marked the exit from the harbor. "I hot-wired it," he shouted back matter-of-factly.

"You *stole* it?"

"Borrowed," Jim replied. "For official police business."

"Whatever you call it, what you did is illegal. I oughta arrest you, man," Felipe said.

"Why don't you go below instead," Jim shouted, "and make sure Winstead and Harper are setting that equipment up right?"

As Felipe started down, Winstead stuck his head up through the companionway. "We have a potential problem," he announced. "The signal from the homing device just went dead."

Jim's knuckles whitened as he gripped the steering wheel tighter. "Phil, take over for me," he said, pulling the throttle back. The boat still skimmed across the water, but no longer at a breakneck speed. The noise of the engine dropped considerably.

"Are you going to call for a helicopter?" Felipe asked as the two men switched places.

Jim nodded tersely. "I want one warmed up and ready to go at a moment's notice."

"When you radio in," Felipe said, squinting out across the glare on the water, "ask if the hospital called with any word about Jewel."

Jim had damn near forgotten about Jewel. He nodded again, touching Felipe briefly on the shoulder, then turned to go below.

Winstead and Harper both had headphones on and were listening intently to the conversation coming in from Emily's radio microphone.

Winstead glanced up at Jim, handing him a third pair of headphones. "They've made physical contact with the second ship," he told him. "Vincent Marino is on a first-name basis with these guys. It appears that he's intending to take his men and Delmore's drug money and depart on this other ship."

"What about Delmore and Emily?" Jim asked, slipping on the headphones.

"Oh, my God! Alex!" he heard Emily say. In a lower voice, surely for their benefit, she added, "He's been beaten up. His face is a mess, and I think his arm's been broken. He can't even stand up."

"See what you get for screwing with me?" Marino's voice said. "See what you get?"

"I'm sorry," Delmore sobbed. "I'm sorry. Please... please, I'll cut you in from now on, I promise."

"Too late," Marino declared. "You had your chance to do business with me. Now I'm doing business with you, and it's in my best interest to cut you out of the picture entirely. You get my drift here?"

"Oh, God," Emily breathed, and Delmore began to cry in earnest. "They're rigging some kind of bomb to the yacht's engine."

Jim pushed the headphones off one ear, reached for the radio and keyed the mike that connected him directly to St. Simone's police headquarters. Briefly he explained about the bomb, and how they'd lost the signal from the homing device. "I need a chopper," he said, "up and over these waters, helping us find the *Home Free.*"

"We've got a chopper standing by," the dispatcher replied over the squawky radio speaker.

Jim passed the microphone to Harper. "Give them the last known reading and heading of the vessel, so at least they'll know where to start looking."

Over the headphones, he could hear Marino say, "Take care of the shortwave radio. We don't want them sending out any SOSs."

"You're just going to leave us here to die?" Emily asked.

Chapter 17

"Actually, no," Vincent Marino said. "I'm going to leave you and your fiancé already dead."

His words came as an icy shock, even though Emily had been waiting for them ever since Marino had come aboard the yacht. She hadn't been thinking about *whether* he was going to kill them, she'd been thinking in terms of *when*.

Now all of the crew were on the other boat, an enormous speedboat, with the exception of Marino and one other man. And Alex and Emily.

Alex had crumpled into a pile on the deck. At Marino's words, he cried even harder.

"Looks like you didn't really need that sunblock after all, did you?" Marino said to Emily with a laugh, ignoring Alex's pleas for mercy. He turned to the man standing next to him. "Waste them."

Emily had never faced death before, but she knew right now she was looking at it dead-on, straight in the eye.

Death wore sunglasses and a conservative dark suit. Death had a long, dangerous-looking gun that he pulled from the holster nestled under his right arm. Death was left-handed, Emily thought inanely.

But he wasn't death. He was a man. He was human.

The man turned his head slightly and looked from her to Alex, and Emily knew in that flash of a moment that he was squeamish about shooting a woman. As he pointed his gun at Alex, Emily dived for the companionway doors and threw herself down the stairs into the yacht's cabin. She tripped and hit the wall with her shoulder and chest. The pin that held the microphone and the miniature radio dug painfully through her shirt and into her skin.

She heard the gunshot, felt the recoil, and heard Alex scream in pain. God, they'd shot Alex, and she was next.

"Go after her!" she heard Marino say as she scrambled down the hall and into the room Alex used as an office.

"The clock's running, Mr. M.," she heard the other man say. "We have less than ten minutes. She's not going anywhere. Let's get out of here."

Were his words a trick to make her relax, to make her believe he wasn't coming after her?

Alex kept a gun in his office. Emily knew he kept a gun in here. And, by God, if they were going to kill her, she was going to go down fighting.

Her breath came in sobs as she searched Alex's desk. The front drawer was locked, and she used a letter opener and a paperweight to pry it open.

And there was Alex's gun, small but deadly, lying amid the paper clips and pencils.

It felt cold and hard in her hands.

She held it up, supporting her right hand with her left, aiming it at the office door, praying it was loaded.

But then she heard the hum of an engine, and felt the *Home Free* rock slightly in the other boat's wake. She peeked out one of the portholes.

They were leaving!

Still holding the gun, she opened the door and slowly went out into the corridor. The yacht was silent. But not dead silent. There was a hissing sound, the sound of white noise, or interference. It was coming from the shortwave radio.

The yacht's radio had been smashed, hit with some kind of heavy object, the microphone pulverized. But it was receiving *something*. She turned the knob marked Volume, and the hissing got louder. She tried to adjust the tuning, but nothing happened. The hiss didn't subside, and the needle didn't move.

Jim's hands were shaking. He was going on faith here, purely on faith. He'd heard only one gunshot. He'd heard someone try to talk Marino into leaving. But all he'd heard from Emily in the past two grueling minutes was silence.

"Come on, Em," he muttered. "Tell me what you're doing. Tell me you're okay. Tell me you're not lying somewhere on that boat, wounded...." Or worse.

"The chopper pilot is leaving the airport," Harper said. "He'll be over the harbor in about ten minutes."

"That's not soon enough," Jim said.

"He's fighting winds coming in from the west," Harper said apologetically. "He's doing the best he can."

"Emily, talk to me, damn it!" Jim growled. Adrenaline was surging through him, but there wasn't one damned thing he could do to help her. She was out there, somewhere, on a boat wired to explode any minute, any time.

"Jim? Felipe? Are you receiving me?"

Emily was alive.

Both Harper and Winstead cheered. Jim closed his eyes briefly. Thank God. Her signal wasn't the greatest—it was as if she were speaking from a long way away, rather than into a microphone that was located just underneath her chin.

"I fell and landed on the mike," she said, her voice shaking slightly, "and I don't even know if it's still working, but I'm hoping that it is. Marino and his men are gone, Alex was shot in the chest. He's bleeding all over the place. He's still alive, but just barely."

The signal from her mike faded slightly, and Winstead worked furiously to bring it back in.

"There's a digital clock on the bomb," Emily reported, "and it's counting down by seconds. Right now it says seven minutes and forty-eight seconds. Forty-seven. Forty-six."

Jim synchronized his watch to the sound of her voice.

"The shortwave radio is receiving *something,*" she said, "but there's a lot of interference. It seems to be stuck somewhere around the 20."

Jim quickly flipped the shortwave to that frequency and keyed the mike. "Emily, can you hear me?" he said.

"Jim! Oh, God, you're there! You're really out there! I can hear you! The reception's not great, but I can hear you!"

"Emily, we're more than ten minutes away from you. We're not going to reach you before the bomb is set to blow. Does the *Home Free* still have a dinghy? Or a lifeboat?"

"Oh, Jim, I'm so sorry about this—"

"Em, we don't have a lot of time here," Jim said. "I need you to stay calm and fill me in on the situation."

"Jim, I love you—" Emily's voice broke. "For a while, I didn't think I'd get a chance to tell you that ever again."

"Yeah, I know," he said hoarsely. "I didn't think I'd get a chance to tell you that I love you, too. And I do, Em. I love you so much that it's killing me. I don't think I can live without you, Emily, so help me out here, please. Is there a lifeboat?"

"No," she said. "There was a dinghy, but they took it with them."

"Okay," Jim said. "Listen carefully, Em. I want you to find a life preserver, put it on, and swim as hard and as fast as you can, away from the ship. Do you hear me?"

"And just leave Alex to die? Jim, I can't do that."

"Emily, damn it, save yourself," Jim rasped. "You can't take Delmore into the water with you. If he's bleeding the way you said he was, you'll be shark bait. Hell, if he's bleeding the way you said he was, he doesn't have a chance.

So *save yourself.* Don't die for a man who's already as good as dead."

"You don't know his condition," Emily said. "Maybe he is going to die. But maybe he's not. Maybe he'll make it. He deserves—"

"He deserves *nothing.*"

"You're wrong," Emily said. "Everyone deserves a second chance. Even Alex. Maybe . . . maybe I can disarm the bomb."

Fear made the hair stand up on the back of Jim's neck. "Don't touch that bomb!"

"Isn't there someone who can talk me through it?" Emily asked. "Don't the police have a specialist or someone who can tell me what to do?"

Seven minutes and two seconds. One second. Seven minutes even.

"Emily, get away from the boat. Do it *now.*"

Harper leaned over to Jim. "We have the bomb squad team leader standing by at police headquarters."

Six minutes fifty-four seconds.

"Em, please," Jim said desperately. "Delmore doesn't deserve the effort."

Emily didn't answer.

"Emily? Are you there?"

"I'm here," she said. "And I disagree. Are you going to let me talk to the bomb expert or not?"

Jim gritted his teeth. "Connect them," he ordered Harper.

Emily leaned over the engine, staring down at the bomb. The digital clock read six minutes and three seconds. She'd spent thirty of her precious seconds describing the bomb to the demolitions expert, a man with a slight French accent, named Jean Dumont.

"Carefully remove the housing," Dumont said in his elegant voice, over the crackling interference of the radio, "but don't touch any of the wires."

"Okay," Emily said, brushing the sweat out of her eyes. "I did it."

"Emily, are you there?" Dumont said. "Your last transmission was breaking up."

Emily tapped at the microphone in the pin she was wearing. "Hello?" she said. "Do you read me now?"

Jim's voice broke in over the radio receiver. "Emily, we've lost your signal. Dumont is going to continue to give you instructions, but he can't hear your reply. None of us can—the mike has gone dead. Please, I'm begging you. Get off the yacht. I love you. Do you hear what I'm saying? Now get *out* of there."

"I love you, too," Emily whispered, feeling her eyes fill with tears.

Dumont's voice came back on. "Emily, inside the housing you will see four wires. Red, green, blue and yellow. Do not touch the red or the yellow, do you understand?"

Emily stared at the bomb. Yes, there were four wires.

But they were all blue.

Jim stood on deck with his legs spread, braced against the up-and-down motion of the powerboat. He scanned the horizon with a pair of field glasses, searching for any sign of the *Home Free*.

The numbers on his watch ticked down, faster and faster now, heading toward zero.

Forty-seven seconds. Forty-six. Forty-five. Forty-four…

In the distance, he could hear the sound of the approaching chopper. He swung his binoculars back toward the east, and he could see it, still too far away, coming in low to the water, and fast. But not fast enough.

Felipe doggedly held the powerboat in a southwesterly direction, following the course heading that the location signal on board the *Home Free* had indicated before it had gone dead.

Harper stuck his head up from the companionway. "Dumont's finished," he said. "If Emily was disarming the bomb, and if she did everything Dumont told her to do correctly, they've got the job done in time. Oh, and Salazar, the hospital called the precinct, looking for you. Your friend's condition's improved."

Felipe said a quick prayer of thanks in Spanish, and Jim glanced over at him.

"Send an extra word or two up there for Emily, while you're at it," Jim said.

"I have been," Felipe said.

Jim looked at his watch. Seventeen seconds. Sixteen. Fifteen. Fourteen.

Out on the horizon, farther south than west, Jim caught sight of what might have been the tip of a mast. He shouted at Felipe, pointing in the mast's direction.

Ten. Nine. Eight.

As they roared toward the ship, more and more of it appeared above the line of the horizon, as if the sea were opening up and spitting it out.

Seven.

Please...

Six.

...God...

Five.

...let...

Four.

...her...

Three.

...be...

Two.

...safe.

One.

The *Home Free*—and it was definitely Delmore's yacht that Jim had spotted—sat at the edge of the horizon, facing into the wind, perfectly still, perfectly calm, perfectly—

The yacht exploded, sending a column of fire up into the air. The sound followed several seconds later, a rumbling roar of noise that echoed across the water.

Jim slowly lowered the binoculars and stared numbly at the thick black smoke that poured from the debris where the ship had once been.

Harper and Winstead came up on deck and stood there silently.

Felipe was the first to speak. "Do you think she got off in time, man?"

Jim shook his head. "I don't know," he said quietly. "God, I honestly don't know."

The thought of Emily dead was overwhelming. Jim felt shockingly empty, totally bereft.

How could the sun be shining so brightly? How could the sky be such a deep shade of blue? Without Emily, colors couldn't possibly exist. Without Emily, life was a single shade of gray.

The powerboat bounced higher over a large swell, and Jim stumbled. His legs felt useless and weak, so he sat down heavily on the bench that lined the deck.

"Hey!" Felipe said. "Are you giving up on me, man? Come on, get those field glasses working. We're getting closer. I know she's out here somewhere. I feel it in my bones, Diego. God's gonna give us a two-miracle day."

Overhead, the chopper made ever-widening circles around the smoking debris. Harper went back down into the cabin to talk with the pilot on the radio.

Jim stood up as Felipe slowed the boat to a crawl.

A two-miracle day? Why not try for three? Because if Emily was still alive, Jim was going to make damn sure he never walked away from her again.

He had told her not to throw her life away for a man who was as good as dead. But wasn't that exactly what he himself had been doing all these years? Because Bob was dead, Jim had been depriving himself of happiness. He'd been walking around more dead than alive himself, letting his guilt control him.

But that hadn't brought Bob back. He could spend the next four hundred years in hell, and that *still* wouldn't bring Bob back.

Bob was dead. End of story. End of Bob's story, anyway. It didn't have to be the end of Jim's.

"Come on, Emily," Jim murmured, using the binoculars to search the water. "Where are you?"

Harper burst up from down below. "The chopper pilot says he's spotted something to the south."

Felipe gunned the boat, turning sharply toward where the helicopter was hovering.

Jim's mouth was dry. Through the binoculars he could see *something* in the water. Something orange and brown. Was it a life jacket? Was it Emily? Or was it just some debris from the explosion?

Everyone deserves a second chance, Emily had said. Please, God, Jim thought, let me have mine. Prove to me you think I'm worth it....

"Can't you make this thing go any faster?" he shouted at Felipe.

"Hang on." His partner rode the throttle, giving the boat surges of even greater speed, and creating a very rocky ride. Jim steadied himself against the railing, focusing and refocusing the binoculars on that floating splotch of orange.

There was definitely something brown in the middle. No, now it wasn't brown, it was lighter. Skin colored. A flick of his finger brought it sharply into focus.

It was Emily's face. She was looking directly at the powerboat.

"She's alive!" Jim grabbed Winstead and kissed him on the top of his shiny bald head.

"All right!" Felipe shouted, holding up one hand to Jim for a high five. "All *right!*"

Jim leaned down and shouted into the cabin, "Harper, we found her! She's alive!"

He no longer needed the binoculars to see her. He leaned over the rail toward her, as if those few extra inches would get him to her faster.

As they drew nearer and Felipe slowed the boat, Jim dived over the side and swam under the water, toward Emily. He surfaced four feet away from her and flicked his wet hair back, out of his eyes.

"I knew you'd come," she said.

He swam closer. "I love you," he said.

Her hair was wet and lank against her pale face. She had smudges of soot on her forehead and her cheeks. But her eyes were the color of heaven, and Jim had never seen her look so beautiful.

She met his eyes steadily. "Do you love me enough to forgive yourself?"

Jim didn't hesitate. "I sure as hell am going to try. Will you help me?"

Emily nodded. "Every day, for as long as you need me to."

He moved even closer. "How about every night?"

She smiled at him then, with her pure, sweet, sexy-as-hell smile. "You don't need any help there, Detective."

The powerboat drifted closer, and Jim reached up and grabbed the side. Pulling Emily close with his other arm, he kissed her.

By the time Jim drove Emily home, it was sunset. With his arm around her shoulders, they climbed the stairs to the second-floor landing—and nearly got run over by Carly Wilson.

"Oops! Sorry," she said. "I'm in a real rush. Mac's waiting for me downstairs."

A truck horn sounded, as if emphasizing her words.

Carly rolled her eyes. "What a romantic guy. He couldn't even get out of his damned pickup truck and walk me upstairs—tonight of all nights."

"What's happening tonight?" Emily asked.

Carly sighed dramatically. "I know I said I wasn't going to do it, but...Mac and I got married today," she said. "Isn't that the stupidest thing you've ever heard? We're driving down to Key West for a two-week honeymoon." She laughed. "At least I know the marriage will last *that* long."

"Maybe this time it'll work out," Emily said.

"Yeah, sure," Carly said with a laugh. She looked from Emily to Jim and back. "Well, look at you two." Carly crossed her arms and leaned against the railing, apparently forgetting that she was supposed to be in a hurry. "Aren't *you* friendly? Jeez, my sister and I still can't get within six feet of each other."

"He's not my brother," Emily said.

Carly leaned forward. "Come again?"

"Carly, meet Jim Keegan," Emily said. "He's a detective on the St. Simone police force. When you met him before, he was undercover. He was only pretending to be my brother."

Carly looked from Jim to Emily. "What's he pretending to be now?"

"I intend to be Emily's husband," Jim said. "And I'm not pretending."

Carly nodded slowly. "When I get back from Key West, you're going to have to tell me the whole story," she said to Emily. "I have a feeling it's going to be a *real* good one."

The horn beeped again, and with a wave Carly was gone.

"She doesn't honestly think her marriage is only going to last a few weeks, does she?" Jim asked as Emily unlocked her door and pushed it open.

Emily shrugged. "With Carly, you never know. Her usual average for a marriage is only about fifteen months."

Jim closed the door behind them, then led Emily over to the couch. He sat down, pulling her onto his lap. "When *we* get married," he said, tracing her lips with his thumb, "I intend for it to be forever."

Emily smiled. "That sounds just about long enough."

She leaned forward and kissed him.

His smile faded, and his eyes became serious. "I was really glad that you got off the *Home Free* when you did."

Emily laced her fingers in his hair. "Alex died," she told him quietly, "while I was talking to Dumont, the bomb expert." She met his eyes. "After my microphone stopped working, and I realized I wasn't going to be able to defuse the bomb, I was going to put Alex into a wet suit and take him over the side with me, but . . . he was already dead."

"Four SWAT teams intercepted Marino and his men," Jim said. "He resisted and was killed. The boat they were in was loaded with cocaine. The other men are going to get sent away for years."

"So it's over," Emily said. She smiled ruefully. "Until the next drug lord comes to town."

"The fight goes on," Jim said. "We do the best we can. And today we did one hell of a lot. Thanks to you." He smiled at her. "Of course, thanks to you, I've also got one hell of an ulcer starting."

"I'm sorry," she murmured.

"It's okay," he said, kissing her gently. "But next time you decide to make a major decision that involves risking your life, I'd appreciate it if you'd at least talk to me first. This relationship *is* a partnership. Do you hear what I'm saying?"

Emily laughed. "Loud and clear."

Jim leaned his head back, nestling her head underneath his chin. He closed his eyes and sighed. "Did we sleep last night? I don't think we slept last night. I'm exhausted."

Emily kissed his neck, then stood up. She held out her hand to him. "Let's go to bed."

Jim took her hand and kissed it lightly. "I'll be in in a second," he said. "I have to make a quick phone call."

The pain was back in his eyes, and Emily felt a wild burst of frustration. Was she going to wake up in the middle of the night and find him sitting out here again, all alone, in the dark?

She went into the bedroom and, leaving the door ajar, began to undress. If that happened again, she vowed, she was going to get up and sit with him. She was going to hold him and love him and...

From the living room, she heard Jim's voice as he spoke on the telephone. "Hi, uh, Ma? It's Jimmy," she heard him say, and she froze.

"Yeah, *Jimmy,*" he said huskily. "Surprise, huh? Yeah, look, I, um...I'm getting married." There was a long pause, and then he laughed. "Yeah, *married.* Can you believe it? Her name's Emily, and you're gonna love her, Ma. God knows I do. Look, I was wondering if, um, if you'd maybe want to come to the wedding— You *would?* That's *great.* That's really great. And Molly and Shannon, too? You really think they'd— They'd want to come, too, huh? That's...that's great. Look, Ma, we had a really rough day, and I've got to go, but I'll call you in a few days, okay?" Another pause. Then Jim's voice caught slightly as he said, "I love you, too, Ma."

Emily slipped quietly into bed, using the sheet to wipe away the tears of happiness that had suddenly filled her eyes.

And when Jim came into the room and climbed into bed beside her, she welcomed him with a kiss and an embrace.

The healing had begun.

* * * * *

INTIMATE MOMENTS®
™ Silhouette®

COMING NEXT MONTH

He's Too Hot To Handle...but she can take a little heat.

SILHOUETTE

Summer Sizzlers

This summer don't be left in the cold, join Silhouette for the hottest Summer Sizzlers collection. The perfect summer read, on the beach or while vacationing, Summer Sizzlers features sexy heroes who are "Too Hot To Handle." This collection of three new stories is written by bestselling authors Mary Lynn Baxter, Ann Major and Laura Parker.

Available this July wherever Silhouette books are sold.

ANNOUNCING THE

PRIZE SURPRISE SWEEPSTAKES!

This month's prize:

L-A-R-G-E—SCREEN PANASONIC TV!

This month, as a special surprise, we're giving away a fabulous FREE TV!

Imagine how delighted you and your family will be to own this brand-new 31" Panasonic** television! It comes with all the latest high-tech features, like a SuperFlat picture tube for a clear, crisp picture...unified remote control...closed-caption decoder...clock and sleep timer, and much more!

The facing page contains two Entry Coupons (as does every book you received this shipment). Complete and return *all* the entry coupons; **the more times you enter, the better your chances of winning the TV!**

Then keep your fingers crossed, because you'll find out by July 15, 1995 if you're the winner!

Remember: The more times you enter, the better your chances of winning!*

PTV KAL

PRIZE SURPRISE
SWEEPSTAKES
OFFICIAL ENTRY COUPON

This entry must be received by: JUNE 30, 1995
This month's winner will be notified by: JULY 15, 1995

YES, I want to win the Panasonic 31" TV! Please enter me in the drawing and let me know if I've won!

Name_____

Address _____ Apt. _____

City_____ State/Prov._____ Zip/Postal Code_____

Account #_____

Return entry with invoice in reply envelope.

© 1995 HARLEQUIN ENTERPRISES LTD.   CTV KAL

PRIZE SURPRISE
SWEEPSTAKES
OFFICIAL ENTRY COUPON

This entry must be received by: JUNE 30, 1995
This month's winner will be notified by: JULY 15, 1995

YES, I want to win the Panasonic 31" TV! Please enter me in the drawing and let me know if I've won!

Name_____

Address _____ Apt. _____

City_____ State/Prov._____ Zip/Postal Code_____

Account #_____

Return entry with invoice in reply envelope.

© 1995 HARLEQUIN ENTERPRISES LTD.   CTV KAL

OFFICIAL RULES

PRIZE SURPRISE SWEEPSTAKES 3448

NO PURCHASE OR OBLIGATION NECESSARY

Three Harlequin Reader Service 1995 shipments will contain respectively, coupons for entry into three different prize drawings, one for a Panasonic 31" wide-screen TV, another for a 5-piece Wedgwood china service for eight and the third for a Sharp ViewCam camcorder. To enter any drawing using an Entry Coupon, simply complete and mail according to directions.

There is no obligation to continue using the Reader Service to enter and be eligible for any prize drawing. You may also enter any drawing by hand printing the words "Prize Surprise," your name and address on a 3"x5" card and the name of the prize you wish that entry to be considered for (i.e., Panasonic wide-screen TV, Wedgwood china or Sharp ViewCam). Send your 3"x5" entries via first-class mail (limit: one per envelope) to: Prize Surprise Sweepstakes 3448, c/o the prize you wish that entry to be considered for, P.O. Box 1315, Buffalo, NY 14269-1315, USA or P.O. Box 610, Fort Erie, Ontario L2A 5X3, Canada.

To be eligible for the Panasonic wide-screen TV, entries must be received by 6/30/95; for the Wedgwood china, 8/30/95; and for the Sharp ViewCam, 10/30/95.

Winners will be determined in random drawings conducted under the supervision of D.L. Blair, Inc., an independent judging organization whose decisions are final, from among all eligible entries received for that drawing. Approximate prize values are as follows: Panasonic wide-screen TV ($1,800); Wedgwood china ($840) and Sharp ViewCam ($2,000). Sweepstakes open to residents of the U.S. (except Puerto Rico) and Canada, 18 years of age or older. Employees and immediate family members of Harlequin Enterprises, Ltd., D.L. Blair, Inc., their affiliates, subsidiaries and all other agencies, entities and persons connected with the use, marketing or conduct of this sweepstakes are not eligible. Odds of winning a prize are dependent upon the number of eligible entries received for that drawing. Prize drawing and winner notification for each drawing will occur no later than 15 days after deadline for entry eligibility for that drawing. Limit: one prize to an individual, family or organization. All applicable laws and regulations apply. Sweepstakes offer void wherever prohibited by law. Any litigation within the province of Quebec respecting the conduct and awarding of the prizes in this sweepstakes must be submitted to the Regies des loteries et Courses du Quebec. In order to win a prize, residents of Canada will be required to correctly answer a time-limited arithmetical skill-testing question. Value of prizes are in U.S. currency.

Winners will be obligated to sign and return an Affidavit of Eligibility within 30 days of notification. In the event of noncompliance within this time period, prize may not be awarded. If any prize or prize notification is returned as undeliverable, that prize will not be awarded. By acceptance of a prize, winner consents to use of his/her name, photograph or other likeness for purposes of advertising, trade and promotion on behalf of Harlequin Enterprises, Ltd., without further compensation, unless prohibited by law.

For the names of prizewinners (available after 12/31/95), send a self-addressed, stamped envelope to: Prize Surprise Sweepstakes 3448 Winners, P.O. Box 4200, Blair, NE 68009.

RPZ KAL